W9-CCD-887

MARK S. GESTON

An AvoNova Book

William Morrow and Company, Inc.
New York

MIRROR TO THE SKY is an original publication of Avon Books. This work has never before appeared in book form. This work is a novel. Any similarity to actual persons or events is purely coincidental.

AVON BOOKS
A division of
The Hearst Corporation
1350 Avenue of the Americas
New York, New York 10019

Copyright © 1992 by Mark S. Geston
Published by arrangement with the author
Library of Congress Catalog Card Number: 92-14991
ISBN: 0-688-11138-6

Library of Congress Cataloging in Publication Data:
Geston, Mark S.
  Mirror to the sky / Mark S. Geston.
     p. cm.
ISBN 0-688-11138-6 : $20.00
I. Title.
PS3557.E83M57   1992
813'.54—dc20   91-14991
                                                            CIP

First Morrow/AvoNova Printing: December 1992

AVONOVA TRADEMARK REG. U.S. PAT. OFF. AND IN OTHER COUNTRIES, MARCA REGISTRADA, HECHO EN U.S.A.

Printed in the U.S.A.

ARC   10   9   8   7   6   5   4   3   2   1

To Marijke
and our children,
Camille, Bob and Emily

THEY ANNOUNCED THEMSELVES SIX MONTHS BEFORE THE ships were resolved as physical entities, the mannered, apologetic voice transmissions reassuring the world that there was no reason for concern. They would, they said in absurdly stilted English, do everything possible to minimize the shock of their arrival and, afterward, their presence among mankind. There would only be a few hundred of them, anyway.

The largest ships remained in orbit. Those that descended were up to a kilometer long and fashioned with a cunning that prevented visual appreciation of their shapes. Their outlines flowed and bent at the edges when closely observed, and this uncertainty persisted in memory such that there was no surety that a given ship had even been present a day after it was seen departing from a landing field.

They never cast shadows unless actually resting on the ground. Localized gravitational fields warped sunlight around their hulls. That was presumed to have been the reason for the seeming fluidity of their shapes.

The newcomers' language was similarly elusive. It was

largely sung, demanding at least two full octaves to complete a sentence. Paragraphs sounded like ballads and speeches like arias. It was enchanting but physiologically and psychologically beyond human duplication. The aliens graciously recognized this and went out of their way to learn the Earthly languages.

They appeared physically human, but idealized according to a strict artistic standard. None were over six feet tall or under five feet eight. None were obviously young or old; not one of those that landed on earth was fat or notably thin. All the males had the strong, world-weary features of late Hellenistic sculptures, while the females suggested a softer Classical model.

Once they acquired fluency in the terrestrial languages, they displayed an earnest, labored sense of humor that was not without irony. They were invariably polite, solicitous and deferential, as if self-conscious about their power and achievements.

The *Times* declared them to be "the new Englishmen of the universe." *L'Express* judged them Gallic in nature, and, stepping back only slightly from the level of British presumption, declared that the French must be their spiritual descendants on Earth. The Americans were disturbed by their sameness and, as usual, hid it poorly. Germany loudly, wearisomely admired it.

The aliens bore all this with the same graceful reserve they had shown when thousands of cultists in West Africa murdered each other before their ships, pleading with them to open the ports and allow the souls of the dying to enter and thus fly up into heaven with them. The rationale of those tedious episodes had been that only the sheer weight of spiritual suffering could force its way into the ships; the scale of self-massacre that was required to disprove it briefly sickened the world. But as the mobs butchered themselves, the news cameras often caught the aliens on the bridge of a hovering ship, expressing such precise compassion and bewilderment that the television watchers became more absorbed with them than with the spectacle on the ground.

In saner parts of the world, the aliens performed the expected tricks and wonders which almost, but never quite, entered decisively into the realm of miracles. Some dying humans, the victims of either disease, misfortune or their own lunatic efforts to win the gods' favor, were rescued, but the dead were always left to their own decay. Earthquakes were occasionally predicted but never stopped. Mathematics and physics were refined and extended under their guidance, but they never hinted that they might uncover new conceptions of reality for mankind. They would not talk at all about their ships or if these vessels routinely violated special or general relativity.

Resentment began to form beneath the gratitude for their favors and astonishment at their existence. It was fed by the conviction that the price for all of this could not possibly be the trivial concessions of privacy and cooperation in the establishment of the diplomatic and scientific stations they requested. Their very aristocratic isolation in these establishments and in the mansions and country estates their human agents discreetly acquired for them aroused inarticulate suspicions in people who should have known better.

The same people surmised that, because they could come so near to reversing death, manipulating the Earth and travelling across stellar distances, immensely greater abilities were concealed behind their humility. People were drawn to the conclusion that they *did* partake of different realities but archly hid them from mankind like a magician at a children's party.

They came to be referred to as "the gods." They said they were embarrassed by that, professing unworthiness and explaining their wonders as if these were things they had accidently stumbled upon instead of fashioned themselves. When this did not end the term's use, they became impatient and made it clear that it could be considered an insult if it persisted.

"We have no wish to place ourselves above you. Nor will we allow you to do this yourselves," they said in a memorandum delivered to the State Department in June, four years after their first landing. "We only wish to maintain our limited presence on your world for our mutual enlightenment and protection.''

The last word naturally caught the eye of governments and other paranoids. ''Protection from what?'' was the essence of State's answering note. ''Protection'' had never been mentioned before; until then everything had been toys and experiments, comic misunderstandings and the indefatigably polite requests to be left alone to pursue their observations.

''Protection from what?'' Timothy Cavan's mother repeated the question to his father at the dinner table.

Andrew Cavan's mouth was full of pot roast, so he waved his fork in the air until he could answer. ''A figure of speech. Means nothing. Same kind of hot air we use on them and each other all the time. You, of all people, should recognize that, Linda.''

''But have they ever deliberately used the word before?''

''Beats me. No one can speak their language. Even NSA's dictionary's stalled at twenty or thirty words. Wentworth told me it's worse than Cretan Linear-B.'' His son looked at him carefully to see where the lies began; the father returned the glance briefly enough to show that he knew what Timothy was thinking and wasn't going to make it easy for him. ''Anyway, just because they've become fluent in English doesn't mean that what they intend by that particular word—and I don't think it's worth dwelling on—is what we'd normally read into it. I mean, Christ, dear, the arrival of these creatures has been the greatest thing in history. Ever. They've ennobled our generation just by landing when they did. And now, after years of offering us nothing but enrichment . . .''

''You can't call what happened in Sierra Leone 'enrichment.' ''

''Don't be silly. The locals did that to themselves. The gods had nothing to do with it.'' Timothy saw his father flinch at his own unintended use of the name. He had made a point of how he disapproved of its use. ''So now, after all the years that they've been here, what we're mainly seeing is jealousy and hurt feelings. And a lot of hysteria over one badly chosen word in one minor note to State.''

He resumed eating, but his wife kept glaring at him. ''But your people *are* looking into it? They're looking into the exact use of that exact word, aren't they?'' she persisted.

''We'd be foolish not to,'' Andrew Cavan answered dispiritedly. Then, after a while, ''But you've got to believe that they can only be good for us. If they had conquest on their minds—and Christ knows how *that* chestnut's been worked over from the moment they hit the atmosphere—they could have pulled it off a hundred times by now.'' This was obvious patch-up; all three of them knew it.

''Probably,'' she said after a while, smiling softly toward him now that she had won the exchange.

Her father was an Under Secretary of State and had warned her about the intrinsic allure of exotic societies, how easy it was to be corrupted by sympathy for foreign perspectives and how constantly one had to guard against it if the nation was to be served professionally. She had decided some time ago that her husband was succumbing in such a way and resented him thoroughly for his weakness.

THE GODS STROVE ENDLESSLY TO LESSEN THE CONSTANT shock of their presence on earth. Their stations were located in remote regions or designed to appear as ordinary as their sensory arrays allowed. Diplomatic missions and residences that were unavoidably located in cities were scrupulously ordinary. They joined the correct clubs, contributed to the correct causes, and never once sought to be chairpersons of anything at all. Numbers were never discussed, but it was assumed that there were never more than a thousand of them on Earth at once.

They exhibited an ambivalent compulsion to conceal themselves but still permit some insight beyond the requirements of strict diplomacy. Stores and cultural missions were often attached to their embassies, but the books available there were invariably opaque and never dealt with anything more intriguing than their home worlds' geologies and fauna; there was never even a star chart to locate them in the constellations. Lectures, devoted to obscure dynastic histories that may have been myths or to other alien cultures, had the dusty smell of racial extinction about them. Readings of their lyric poetry were given during the two months following their arrival, but ceased before too much of their language was exposed to human analysis.

The gods were most willing, however, to share their visual arts. They were naturally proud of their works, no matter what the New York critics said about its "archaic representationalism," and strangely acted as if it should pose an even greater mystery to mankind than their science or language. They appeared unconcerned over the negligible possibility of human understanding.

For this reason, Andrew Cavan examined the pictures on their missions' walls and the sculptures in their foyers as closely as he did the readouts from the surveillance nets around each of their known Earth stations. He came to believe that the gods were flaunting something of great significance, almost against their will, as if they derived a contradictory thrill from the remote chance that one of their works might be understood by human beings.

He sometimes took Timothy to look at the gods' art when it was convenient to his normal business. He had brought Linda along too at first, but she refused to go any more once she detected how he slipped away from her in the presence of their paintings.

In the fifth year after their arrival, Andrew Cavan brought home a small fractured bust, consisting only of the left quadrant of a head, from mid-forehead, down around the eye and below the cheek bone. It was obviously of a god, fashioned by them. This was surprising, both because it was against the law and the Department's own protocols for individuals to keep anything the gods created and because they almost never let anything out of their possession.

He placed it on a bookcase in the living room, between two shelves of history books, where he could look at it while pretending to read on the sofa. The object produced enough unease for his wife to avoid the room, just as she had refused to accompany her husband anywhere he might encounter gods or their larger works.

Timothy was initially disappointed, but as he continued to look he discerned creases and folds which implied that the subject's mouth had been drawn back in a feral grin, an expression impossible to conceive on any living god he had seen. After more examination, he thought he could sense the tension of the muscles sculpted below the fired surface. Intimations of a particular time, a finite number of years embedded in conflict, radiated from the bust along with profounder emotions from which his youth and inexperience protected him.

HIS FATHER CAME HOME ONE EVENING IN EARLY SPRING, flushed with booze and success. He had, he announced to his wife and son, pretty much wrapped up the first formal exhibition of godly art. His wife said deliberately that this was very good and left them.

Timothy watched his father make the conscious decision that this reception should not diminish the moment; he had been foolish to expect admiration from her at all. So he reconstructed his smile and unloaded his triumph on his son. Timothy tried to understand in the hope it would make up for the unidentifiable thing which had walked out of the room with his mother.

His father said that State and Commerce had just cleared the project. CIA and Defense Intelligence had disclaimed any interest in something so emphemeral. The gods themselves had been reluctant, but he had imposed upon a particularly ambitious and receptive fellow named Slate, and they had finally committed themselves to produce not only a representative group of fifty pieces but some of the artists as well. Most of the works and artists, his father said, his voice regaining its excitement, *must* be coming from their home worlds, so, even while they were speaking, the very paintings and statues they would see that autumn were doubtlessly being packed in strange excelsiors and loaded into the holds of starships. Perhaps they were even moving through the constellations now, necessarily at superluminal speeds if they were to arrive in time.

But, he continued, that assumed the exhibition had not really been planned and the works dispatched centuries ago, and the gods' agreement was merely a charade designed to subtly reinforce the erroneous belief of gullible humans that they had mastered faster-than-light travel.

"So which do you believe?" Timothy asked carefully.

"Ah," his father delayed, looking toward the study where his wife had retired. "That really doesn't matter right now, does it, Tim? If they can't outrun light, then we can't. And if they can—as seems to be the case—we couldn't grasp the technology for another five hundred years. We'd burn ourselves up trying. The important thing is that they might show us something we *can* understand, even if they don't mean to or can't stop themselves from doing it. I think we'll be able to look at one or two of the pictures, all alone." Then he whistled to himself as if only now struck by the implications of his thoughts and lurched off to the kitchen.

Timothy waited all that night for the shouting to start, but nothing erupted. His father sat in the living room with the television on, sipping his most expensive wines and staring at the bust. His mother stayed with him and actually seemed to be making some kind of effort to reach him. She sat at the opposite end of the couch with her own glass of gin, filled higher than usual, occasionally touching him and smiling indulgently, but then drawing back when he went for another drink.

Timothy asked her about that the next day, before he went to school. She shrugged in her reassuring, educated way to show that, despite last night's difficulties, she was still making a favorable daily choice. "He's his own person. We're all on our own when we think about it. And we could be back in Zurich, before you were born . . ."

"Before the gods landed?"

"Before they ever came here. Now that was difficult. Exciting. But still difficult."

P EOPLE STILL EXPECTED THE LEAVES TO CHANGE IN October, even though that had not happened for twenty years before the gods arrived. Changes were being made in the geochemical carbon cycle to hasten the return of normal seasons. There was now substantial involvement of the gods' technology in these stupendous efforts, but even they said that the process would take decades and was full of uncertainty. Their hints that the present climate reminded them of their home worlds both reassured and unsettled those who still wished for snow and crops in Iowa.

The leaves were down by the beginning of December. The prediction for the next year moved the date for this back to Thanksgiving, if everything went as planned; a small but gratifying improvement if it happened.

Timothy's mother had declined the invitation for the opening reception, even though it was signed jointly by the State Department, UNESCO's General Secretary and the gods' Chief of Mission in Washington. His father had argued with her only briefly over this. They compromised when she agreed to accompany him to a reception given by the Kampuchean Embassy the following week, a function they would both detest.

Andrew Cavan went to the National Gallery alone and came home early. Timothy listened anxiously against the wall between their bedrooms but heard only strained pleasantries. His father's voice had none of the slurred extravagance that had been there on the night he announced the project.

Timothy positioned himself at breakfast Sunday so that his father could ask him to go to the Gallery, but not his mother. Everyone cooperated in the conspiracy, even to the extent that it was his mother who suggested he and his father take in the show without all the distractions of diplomatic community socializing.

A wing had been set aside at the National Gallery. The National Air and Space Museum was directly across the Mall and Timothy, who had been there often, could not help but place his mind's eye in the cockpit of the X–15 hanging from one side of the entry hall celling or in the *Spirit of St. Louis*, suspended on the other side, and look through Lindbergh's periscope at the alien blue sculpture on the Gallery steps.

The gods translated the sculpture's title as *Promise* and regretted that the sculptor, identified in English as Jess, had been too ill to attend. It seemed fairly standard abstract stuff, hugely graceful in the manner of a Calder. But it possessed the singular power to invoke, specifically and literally for some few people, the day before the gods landed. To the evident dismay of some of the gods present, this had been mentioned during the previous night's diplomatic reception.

The exhibition was opened to the public the next day. The crowds did not seem very large to Timothy, despite the show's overwhelming importance to his father and the mildness of the weather. The Hudson School exhibition in the wing across the entrance hall seemed to be drawing nearly as many people.

His father remarked that perhaps the necessary security measures were keeping things subdued. Everyone entering the Gallery had to pass through standard metal detectors and neutron activation sniffers. Signs in the entrance hall reiterated the government's right to conduct random strip searches. Half the cops posted outside the Gallery and in the cavernous entrance hall had attack dogs and the other half were carrying machine pistols.

Salutes and other signs of deference were offered to his father by the senior officers on duty. They walked into the exhibition and saw nothing immediately remarkable. Three large pictures, rendered in the same style and arranged as a triptych, occupied the far wall. Timothy felt chilled when he first saw them, but that could have been a breeze or the obligatory reaction to his father's buildup about the exhibition's significance.

The walls on either side of the hall were lined with framed paintings; the angle prevented him from seeing them clearly.

A row of freestanding sculptures, including an enlargement of the half-bust his father had brought home, occupied the center space. Timothy naturally walked toward this first. He stood in front of it, expecting the half-imagined emotions the piece at home evoked would be vastly magnified and hurled toward him all at once.

The craftsmanship was even more obsessive than that which had been lavished on the smaller version. He first made out individual pores when he bent close to the surface and then, within them, the vaguely implied presence of individual cells. The lines of the facial muscles were detectable, also, and after a minute's concentration he thought that he could perceive the fragmented section of skull underneath.

He jerked himself away, realizing the impossibility of such perceptions. "Nice trick," he mumbled and was embarrassed that his father heard.

"I should say. They say it's just an extrapolation of our own techniques of perspective. We can manage the illusion of three dimensions on two-dimensional surfaces: height, width and depth on a flat canvas. We always know it's an illusion, although if the artist's using holographic enhancements, the illusion can be pretty convincing. Remember the Ivanov show here last year, Tim?"

His son nodded. The man's renderings of the "Stalin" myth-cycle had been a source of nightmares for weeks afterward. They still interfered at school with his ability to grasp the history of that particular era in academic terms.

"But where we can just do the illusion of depth, their best artists are supposed to be able to convey all kinds of non-visible . . ." Andrew Cavan's speech slowed as he sensed the irrationality of what he was saying. ". . . ah, invisible knowledge like time and the identity of the subjects, mood, emotion. Anything at all, if you want to believe what I was told at the reception last night. And, of course, they have access to things we don't, times and places that are completely foreign to us. Things we don't have any frame of reference for."

"That's what Mother. . . ."

"I know. I know," he continued, his enthusiasm only briefly waning. "But you can see that, in a way, they *are* starting to share such things with us."

"On purpose?"

Andrew Cavan looked at his son approvingly, as he did when the boy achieved a worthy insight. "Their intentions are unclear. They always are," he sighed. "But the risk is being taken. I think they're going to be surprised at how accessible some of this is to us. Like the sculpture outside."

"And how they'll arrive 'tomorrow'? Right?"

The piece next to the bust was distinctly reminiscent of the blue metal stabile in front of the Gallery's steps, but there was no invocation of memory hovering around it. Timothy strained toward some kind of insight, but then relaxed when he realized how ridiculous such a conscious effort was.

Timothy gave the sculpture a last chance at astonishment and then began a slow circuit of the room, heading toward the far end where his father was now talking to a god. He would be embarrassed to appear at his side without any flattering observations about the art.

He passed a row of landscapes distinguished by the polychrome flora the gods spoke of so lovingly when they described their homes. Most were uninhabited. The execution was often hyper-realistic, though the reluctance of the gods to produce photographs of their lands made it impossible to be certain. A few others smeared their way toward the worst of terrestrial abstractionism.

Timothy found one he thought particularly inept and studied it, relieved to discover humanly scaled imperfection. But the painting's contours separated and defined themselves as he looked. A wondrously imagined landscape that could have existed only in a single mind gradually emerged, exercising its speculative powers during a particular month in the course of a specific historical era. There was no sense of *déjà vu*, but he was momentarily convinced that he could locate the painting precisely in the imaginative experience of the painter.

This certainty vanished when he turned away. He could

remember the coloration of the grasses and flowers, as well as the daVincian city on the vague horizon, but the larger elements of the painting's imaginary geography were instantly withdrawn. What stayed with him were the suspicion of having been tricked and the judgment of inferior technique.

He glanced back and rediscovered the land the artist had created, but it slipped away again when he moved on.

The landscapes were followed by portraits, one of a female god and then two of males. One was dressed in some grand uniform, but neither the picture nor the English commentary under the frame disclosed much about him.

The other male portrait showed an elderly god seated in a room filled with books and archaic scientific instruments. The subject had gray hair and features more severe than the gods seen on Earth. The total impression should have been one of scholarship and wisdom, but a faint trickle of insanity began to leak from the painting as he examined it. It ran first from the subject's eyes and then from his hands. Statuettes of gods in philosophic poses on the bookshelves behind him exuded the same frightening mist.

Timothy stepped back and the impression weakened; then forward again, and it intensified as if he were seeing emotional details in the same way as he had seen the microscopic anatomy of the bust in the center of the room, just by gazing more closely.

A woman beside him stared sweetly at the portrait, stepping up close and then backward and showing only polite interest. Her boyfriend or husband joined her, glanced at the painting and abruptly walked away, moving his head as if he had been subjected to a wrenching strain.

The third portrait was of the female god. She was not what a person of Timothy's age and social background would find ravishingly beautiful. The racial divergence between gods and humankind was even more daunting in this picture than it was in real life, but the painting's unseen dimensions thrust an unexpected weight of sexuality at the boy, aimed at his abdomen and crotch. He was abducted so unexpectedly by this sensuality that he did not immediately realize what was happening, and when he did he was more frightened than he had ever yet been with a girl.

Timothy backed clumsily away from the painting. He was breathing hard and his heart was racing. There was nothing false or simulated about his reaction. His friends must know of this! Such a thing!

He kept retreating until he could look back from an oblique angle that distorted the picture's subject. A few men seemed to stare at it and then walk away, but generally the painting did not seem to exercise any special power over other viewers.

But control, control, he told himself, as aware of his Earthly inexperience as of his ignorance of the gods. He walked back the way he had come so he would nearly circle the gallery before rejoining his father.

A guard dog growled at him as he passed, but its master was transfixed by a starscape, two meters square, on the wall to the left of the entryway. Its graphic style seemed better suited to a *National Geographic* illustration than an art gallery. *Surely a spacefaring race could have come up with something more remarkable than this!* He found in it only the dread he customarily sensed whenever he looked into the night. The painter's ability had been squandered, Timothy decided, on trivial clues of menace lying in the tentacled galaxy at the center of the painting. The painting's artifice did nothing more than match what he already believed. It was good that his mother had not come, though.

The other wall was given over to pictures of godly life, so the crowds were thicker there. The first was aswarm with gods, packed together in a brilliant exercise of composition and color. It shimmered tangibly, even though there wasn't a hint why all those astonishing creatures had been assembled by the artist's mind. That was the one his father said the critics would write about first.

Then came a picture of an abandoned temple with vine-encircled columns, luxuriant overgrowth all around and statues shattered in mid-gesture. It would have fit in the Hudson School

exhibit across the entrance hall. Its evocation of antiquity was
clear and precise enough to masquerade briefly as personal
memory. He could follow the lines of chronic perspective back
to a vanishing point located below the picture's center, an-
choring the genteel ruins to a definite era that ended with a
defeat in another place and conquest, three hundred and fifty
years before the picture was made.

"Why haven't they shown us these before?" he mumbled.
A security man who may have shared this sense of recounted
history caught his eye, glanced at the painting, and continued
walking by.

Timothy passed more portraits and landscapes, but they
failed to elicit any particular emotions. This made him feel a
bit more confident of how well he could control his thoughts
against the paintings' assaults, though he still kept moving
deliberately toward where his father was speaking to the alien,
near the triptych on the far wall.

He looked up as he passed its huge middle panel and slowed
against his will. Masses of dramatically posed figures were
arrayed in the lower foreground, barely visible against the
composition's prevailing darkness. Stars sprayed up from the
jagged skyline behind them.

Timothy examined it warily, ready for the impact of unworldly dimensions, and wondered how many purely godly
things were hidden in the other paintings. He had found something in only a few of them. It seemed unlikely that each one
harbored some coiled assault on the viewer's mind, but that
could be the way the gods did things. One had to be careful.
They would have never been meant for human eyes if they
were genuine. It was only luck and his father's persistence that
had brought them here.

The figures in the middle panel refused to define themselves.
Some appeared to be reaching forward while others stood up-
right. Another line on the painting's right side leaned forward
to meet them; these were painted in a deeper blackness, so
profound that they were indentations in the painting's temporal
surface. This second group may have been pointing their arms

or holding weapons. It was impossible to tell which, but the suggestion was of the latter. Timothy thought of Goya's paintings of the Spanish resistance.

The painting's night sky was rendered in wonderful detail and with far more vibrancy than the galaxy at the other end of the room, but it contained the same threat of dread, terribly amplified and descending upon a darkened city and the immobilized gods before it. Its cool, building fear was simultaneously intriguing and unnerving. Timothy played with it in his mind for a few seconds until it grew so large that the sunlight and security men behind him, and then the city of Washington around him, no longer implied enough protection.

The usual remedy: step back and turn away. This time, however, the fear was not diluted. It only shifted from the merely visual into other channels, now carrying with it an inflexible conviction of place and time. The former was very distant, but located within the artist's own experience; it was not imaginary in any respect. Everything must have been observed at first hand by the god who painted it.

The time of the painting was located in the future but with equal precision. It was naturally depicted in alien units, but done so powerfully that the translation into two hundred and seventy-three terrestrial years followed unbidden. Too soon.

Although the constellations were expectedly unfamiliar, he looked up at them from the city in the picture, not from suburban Washington. He started to believe in what the artist had done and glimpsed the dimensions of other unhuman thoughts lined up behind the painting's inscription of time and dread.

Too much, he thought, *too much*. He was beginning to accept things that he might have fabricated for his own amusement. He escaped and passed one more portrait after the triptych before reaching his father. This was simpler than the others and contained only a man-like creature, certainly a god, half leaning out of an old-fashioned bathtub. A towel was wrapped around his head like a turban, but he seemed otherwise naked. One arm was on a board or portable secretary laid across the tub, holding a sheet of paper with the sketch of a galaxy on it; the other hand had fallen to the floor, holding a pen. The background was a finely textured wall of dark gray and white. Timothy was brutally reminded of David's *Marat Assassinated*, even though he had only seen reproductions.

The time the artist had crafted into the picture was *now*. There was nothing more that Timothy wanted to discover in it. Nevertheless, an encyclopedia of other meanings, histories, whole philosophies were worked into the painting's balance of shape and shadow, and the boy saw their erratic flickerings between the physical setting and the conviction of the alien's death.

The idea that the being was not only dead but had, in fact, just been murdered struck him a second time with as much force as it had when he first looked. His attention slipped for a second and when it returned, it hit him again, starting over from the beginning with an imagined memory of the creature having just been alive. The cycle repeated itself, like the unraveling of an especially clever trompe l'oeil, except that this discovery was not blunted by repetition. It renewed itself with every heartbeat, striking him afresh and with the same impact as if he had just come into the room the painting depicted and found the creature newly dead, newly murdered, time after time, instant after instant.

The scene in the picture remained absolutely static, but the recurrent shock of the alien's death hammered against Timothy's chest and built a foundation to receive other knowledge the artist had grafted into the work. He began to sweat. The other things were there; he could see them more clearly now, and none of them were from his own world.

He ordered himself to move away, but he had never seen death this closely before; in three minutes he had now seen it twenty times over. *This* creature had not been imagined; the melody of a name, sung in the gods' own language, unraveled from the bottom of the sketch sheet the alien still held and threatened to entwine him. He had been a hero, one worthy of ruthless enemies. Their names pursued that of their victim through Timothy's consciousness.

"My son," his father said behind him. His hand closed on Timothy's elbow and turned him around, away from the painting. He asked if anything was wrong. "I thought the woman over there might upset you a bit, but not this badly."

The god was still by Timothy's father, and it was almost a relief to see one of that race confined to three ordinary dimensions. "Could it have been the one behind you?" he asked quietly.

Timothy kept his back to the painting. "I saw the person in it as if he'd just been killed. If I looked back now, I'd think the same thing all over again, from the beginning, as if he'd been brought to life for a moment so he could be murdered again."

"Very good." The alien cautiously shook Timothy's hand in the American fashion. "I am flattered. I tried to put a great deal of history into it. There is . . ."

Timothy was shocked. "That's yours? You painted it?"

"Do you like it?" The alien's forehead wrinkled in the most perfect simulation of concern over whether the boy was telling the truth or just being polite in his father's presence. "I did it . . . years ago, by your measuring, and I thought it was quite daring. You see, there is a lot of political weight to its subject. It caused me no end of trouble when I finished it, but that appears to be behind me now." The god looked at his work again, then at the rest of the exhibition hall and radiated a carefully modulated sense of vindication.

The god continued: "He was a hero, the artist who did the triptych here. A copy, of course. The original is safely . . . ever so safely at home where it continues to influence our race, far more than any simple work of artistic genius could. Many of my kind believe it to be the greatest single work in all of our history." The god's words were underlined by contradictory pride and anger.

The creature looked around at the human security agents and the ten or twelve other gods in the room.

Timothy followed the creature's gaze and noted when it hesitated at two other gods. *Government men*, his instincts

informed him. They, in turn, looked back with the designedly
unconcerned expression of men who did nothing else for their
living but watch their fellows.

"That was why the painter was killed—as I painted it. I
believed that if I could ever approach the genius of his work,
then perhaps I could capture his death. That has meant so much,
too much for us." The creature searched for suitable words in
English and began singing when he could not find them. Timothy and his father both looked away, embarrassed as a thin
melody came from the alien's lips, so softly that none of the
humans around them or the alien security types heard it.

He finished quickly and apologized. "I think the word would
be 'passion.' He invested so much passion in the triptych that
he was killed for it. Or, at least, for what it caused."

"By whom?" Timothy's father asked.

"Why?" Timothy followed.

The god answered the boy's question: "Because his painting
revealed to us the necessity . . . the *imperative* that we go out
to where a great threat was certainly stalking us. Something
that would end us, and which was so powerful that the best
we could ever do would be to meet it as far away from home
as possible." The god's expression saddened, as if he had said
something he had not intended to. "He was Blake. That would
be the closest to your speech."

"Blake, then. How was this Blake killed? How'd he die?"

"By unknown killers who either wanted revenge for what
he had inflicted on our kind or who wanted to make sure its
powers would never be diluted by another work of genius by
him. Legend names a woman. I painted her, too, or at least a
picture of how I thought she would have been. That was pure
imagination, and I am afraid it showed. I never thought that
picture was nearly as good as this one." The god looked at
both of them as if it was their turn to continue. "No. It's not
the woman on the opposite wall. I could never have done that."

The question came to Timothy's mind unbidden: "Was he
right?"

The alien waited too long before answering. "About the threat? He must have been. By definition. We have not found it yet, nor has it discovered us. But the triptych has not created it. It has unveiled the truth. The threat, we believe now, predated the painting and Blake only warned us of it. Simple. Correct? Inescapable. So we are allowed . . . required by this destiny to keep looking. Each light-hour that we move outward without encountering it is that much more time and safety for our homes, and is thus considered a victory."

"A threat?" Andrew Cavan replied, still obviously thinking in terms of artistic metaphor instead of literally, as his son nearly was. "We surely wouldn't have anything to do with such a thing, would we?" He put on his best Deputy Under Secretary's smile.

"Your world seems pleasant enough to me." The god surveyed the mostly white, mostly well-dressed crowd. "It agrees with your own kind." That sounded like something he had memorized.

"But we don't have anything to compare it to," Andrew Cavan continued, and the god looked relieved. "You don't tell us much about your home. Everything we see is so filtered that, except for the shock of your arrival, we've learned hardly anything of you or your kind." He flushed a bit. "You've heard that speech before, Rane."

The god nodded indulgently.

Timothy was taken with the suggestion that the paintings could communicate literal truths. He had not been able to understand why the triptych's powers should be so different from the other paintings which so disturbed him. "You . . . your kind don't, ah, broadcast a certain time to one another in real life, like the sculptures. Or death, over and over again, like your portrait there? Or . . . ?" Timothy's voice faded as he looked across the room.

"Or such lust? Even between lovers? No. Putting such things into the form of paintings is a talent that some of us have. I believe I am one of them, however immodest that sounds. But, except for the triptych, they are always just the carriers of illusions that do not always work. They might strike a chord in some watchers and leave others untouched. You surely do not think there are those of us at home like that, throwing off madness like sparks, or that the hillsides at home really melt together as if they were made of butter. Many of my own race would not be as touched by some of these works as I think you have been, Timothy. You should be proud of yourself."

Andrew Cavan was not listening to them any more. Instead, his attention shifted raptly between Rane's painting of Blake and the triptych on the adjoining wall. His expression showed no distress, so Timothy thought his father might not be seeing as much as he had. Either that, or had seen things like them before.

Then Rane began staring at the paintings himself, as if they were suddenly as foreign to him as they were to the human beings he was talking to. "I really do not know why the government let them come here. I asked, of course. I wanted desperately to come. But, still, that they should have favored me so. . . ."

"It's quite powerful," Timothy said, looking pointedly at the portrait of the murdered god.

"Sometimes I think it is something different than what I had intended. I did it when I was young." He spoke straight past Timothy, to the portrait.

Neither Rane nor his father said anything more. Timothy felt the picture battering against the back of his neck and shoulders. He had almost resolved to examine it again when two security men rushed past them, toward a man standing in front of the portrait of the woman on the opposite wall. His knees were bent forward and his slacks drooped comically below his suit coat. His arms were pumping in front of him. People were drawing sharply away from the man, their faces scarlet and their eyes darting between him and every other place in the room. A woman yelled, and that was followed by a rumble of obscenities from the guards who were now on either side of him.

"Oh, Christ," his father hissed. "That's Dennis." Timothy

recognized the Congressman's name and started laughing when he knew he shouldn't.

Rane gestured questioningly at them. "Is the reaction what one would expect for . . . ?"

The man was nearly lifted from his feet and hustled from the room, one security man diplomatically holding his uniform cap over the man's face and the other hitching up his trousers. "It is impossible that he could have. . . . I mean, the painting is nearly two of your centuries old. And of another race! There are similarities, but it should be impossible for it to strike one of you like that!" The god sounded appalled.

Timothy had glimpsed the man's obsessed expression before the guard's hat covered it. He was able to connect it with newspaper pictures of an aristocratic Senator from Connecticut.

"Terrific." his father muttered against the current of Rane's bewilderment. "Chairman of the Foreign Relations Committee. I thought he said he'd seen enough of this stuff last night."

Andrew Cavan scanned the room for more disasters: "Even better! There's Lombard from the *Post*. The bitch naturally has to be here. Just *has* to be here." A tall, flamboyantly dressed woman was stepping quickly after the security men with a recorder in her hand.

Cavan looked questioningly at his son, then at the knot of people following the Senator as he was hustled out of the room. "This is the first day, Rane. Two positive reactions to what your people assured me would be inaccessible to us: Tim's and the Senator's. Two insights. And that doesn't count what I've felt myself."

"*My* people," the god answered, abruptly cold and remote, "were government officials who know nothing about about *my* works and, except for the triptych, little more about any others'. You, or your government, asked for a sampling of our art, Andrew, and both that government and mine naturally assumed such a thing would be perfect because it would be so remote from you as to be harmless. Great works could be risked before your eyes because you were assumed to be blind. I am not surprised they were wrong."

Then he paused while his voice regained its polish. "Can you believe I warned them about this? *Me?* With my political rehabilitation only ten of your years old? I do not believe any of the worlds my kind have visited have ever *asked* for anything like this." He cleared his throat, reaching for memorized phrases. "Our reactions might be just as unexpected when we visit your places of art."

"But your kind won't, will they? You know it's nothing like this."

"It is still possible that your artists might have unintentionally created things that could strike some of my own kind as strongly as some of these." Rane began to drift away.

Andrew Cavan stayed in conspiratory proximity to the god. The boy trailed to one side, observing both of them. His father now seemed to be the one who was making the other uncomfortable, for Rane slowed down and alternately glanced from his companion to the paintings in the room, seeking their advice and often finding that their creators' visions were as closed to him as they had been to nearly everyone else but the politician and the boy.

They passed through security and stepped out onto the portico. "Is there really insanity in there, Rane, or any history beyond your murdered artist and the copy of his masterpiece?" His father was smiling. "How about that racial dread or the reason why you've come here? Will I be able to see any of that before your government or mine closes the show?" Andrew's voice was dangerously tinged with enchantment.

Rane walked down the Gallery steps ahead of them. "This is turning out badly, Andrew. I will inform my censors. I trust you will do the same."

T HE EXHIBITION'S SECOND DAY PASSED QUIETLY, AL-though the absence of any mention of Senator Dennis's libido in the newspapers cast doubt on how closely the press was being allowed to report it.

Timothy knew what was at the Gallery and could not imagine

that he, the Senator and, though to a much lesser degree, his father were the only ones who had been touched by it. The vision of the ancient woman enticed him at night. Her presence alternated with Blake's and his vastly darker instructions for his race. He awoke breathing heavily because he had not inhaled during the time between physical awakening and the seconds required to throw off his dreams.

"Okay. No murders yet," his father reported when he got home after the exhibition's fourth day. That, Timothy thought, did not include the look his mother was giving him. "No fights. Just some organized protests from the usual bunch of xenophobes and climate-creeps, and a favorable review in *The Star*." He turned the evening paper outward to show his son. "See? Even a nice word about our Rane, though I don't think this reporter saw half of what you did, Tim."

"Then he should write something to the paper. Don't you think so, Andy?" His mother's tone was as brittle as glass. She then predicted violence and said she would be unable to find any artistic justification for that when it happened.

At this, her husband launched into a recitation of great twentieth-century artistic misunderstandings, starting with the assault on the *Pietà* and working forward to the acid-throwing spree at the Metropolitan two years before the gods arrived. And, he continued after his wife had lost interest in the fight, there had been the great days of Stravinsky's music, Diaghilev's ballet and the Armory Show when the scale of rioting was the accepted measure of any new talent.

T HE INSANITY WHICH LEAKED FROM THE SCHOLAR'S PORtrait overcame a group of tourists from Columbus that weekend. The disturbance that resulted should have remained a minor scuffle, but the adjoining portraits of the lady and the soldier (which to that time had not touched anyone's emotions at all) had equally agitated groups of admirers clustered before them. It was as if the artist who had done all three paintings had set ancient trip-wires to await such a confluence of mood, place and audience. Four people were sent to Georgetown University Hospital; one man died there that evening.

The gods expressed their regret and withdrew the three portraits from the exhibition. The rest of the paintings had security screens placed in front of them. The sculptures were judged sturdy enough to protect themselves. The show's scheduled run was also shortened by two weeks.

Attendance tripled, and Andrew Cavan reported to his family that the crowds were becoming more "diverse."

A serious disturbance broke out the following Wednesday. Some of the spectators had come prepared for artistic ecstasy, with wooden nightsticks and epoxy knuckles smuggled past security. Three bodies were recovered afterward.

Actually, four had died. Timothy learned this when Rane appeared at his home that night. He looked even more unworldly than before, pacing about their living room and anxiously making sure the drapes were tightly drawn. Gods never visited private residences this way, uninvited and unchaperoned. He apologized for waking them and then for his painting at the Gallery and for any part it might have played in the recent unpleasantness; he apologized for his fellow artists, for the show, for his government and for the day the decision was made to travel to Earth.

But they, "his dear friends," had to understand that he was an artist who was as separate from his own race—or at least from what it had driven itself to become in the years since Blake inflicted his masterpiece on it—as he was from theirs. Only the blindness of the incompetents at home had permitted him to come to Earth; pure irony, however, had led the same idiots to select his best painting, *The Death of Blake*, to accompany the copy of the triptych. "But *that* follows us everywhere. Or, I should say, it leads us everywhere. Everywhere dark and cold and pointless."

Zee artiste! Burdened wiz zee cares of zee Universe, and no one understands! boiled through Linda Cavan's mind as she brought the coffee tray into the room. *Dad said to never let your contempt show. Never let the yahoos know how they look to you.*

Andrew Cavan asked his son to leave, but Timothy acted as if he had not heard. His father was quickly too enthralled to press the point.

Not even the CIA had gotten a god to loosen up this much. They would hardly have picked up the nickname they did if they behaved as Rane was now, sitting on their sofa, his hands shaking so badly that he could barely hold a coffee cup. Something was falling apart before Timothy's eyes.

Rane continued his apologies. He still believed the races to be far apart in their perceptions and abilities, but some obviously had sensitivities that no one at home had anticipated. "And now," he said, his voice constricted with shame, "we have brought one of your kind back from dying." He shook his head. "From death."

"Who was it?" Andrew Cavan asked, missing the distinction the alien had labored to make.

"There was a young girl at the Gallery. She was caught in the last of the fighting and badly trampled."

"The news said only three had been killed, and they were all adults," Linda Cavan said from the entryway where she had been standing, unwilling to stay in the same room with the god any longer than manners required.

"That was true. But there was also this child . . . and someone did not follow instructions."

"Was she badly hurt?"

"She was killed!" Rane said, suddenly righteous. "Her skull was crushed and her neck broken in two places. The body was stiffening by the time it could be removed. It was brought to our Mission, probably because there is a medical facility there." His voice returned to a mortified hush. "All strictly against everything I thought we were supposed to do here."

"How long without vital signs?" Andrew asked.

The alien's voice spiked up again: "Signs? She was *dead*, Andrew! Her head was a *pulp*! There were no signs."

"You saw her at the Mission?"

"I saw her when she was brought in." Rane looked sickened over what he was telling them. "I made sketches. Can you believe that? I was coming up from the library and passed as they brought her in from the garage. I began sketching. None of the doctors had any time to make me go away.

"I thought of doing another *Blake*. I thought for a short while I could remember how I arranged the lines of perspective in that picture, and how the history of the moment I wanted to portray struck me, from all those years ago. I understood much less of this than I did of Blake and his story, but I was standing there now, watching this unfold! Something that was impossible when I painted my Blake.

"I cannot believe I was capable of doing that. To be struck by a thought like that at such a time and actually begin?"

"She was an alien. Remember?" Linda Cavan murmured coldly.

Rane accepted the observation literally. "Of course. As foreign to me as an ape would be to you." He folded his hands over his eyes and found something the woman's comment had never intended to include. "No. That is unfair to us all. The form is there. Your son has seen what I believed would be invisible to your race. The politician saw something else. And now the rioters.

"The death could therefore be the same, too." He withdrew his hands; his eyes had reddened as if he were attempting to cry. "The techniques were ours, and they were successful, so I must assume her physiology is not so far removed from our own."

"And . . . ?" Andrew Cavan prompted when Rane failed to continue.

"And she was brought back from the dead."

"But that's marvelous."

"I think the doctors at the Mission did it because they were able to do it. There was no more thought given to it than that." Linda Cavan sighed disgustedly at this and stalked away.

"Then your higher-ups don't know about this yet?"

Rane shook his head. "Neither do yours. But they must find out soon."

"What will happen then?"

"You are the diplomat, Andrew. You tell me. There was a point to all of this business at the start, but things are becoming undone. As I said they would."

"But you must have some idea?"

Rane firmed his voice to say something that was against his nature. "She . . . *should* be killed. That would be the political solution, would it not?"

"It might be." The skin was becoming stretched tautly around his neck and jaw. When he saw that Rane was appalled by his agreement he quickly changed the subject. "Is this a common thing?" he continued in a different tone of voice. "To recover the dead?"

"It is done."

"How long after the end of life before it's impossible?"

"Hours, usually. Two days at the most. Though the resurrection of beings as long dead as Blake is still left to artists." Rane attempted a smile, but it hardly worked.

"Can you restore sight to the blind?"

"Even your kind can do that."

"With machines. But can you rebuild the eye and reweave the optic nerve?"

"Certainly. That could be done long before resurrection was feasible. Some of the first experiments were on politically disgraced artists. I believe that some of the tricks of perspective you saw at the Gallery were discovered by blind painters who had their sight imperfectly restored."

"And travel . . . ?"

"Faster than light? Your endlessly asked question. I hardly know. I suppose we can. I only know that I left home and arrived here after not too long a time, and that when I return I expect that my friends will have aged only a little more than I will have." Rane stared at the man as if he were truly puzzled by all this curiosity. "Why is that particular ability so important to your kind?"

Impatience infiltrated Andrew Cavan's voice. "Because it means that someday the universe might be as open to us as it is to you. It was the first thing we thought of when your kind arrived. We've believed for years that it was the great secret you've kept from us. But now it looks like there're many others."

"Would you want the universe to be so open? Why? So you could join the community of the stars and follow all those other daydreams your execrable writers make up? So you would be able to see a few paintings that will only upset you, or to see one in particular that might tyrannize your race for centuries?" He put his coffee cup on the table and pushed both hands out against the man's questions. "I leave things like that to those who can build their lives around them. My inclination is to undermine them whenever I can."

He recoiled against his chair, realizing he had to keep talking. "Though always with sufficient irony and indirection to keep the authorities, upon whom I depend, uncertain. So they will risk sending me to a faraway place and think I will be as incomprehensible, and therefore as inconsequential to the native population, as my works."

Andrew Cavan cleared his throat after a moment and mentioned that the "problem" with the girl was comparatively minor when contrasted to the exhibition and the gods' continued presence on Earth. "The exhibition can't remain open much longer. A story, several of them, will have to be put together, but that shouldn't be too hard."

"And your dead?"

Andrew Cavan had forgotten them. "As I reminded Linda, violence isn't anything new to the arts here. If anything—and once the lawsuits are settled—it'll assure you a footnote in the cultural histories. I don't think there's much danger of a human artist picking up the ability to fix times or feelings so literally within a painting." He looked over at the little bust on the bookshelf. "Things have been changed, but they can be managed."

Rane seemed content with that. Both of them relaxed, settling back into their seats, ignoring Timothy until he asked, "The girl won't be killed, will she?"

"She died at the Gallery, Rane? There's no question about that, is there?"

"None."

"Then . . . it'll be delicate, we don't want to make a bigger fuss than the one the papers'll make if they get hold of this, but I'm sure the right decision will be made. By your people or ours. It doesn't sound like a problem for State anyway. . . ." His father's voice trailed away. His eyes stayed on the bust while Rane looked at the carpet.

"But that it can be done at all . . ." Andrew Cavan said dreamily. "How odd that such information should be dangerous. I know that it is. But, still, such wonder . . ." He shook himself from his reverie. "In any event, I can't see how dealing with the girl herself is any of State's concern. Sounds more like something for goons like Tony Marinetti."

"IT'S THE GODDAMN UN AND THE MORONS IN PARIS," his father was muttering as he walked through the door Friday evening. "And we've got to have a goddamn working group session tomorrow because they can't make the obvious decision and just close it."

His wife knew he was talking about the Gallery exhibition because he had spoken about nothing else for weeks. "It was, after all, Andy, . . ."

"Sure. My bright idea. But only at first and within limitations. I should get a medal for that much of it. It worked, Linda. Didn't it? We got more insights about our friends than we'd collected during all the years before."

"We also got four . . . no, five dead people, a career that'd have been ruined if strings hadn't been pulled quickly enough by family friends, and a son with more problems than he needs right now," she said evenly. "Have you looked at him this week, Andy? Spoken to him about anything except your pet gods and their paintings? *Have* you?" She moved into the entryway and pointed to where Timothy was reading. "He's said a hundred words since you took him to that show. And they've all been about the gods and the poor murdered child they couldn't leave alone."

Her husband braced himself at the mention of the girl, and she pursued her advantage: "Have we left her alone?"

Andrew Cavan dropped his coat on a chair and walked into the kitchen. He poured himself a drink and came back into the hallway. "You've read the paper? I don't know if it's made the television yet."

She moved closer, suppressing a smile. " 'They' couldn't keep it quiet, huh?"

"No. Someone didn't think things through or recognize what was required." He realized his hesitation was only adding to the drama; the episode should be minimized, and it was no longer his direct responsibility anyway.

"So she wasn't eliminated, or re-eliminated, was she?"

Andrew Cavan tried to affect unconcern; neither the Earthly "theys" nor the godly ones had done the wise and expedient thing. He stepped down into the living room and dropped onto the sofa. Ms. Lombard's bylined story occupied the front page of the paper he had with him: "Girl Resurrected by the Gods." Lombard was making up for ground lost when the Dennis story was spiked: "Miracle . . . Death vanquished . . . Parents consumed with gratitude. Verified reports nevertheless greeted with skepticism by National Institutes of Health . . ."

He opened the first section and pointed to other articles. "Here. The really good reactions are starting already: 'Vatican and Canterbury Outraged.' 'Patriarch of Eastern Church Warns of Heresy.' 'Burmese Sect Followers Hail Incarnation of Buddha.' And look at this one: 'Hundreds Killed in Sri Lankan Celebration of Life over Death.' That's my favorite." He dropped back against the cushions and emptied his drink. "Ah, Christ! What will they think of us now? The poor bastards've committed their miracle. They let their divinity out of the bag. Years of playing it safe, staying out of our way, showing us how really civilized creatures should behave until a couple of pea-brained doctors decide to show off. So now *everyone* knows how well they're named! And where the hell does that leave us?''

It took a moment for Timothy and his mother to realize that he was really asking them a question.

"Out of the million things we need from them, this is *not* one of them. At least not now.'' He went back to the kitchen for another drink and was slightly comforted when his wife joined him.

RANE APPEARED AS UNCOMFORTABLE IN ANDREW CAvan's office as he had in his home two weeks ago. A physically similar god accompanied him. Cavan noted how much they looked alike, as well as how the second alien's vastly more self-assured manner set him apart from the artist. The other creature was attached to their New York Mission and had been on Earth for three years. Andrew Cavan had met him when he was negotiating for the first exhibition. He had even been something of a key in reaching an agreement on the terms.

His Anglicized name was Slate, and he worked hard to play the part of an Earth-man. His suit was better cut than Cavan's. He colored his musical speech with diplomatic corps English phrasing that highlighted professional code words, trade talk and parenthetical asides. He was obviously used to being carefully listened to.

Slate explained that he had been asked to try and ease of the recent "misunderstandings" about the National Gallery exhibition. Because he had worked with Cavan on it and was now just as unable as the human was to escape responsibility, it was thought that they should try to repair the damage. "After all, we still believe in the wisdom of the original concept, don't we, Andy?''

Cavan was alert to a set-up. Rane's expression showed that the artist had reached the same conclusion. Slate continued to smile as politely as he had from the moment he entered the office. "The business with the girl was regrettable. People will realize we acted out of the best motives."

Cavan tried to be formally correct but was unable to keep the wonder out of his voice. "It wasn't saving her that was the problem. It was just that your race could do it at all. It's as startling as your arrival, years ago."

"But surely you realize the procedure is considered extraordinary by us, too. It's difficult and can only work within strict limitations. It is not as if we can just pronounce a magical spell . . ."

Cavan interrupted. "The girl was a bloody mess when she was brought in. We got the pictures your staff took, the originals, before the press could. She was dead. Now she's alive in the spotlight, so we have to either explain or credibly ignore it."

The god was unconcerned. "People will forget. Or they will accommodate. Even for this. You've accepted us and our spacefaring without going seriously to pieces over it. I imagine the recent advances of your own medical science would appear just as miraculous if they were taken back a hundred years. You have the resiliency of all reasonably intelligent species. There'll be some short-term problems, of course: cults and some religious disruptions and the like, until this can be put in perspective.

"Now, Rane and I have some ideas that may help." He looked at the other alien who, in turn, appeared to wilt. Slate reached into his portfolio, withdrew a sheet of paper and put it on the desk in front of Cavan. It was a pencil portrait of a young woman of indeterminate race; initially, her features implied both the gods and humankind.

"Is this new?" Cavan asked, pleased by the thought. Rane acknowledged that he had done it yesterday. Cavan admired the draftsmanship as he half-waited for the picture's trap to spring.

He blinked once, and the face on the paper shifted. He saw Linda as she had been when they first met in Amsterdam; then a complete tapestry of her life before she met him telescoped out behind her picture, accurate in the most minute detail.

Andrew Cavan suppressed a gasp of recognition, distracting him long enough for the portrait to blur and re-form itself into the face of his first wife, whose name he never mentioned aloud. The picture's history of her life was, during the instant he indulged himself, equally complete.

Each time he disengaged himself from the drawing, it revised itself to suggest another woman he had loved or desired beyond the limits that his age and circumstances had permitted.

Finally, he blinked and thought he saw a tall, coltish girl in the sixth grade in a small Idaho city. The life before she met him was no more than two or three heartbeats tucked behind a mane of blond hair. That elicited a peculiar light that flared briefly and then shrivelled to a firefly of sentiment.

"Is it acceptable?" Slate asked with polished sincerity. "The idea of a gift was mine but the work was naturally Rane's." He turned his aristocratic face toward the artist. "Genius, don't you think?"

Cavan nodded, shaken by Rane's talent. *This was done on Earth!*

"This should be considered part of a new first step. I believe it was wrong to hide our individual selves for so long. No wonder this exhibition is such a shock to so many of you. We must prove to your race that we have hearts and feelings as diverse and idiosyncratic as your own. By staying so aloof, we've unintentionally let ourselves be seen as an undifferentiated mass of supernatural creatures. A . . . ." He searched for a word.

"Pantheon?" Cavan suggested.

"Exactly. All gods look alike. Therefore, all gods think, feel and believe alike. That's the way we must appear to you and especially to societies on other parts of the planet that have a collectivist way of looking at race anyway. If a person believes one is an interchangeable part of a larger mass, then one partakes of all the larger than, ah, human powers and deficits of that group.

"So, how are we, each one of us, perceived? I would think

that each of us is credited with all the outward abilities of everyone else. I wouldn't be surprised to find an absolute resistance in the ordinary human mind, nowadays, to seeing me, for instance, as a distinct, moral being. Instead, I'm probably, if subconsciously, credited with Rane's artistic talent, just as he is probably credited with the ability to understand superluminal travel. And all of us may now be credited with the recovery of that unfortunate girl. This is wonderful for our self-esteem, but it is wrong and it is dangerous. It is not why we are here.''

Cavan suppressed the urge to ask the reason, but it was clear that Slate would not answer. His speech was not directed at that issue.

"The National Gallery exhibition was too limited. It must be expanded.''

Cavan started to object.

"If we did anything less, it could appear that we really do have something to hide.''

Cavan wondered if this preposterous idea came from home or if Slate had cooked it up all by himself—perhaps to vindicate what had already been done, no matter how badly it had turned out. That was a common enough approach among Earthly politicians. But Cavan was not sure if he wanted the gods to disavow their divinity, no matter how they thought about themselves.

Slate nevertheless seemed pleased by the reception he was getting. Rane stayed slouched in his chair, his eyes fixed on a spot on the front of Cavan's desk.

He next took a sheaf of engineering drawings and a book from his portfolio and placed them on the desk beside Rane's sketch. "Now, this may seem unnecessarily dramatic, but I assure you I've thought about this a great deal. These should be sufficient to understand and begin pilot production of our small fusion engines, the ones you seem to admire so much.''

Cavan was naturally pleased, but this did not seem all that momentous. "The theoretical basis for those devices was disclosed by your scientific attaché last year in Stockholm.''

"This isn't 'theory.' This is practical information to build them. 'Applied technology' would be the correct term. The 'nuts and bolts.' '' The alien diplomat smiled indulgently, aware that he was again achieving his desired effect.

Cavan stared back at him, elevating his kind back onto the very pedestal Slate had descended from to dispense all that talk about mortality a few moments ago. He carefully picked up the papers that had been placed in front of him. The drawings looked like conventional engineering blueprints; except for elaborately encircled blocks of alien script, all the notations were in English. He opened the book and leafed through enough of it to see that it was basically in English too. Passages of mathematics and symbolic logic seemed to employ conventional terminology.

Is it happening now? he thought carefully. *Why have they chosen this moment? Now they're placing this in our hands. . . . In my hands.*

Slate read his reaction perfectly: "We thought it simply easier to give it to one of our friends, and trust in his good sense to make the proper people aware of this, than to make a fuss over it ourselves and risk creating the wrong impression. As we have by waiting too long before revealing our art.''

They've made my career. The venality of the idea did not repel Cavan as he thought it should. He rationalized: *Perhaps because they are drawing me past that already.* It may also be that, as Rane so clearly believed, the whole tactic of artistic revelation was misguided and dangerous. But even if it was, he could not help but join Slate in this colossal error.

CAVAN CALLED WENTWORTH AT NSA AND JUDY IRELAND at the Defense Advanced Research Projects Agency as soon as the two gods left. He had lunch brought in for all of them and made as big a deal as the time allowed over the fusion engine design material.

They looked as he imagined he had when Slate gave him

the information that morning. They were not the first to touch the book and drawings, but being the second and third to do so was good enough to ensure that their personnel files would be illuminated for years to come it.

Rane's sketch stayed in Cavan's office safe and was not mentioned.

Andrew Cavan told them there were plans to expand the exhibition at the National Gallery, rather than shutting it down as everyone had supposed would happen. He outlined Slate's thinking behind it and found himself arguing more forcefully than he had intended that the risk was worth taking.

Ireland was a person of such natural severity that she would not have thought the prospect of more alien art of much importance even if her attention had not been so completely absorbed by the material on the engines. She said it was a thoughtful gesture by the aliens, questioned whether it was necessary and returned to the drawings.

Wentworth, an academic with specialties in philology and cryptography, had been working on the gods' language since they arrived. The book and drawings could be a Rosetta stone for him. Or perhaps it was only Cavan's desire to share the moment immediately with someone who *knew* about such things and had hungered for a breakthrough as Wentworth had for years. Anthony Marinetti had too, but neither he nor his bosses could be trusted to do the *right thing*. Their concerns were always elsewhere.

"THIS," LINDA BEGAN, TAPPING THE PRESS RELEASE with her fingertip, "is not going to work. They're going to have something uncontrollable on their hands." She was usually in an analytical mood in the morning, and especially so on Sundays.

Her husband answered as he had during each of their prior conversations, explaining Slate's reasoning and that it had been endorsed with varying degrees of enthusiasm at the highest levels of contact between men and gods. They looked at him as if he were a great distance away instead of sitting just across the kitchen table. His son moved closer in response while Linda carefully pushed her chair away.

T HE SHIP LANDED ON FEBRUARY 25 WHEN THE WINTER'S only snowfall was still on the ground. The reflected sunshine combined with its customary optical distortions to make looking at it difficult for more than a few seconds at a time.

Security was heavy, as both the gods and the government had desired. A double cordon of D.C. riot police marked off the five-hundred-meter stretch of the Mall across from the National Gallery where the ship had descended. Quiet lines of people, bundled against the unusual cold, pressed against temporary barriers blocking the cross streets. Silenced helicopters hovered discreetly above the nearest buildings.

Andrew Cavan and his son were in the group of dignitaries directly under the bow of the ship. Linda had declined his invitation to attend.

Cavan was flattered when Slate, resplendent in a dark shearling coat, sought them out in the dignitaries' section below the bow of the ship. Rane accompanied the diplomat, appearing a little happier than he had the month before when Andrew met him at the Department. He even took Cavan and his son briefly away from Slate to introduce them to several other artists. Although these others exhibited the monotonous perfection of their race, they still looked at both humans and other gods with measurable unease. Two of them were the first aliens Cavan had met who could not speak English.

There was a cluster of microphones placed by the ship's extended landing ramp. The Secretary of State made a speech about the new era of understanding between the races, parroting Slate's rationale for expanding the exhibition but omitting mention of the fusion engine designs even though reports of their disclosure were already leaking to the press.

The alien Chief of the Washington Mission confined himself

to similar generalities. He had the same trouble as the Secretary with his speech writers' euphemisms describing the works of art that had just been brought down. The public landing and the new art should, they explained in simplistic terms, de-mythologize the gods; but the echoing speeches, the ship's coruscating image and the cold, dense winter air invested the moment with sufficient mystery to defeat this rational intent. The effect was tinged with something Timothy guessed he could hate once he understood it.

When the Chief of Mission finished his speech, he gestured toward the ship's landing ramp, and two gods in blue coveralls emerged, carrying a framed painting between them. Andrew Cavan had assumed the works would at least be crated; their immediate exposure seemed precipitous and needlessly pro-vocative. He looked over at Slate and found the alien diplomat smiling as serenely as he had all morning, glancing at Rane and the other artists with contrived admiration.

Andrew Cavan examined it as it was brought past and found only an ordinary landscape of an ordinary world. His arm was pressed against his son's shoulder, and he was further reas-surred when the boy betrayed no reaction.

The next work carried out was an oil portrait. Cavan braced himself again, but it was without sufficient power to assault him. His son might have tensed or inhaled too sharply, but it was hard to be sure.

The Secretary and the Chief of Mission looked on approv-ingly as more pictures and sculptures were unloaded. Slate occasionally guided one or another of the artists to the podium, presumably to take credit for a particular work. Several of Cavan's colleagues from State or Defense stifled yawns, and even some of the gods seemed distracted.

The works grew in size and complexity as they emerged from the ship. Large sculptures were brought out on tracked carriers. Cavan thought that his son was reacting directly to some of them, and even the Secretary once rose unnaturally on the balls of his feet when a certain work paraded by.

Anticipation was building up in his chest. *All this should've been previewed by State psychologists.* There would have been time for something like that.

Then Cavan heard a shout. It was sharp and implied both recognition and profound misunderstanding.

A figure broke away from the crowd at the end of 7th Street. The man dodged around the security barriers, followed the street and then ran onto the snow, toward the corridor of Park Service police and the gods carrying art to the Gallery.

He was powerfully built, and none of the Park Service guards were armed. He reached the line and knocked over the two nearest humans before lunging at a tracked carrier with a sculpture on it.

Andrew Cavan blinked and tried to understand what was going on. None of it was happening too quickly enough to be grasped, but he had lost the ability to move. Slate's expression reflected the same paralysis. Only Rane and a few of the other artists seemed able to do anything, and they were simply turning away from the man's assault on their works or looking embarrassedly at the ground.

"Fanatic," Cavan murmured with absolute conviction as he focused on the man's face. *Because of that?* he added involuntarily, shifting his attention to the sculpture's monstrous tangle of limbs.

The man leaped onto the carrier and threw himself against it. Andrew Cavan, Timothy and every other human gasped as a shock wave of morbid possession radiated from the impaled figure. The impression of unlimited wealth, great enough to overpower every restraint of manners, taste or practical feasibility, suddenly focused through the man's body and out toward the human mob. Detailed catalogues of self-indulgence and whim, all leading instantly to hedonistic decadence, became desires for which Andrew Cavan reflexively decided he had a right to demand satisfaction. And, more appealing still, there was a sensation of immortal confidence and ease, such that one could recline at leisure and dissect every corrupt pleasure into its parts and prices, and easily pay for each one. Lace and cloth-of-gold seemed draped across Andrew's shoulders, and he recoiled from the uncouth pressure of his son's skin (as his son did from his own) before he tried to arrest his descent.

It was too unexpected to prepare any emotional defenses. Only the gods and several of the ranking human soldiers around him seemed unmoved.

Timothy shrugged his father away when he tried to shield his eyes from the spectacle. Then the slabs of plastique sewn into the man's overcoat detonated. The blast was initially white, so it looked as if the trampled snow had abruptly risen to engulf the carrier. He thought he could see the shock-globe devour the Park Service people and gods closest to it.

Andrew Cavan was instantly returned to familiar territory. He was able to grab his son with all his strength and drive him to the ground. He had seen such things often enough in Earthly cities. His calm was now the same as it had been during the worst days in London during the IRA's proclaimed Last Summer. The shock front and the deafening report arrived carrying fragments of metal and body parts.

Then there was the usual theatrical pause while the immediate landscape returned to the horizontal, revealing the inevitable crater with the twisted chassis in the center of it. In Zurich it was often a Mercedes with the bomb in its trunk; in London, always an Alvis Saladin IV which hit a street mine. The immediate, consuming idea of wealth the sculpture had projected was now a remote memory, like the idea of a squandered inheritance.

Bodies were arrayed in roughly concentric circles, the degrees of mutilation increasing with proximity to the crater. Those nearest the blast were in pieces. Complete corpses did not appear until midway between the blast center and where Cavan had been standing. A neat line of gods, most of them still grasping the works of art they had been charged with, had been blown down like a row of dominos. Only those more than sixty meters from the crater were attempting to stand up.

A squad of Secret Service agents, some visibly bleeding from scalp wounds or impassively bracing broken arms, pushed through the stunned crowd to look after the Secretary and other dignitaries. Groups from the uniformed security perimeter and gods from inside the ship began moving with perceptible acceleration, though only some of their actions made any immediate sense to Cavan. It was as if the people and gods on the Mall, himself included, were gradually freeing themselves from entrapment in winter amber, moving their heads and then their arms and legs until they shook off the afterthought of the man and the sculpture's incandescent truth.

A wind loaded with ice crystals, kicked up by descending helicopters, abraded his cheeks. Six landed around the spaceship, rotary cannons pointed outward, while six more hovered at fifty meters, each covering a different sector of the perimeter.

All right, he thought, *all right. Protect the kid. Thank God Linda's not here. Scan the rooftops. Look for the follow-up.* All by the book. But he was articulating this only to himself. His attention was not where correct counterterror procedures dictated, but on the blast crater in front of him.

Now gods came running out of the ship and hurried toward the bodies nearest the crater. Some were carrying instrument cases while others pushed levitation pallets with stretchers and elaborate machineries on them.

The realization came to Andrew Cavan as suddenly as the sculpture on the carrier had closed its trap, just as the man was hurling himself upon it: *They're going to save them! Bring them back to life in front of all of us! Oh, Jesus! This can't happen now! Please don't let it happen!*

He left his son and ran over to Slate. The diplomat's beautiful coat was stained with mud and a glistening, ichorous liquid seeping from a wound on his right shoulder.

"Stop them," Andrew Cavan hissed.

"From doing what?" Despite the clarity of his voice, Slate had trouble standing and focusing his eyes.

"They're going to do it again, aren't they?"

Slate surveyed the blast area. "They'll only bring our own kind back. There won't be another mistake."

The podium had been blown down and the elegant figure of

their Mission Chief was on the ground beside it. One arm was bent entirely around his back, and the snow was melted beneath his abdomen.

"That's going to be almost as bad!" Cavan knew he was starting to yell, but no one around seemed to notice. "The secret's out. Remember? That's what we're trying to keep the people from thinking about. Can't you just . . ." His words trailed away as he realized there was no civilized way to put the matter.

"We'll assist our own kind, Andrew. Concern for your people's sensibilities can't stop that. If you see any of our personnel foolishly helping a human being, please feel free to ask them to stop." The modulated accent slipped from Slate's voice, leaving only a mechanically correct assemblage of syllables.

The gods had come up with a stupid answer to a problem they had not understood—and Cavan had joined them in it. Now they were going to compound it; their planned revelation of individuality and mortality was going to be the accidental stage on which they would—with only the most commendable intentions—demonstrate that they could overcome death as easily as they could probably overcome the laws of physics.

One team already had their Chief of Mission on a levitation pallet with boxes of various shapes plugged into him. Others were retrieving body parts and then going from one nearby torso to another, roughly trying the fit of this limb or that together until they had reassembled a complete body. At least they were discarding arms or legs flowing blood instead of ichor.

Andrew Cavan trotted uncertainly toward the blast crater. It was every bit as bad as London had been. But then he had not had this fustration to deal with nor had there been the bizarre winter scene, the glittering spaceship, the orbiting helicopters and aliens dispensing life to selected victims.

A god in coveralls splattered with blood and ichor emerged from the blast crater with a human head in one hand, held it up for critical examination as if it were Yorick's, and then tossed it back in the hole. The hair color was right, and it might have been the bomber's.

Human medical personnel were arriving by now. They bent over the human survivors with the usual paraphernalia, but the EMTs and doctors frequently looked up from their work to see what the gods were doing with their fellow creatures. Andrew Cavan watched as one physician even stopped what he was doing and, despite the protests of the technicians who were assisting him, walked over to a group of aliens. They were clustered around a barely recognizable form with the entire left side of its torso ripped open; unfamiliar organs spilled out onto the snow. They were unaware of the doctor's presence, so he could watch with an expression of childish delight as a leg was found and placed into rough alignment with the shattered hip joint; entrails were gently fitted into a fiber harness that anchored itself to the edges of the long wound, became opaque and then slowly tightened, drawing the tissues back into the body. Tubes were inserted into exposed arteries and granular substances, rather than fluids, fed into them.

The doctor drew back when the half-reconstructed torso jerked and a bar of music that resembled the gods' natural speech came from the pulverized mass that had been its head. The physician tore himself away, worshipful fear written on his face, and went back to his human patient.

The area was becoming overrun with aliens and humans. Press and television helicopters had replaced the military ships over the buildings lining the Mall, although their wavering flight indicated that they were being warned away.

Cavan felt his emotions returning to a manageable level. He now believed he had always known the gods could perform miracles. This only confirmed his judgment.

He finally took inventory of himself, the first thing he should have done after it was apparent the attack would not be followed up. Everything felt fine, although his overcoat was smeared with blood and fragments of tissue. He undid the buttons, pressing his fingers tenderly against his chest as if the lack of pain might have deceived him and his guts would burst out from some internal pressure if he tested them too roughly. He had taken a small-caliber bullet during London's Last Summer and remembered that the momentary excitement had so obscured his pain that he had not even seen a doctor until the evening after the attack. Again, everything seemed normal.

He resumed walking, faster now. The blood could not have been Slate's because theirs was honey tinted or almost clear, as mythic ichor was supposed to be; proof of that was lying all around him. *Could it be Tim's?* He had not checked the boy.

Andrew Cavan sprinted the last ten meters to where he had left Timothy. A medical technician in a green Georgetown University Hospital parka was bent over the boy's body, cutting away pieces of shredded clothing. The man looked up at Cavan but gave no outward sign of recognition or concern. He returned to his work, inserting an IV feed and cannister into the exposed subclavian artery.

There was major damage to his upper chest. Something had hit the boy there and driven inward; rib ends and a fractured sternum protruded into the ragged cavity. Cavan could not believe he had missed the impact of something like that. He had been either standing next to the boy or actually covering him as he tried to pull him to the ground. A random fragment of the sculpture or the carrier, turned into shrapnel, must have passed between them.

The boy's face, speckled with blood, was absolutely white. The clinical details of the London episode kept returning to Cavan: *Listen for the whistling of air through a punctured lung; eye movement or pupil dilatation; smell of bowel release.* He ran through the checklist, pushing the thought of the boy himself further back from his consciousness as each item was checked off.

Andrew Cavan knelt down carefully. He had to move each muscle individually or risk collapsing. He tried to ask the technician a question, but his throat had closed too tightly to allow anything but a choking sigh to escape. The man looked up anyway: "This is pretty bad. See anyone around with equipment?"

Andrew Cavan found his voice: "What kind?"

The man actually had three fingers of his right hand inside the boy's chest, probing underneath the edge of the split sternum.

"Ah, shit! Uh, chest vacuums. Although. . . ." He withdrew his hand and moved the IV neck cannister so he could read the tiny LED display. "This guy's got about five more minutes before there'll be too much damage to keep trying. He's probably already got cognitive impairment that'll take a resident micro to handle."

The technician went back inside the chest. He kept working with the same methodical gestures, but his features were going soft and his voice rose in pitch until it began to sound like Cavan's. "Oh, please, Jesus, please," he said, entirely to himself while his hands tried to find enough intact artery to insert a self-contained linear pump. "Goddamn. Damn."

The cannister began a delicate chiming. A doctor came over and reminded the EMT that he was now working outside of protected ethics: "I can't stop you, but I won't help, and even if you win you'll have to account for it if the kid's worthless."

The technician abruptly jerked his hands away. "Right. Right!" His voice went back down to normal. He had been following the boy down, too, but the doctor broke the tie and released him. "Can't win by now anyway." He hurridly unclipped the neck cannister and withdrew the equipment he had emplaced in the chest. Connecting tubes and wires were left hanging out of the wound.

The technician gathered up his equipment and nearly stumbled in his haste to get away from the corpse. He said nothing to Cavan and had probably not guessed he was anything but a spectator. There was no reason for any anger with the man's behavior; he had presumably done what he was supposed to and, it seemed, had tried to do a bit more. The doctor was correct: bringing Timothy back would have been wrong; three minutes ago it might not have been; now it was.

A breathlessness filled Andrew Cavan's mind. The carnage around him was no longer like London but as foreign as the gods' home worlds; the milling crowds around the Mall and the helicopters behind him were as indistinct as the spaceship— they all partook of realities that had slipped from his grasp.

He touched the boy's face tentatively, and then roughly when he was unable to accept how cold it was. The head had an unaccustomed weight to it; it lolled back into the churned-up snow at his touch. He thought he should be remembering scenes from their lives, from *his* life, but could not. He could barely recall the boy's name, let alone the last thing they had done together before coming to the Mall. That was the extent of it until the death found a way to explode the vacuum with the energy of tears and panic.

Andrew Cavan tried to rise as suddenly as the medical technician had. This time he did fall over. His head landed on a soft lump of tissue which he recognized as a section of a god's hand, cut neatly down from the intersection of the middle and ring fingers to the wrist.

He stood up and started moving away from the boy, without any idea where he was going. The glare was less now that the afternoon was coming on, and much of the Mall had been churned into a frigid bog by victims and rescuers. There were knots of frantic activity along the crowd's perimeter, especially near the steps of the National Gallery where the works of art that had not been carried inside before the blast had been dropped. Some figures in blue coveralls, presumably gods, were struggling with the larger works while other figures leapt over barriers and ran toward them, until these humans were either tackled or ridden down by Park Service police.

Cavan thought he could see specks of light, like photo flashes, appear against the encircling lines of people. The crackle of gunfire followed, but he was ready to believe that he had constructed this out of his own irrationality.

The flashes continued. He slowed and watched more carefully. London's Last Summer reappeared as a subtext to the unbearable acknowledgement of Timothy's death. It refused to vanish this time as he recoiled in shame from its distraction. The frequency of the lights increased and nearly each one was accompanied by a sharp retort. Waves of furious yelling underlay the gunfire.

Several of the blue figures fell and rolled down the Gallery's steps. A government rider was jerked from his horse by something unseen. Cavan felt a calming horror as other riders moved toward the building, unmistakably drawing riot guns from saddle scabbards. "Crystal Palace riots all over again," he murmured to himself: *Before he was born.*

The groups of Park Service, Secret Service and regular Army people who had rushed to help the dignitaries now regrouped and ran to position themselves across from where the crowds were most turbulent.

I must bring him home, he thought. He could form a recognizable picture of his son, either alive or dead, only with conscious effort. He also imagined dishonor when he next asked himself why he should risk anything for that. *Linda's heart would demand it. Even though she's as lost to me now as the boy is, anyway.* That was enough of an answer.

Cavan walked as quickly as his sense of unreality allowed, stepping over corpses and around godly and human medical teams. The crowd along the eastern edge of the Mall seemed calmer, but they were farther away, and the roaring and irregular gunfire behind him could easily be hiding what was going on over there.

The alien ship loomed over him. The image of the sun rested just on top of its wavering outline but did not drop behind it as he approached. The gravitational forces necessary to cause such lensing must have been stupendous, but he felt nothing unusual in their presence.

He slowed as he spotted Slate again. The alien was standing beside the pallet with their Chief of Mission on it. Another pallet carrying machinery was beside it, and clusters of gods anxiously tended the controls.

The right sleeve of Slate's coat had been cut away at the shoulder. Enough flesh and muscle had been torn away to reveal the shoulder joint's contours. A technician was fitting an articulated brace to the exposed bones and gluing it in place. He was transparently irritated with his patient.

Slate, on the other hand, was standing absolutely still, starring fixedly at the alien on the pallet and evincing no pain at all. He had consciously elevated himself above that. Cavan had watched some humans transport themselves past physical agony during the Last Summer, especially when they knew their own miscalculation had helped cause the disaster.

Slate nearly smiled at Cavan when he was a meter away. The technician working on the diplomat's shoulder dropped some tiny mechanism he had been trying to implant in the exposed shoulder joint and sang a curse.

"Andrew! Are you all right? My apologies for being rude, but all of this. . . ." He waved his left hand to take in the terrible scene. "I can't believe such a thing could happen here. In your city, of all places. And especially now, when we're trying so hard to . . . to fix things. . . ."

"Is the Ambassador badly hurt?" That was easier to talk about.

"There's critical damage to his left arm and spinal column. He'll require a lot of reconstruction before he can even be moved. I'm sorry we have to do this out here. They'll take him inside the ship as soon as they can."

Slate paused until he saw the rest was inescapable. "Your son isn't here. He was standing with you during the speeches. Is he all right?"

"He's dead."

"That should not have happened. Your son understood Rane's painting and others at the Gallery." Then he smiled wanly. "His understanding probably exceeded my own."

"Would it be possible . . . ?" Andrew Cavan's voice ran dry. He was at war with himself and prayed that Slate would not sense it. "Could your people . . . if they can be spared . . . look at him?"

"But why?" Slate asked with complete innocence.

Cavan felt all the restraints break at once. "Maybe he can be saved."

He expected an expression of smug vindication from the god. Instead, Slate's idealized features saddened until he almost looked the way Rane had at his home, weeks before. He looked at his own wound, at last acknowledging the medic's existence. The other god began ladling synthetic tissue into the wound with a surgical trowel.

The Chief of Mission's pallet passed by them, floating a meter above the ground. A segmented metal spine with arrays of tubes and wires emerging from either side into the torn, glistening flesh had been placed along his back. Two godly technicians guided it up the entry ramp and into the ship.

"Could you at least see if there's something left to save?"

"And do the very thing you told me was going to ruin us here. I know how you feel, Andrew, but that would only make things worse. There're bad enough now as it is. I think we should just collect our dead, pull back to our castles or back into space entirely, and be the gods you saw us as all along. Then we could pursue our work and leave when we're done."

Slate's mention of departure shoved aside all thoughts of his son. *Leave? The world without them?* It was momentarily less tolerable than a world without Timothy or Linda. Cavan willed his dead son back into the center of his mind. "Then there's nothing to be lost from another miracle. I know, I know. They aren't miracles. They're just what you're able to do, and I'm betraying . . . something by asking you to do this." Cavan was disturbed at how easy it would be for him *not* to ask the god this favor.

"Then we would be doing you or him no great favor," Slate replied bitterly. Then he waved it away: "Where is he? I don't know anything about how these things are done. This conversation may be putting him beyond the reach of useful recall."

Cavan ran back to his son. Slate sang a short melody to some godly technicians who fell in after him with a levitation sled.

All the bodies left on the snow were human. A dark line of

people had crossed in front of the National Gallery. Mounted police were trying to cut off the stream of figures ascending the steps.

The National Archives was just across 7th Street from the Gallery. It was a smaller building, concerned with merely human history. There were no signs of violence there, aside from two orbiting helicopter gunships.

Andrew Cavan finally pushed away Slate's remark about the gods departing and replaced it with emotionally correct grief for his son. The boy's corpse had been trampled during the short time he had been away. His arms were twisted grotesquely away from the shoulders. A large oval depression was centered over the ear on the right side of the skull, and his eyes had been partially forced from their sockets by the impact that caused it.

The two medical types who followed Slate let their pallet sink to the mud beside the boy. Slate stepped closer to look, but then drew back, repelled by the sight.

"The pictures of the young girl you saved after she was brought in from the Gallery weren't much better." Cavan tried to sound analytical. "Your ship's here. You have all the powers of your fleet. If that's not enough, there's the ship orbiting behind Jupiter. The big one inside the magnetic bow shock." He had not meant to mention that last part; Wentworth had sworn him to secrecy over it, but mentioning it now had been part of a logical progression.

The medics placed the same pillowy capsules they had used on the Chief of Mission around the boy's arms.

Slate looked at Cavan with disciplined indecision. Cavan recognized his expression: *The locals are confounding you because they are beginning to love you as you always secretly wanted.*

The two gods worked on the boy for several minutes before one of them sang softly into a radio. Another pallet was brought up by three more technicians, this one freshly splattered with ichor. Globes the size of softballs were taken from it and attached to the boy's head; another with a perforated lower hemisphere was inserted into his chest wound.

The rioting around the Mall perimeter was losing momentum. Knots of people would cluster together, move from one side to another; there would be a brief spray of muzzle flashes, or a more intense light when someone dropped or threw a Molotov bomb. Then mounted police broke up the knot, and the process would be repeated somewhere else.

Whenever he returned his attention to the boy, he found that something had been closed, healed, or covered with a device. Brief verses of song passed between the technicians, interrupted by sounds that could have been amusement.

Rane found them, surveyed the work with a look of incomprehension and then put his hand on Cavan's shoulder. "This is more important..." It was obvious he did not know how to finish the sentence.

T HEY TOOK THE BOY INTO THE SHIP AS IT WAS BEGINNING to get dark. The northern side of the Mall had been cleared, but a group of rioters still played tag with the police around the Gallery. Two of the helicopter gunships remained, and a detachment of National Guard armored cars had been brought up for the night. No one knew if the gods would remove what the Mayor stupidly called their "blatant provocation," but the hope was that they would.

Cavan watched the late news in his office. No one was answering the telephone at home. He tried to focus on the boy's mangled body, and at intervals sufficient grief emerged from the stillness of his heart to drive his head down into his hands. But an irrational hope asserted itself between these attacks. What the gods had done with his son, how they had patched and straightened him and acted as if he was not yet beyond their grasp, began to affect Andrew Cavan. He welcomed it against all his training.

He took a copy of the book and design drawings Slate had given him from his office safe. Wentworth had highlighted the pages where fragments of the gods' native script was embedded in the English text.

"This is the first opening. Know that, Andy?" he had told him the week before. "The first chance to get a fix on their grammatic structures. Doesn't look like the Rosetta stone yet. And they couldn't have done this on purpose, could they?"

The basis for Wentworth's excitement eluded him, but at least there, in plain English, were promises of unlimited electrical power. There were even cost projections for prototypes and graphs showing economies of scale for mass production, all reduced to constant, current-year dollars. It seemed unaccountably trivial to Andrew Cavan.

A news bulletin jolted him awake at 3:00 A.M. The ship had departed. There was no mention of anyone having emerged from it during the evening. Andrew Cavan called the appropriate people. Nearly all of them were at their duty stations but no one knew anything about his son; he was careful not to imply that the gods had taken him.

A D.C. police lieutenant answered his call to the gods' Mission. After Cavan convinced him of his importance, the officer said that the embassy staff had left around seven the prior evening and gone to the Mall. Two had been beaten when their car was stopped by rioters on the north side of the Mall; police had intervened and delivered them to their ship.

The lieutenant asked him if that had been the right thing to do, as if anyone had been in a position to do anything else. Cavan assured him that, from State's point of view, it unquestionably was.

The lieutenant remarked upon the piles of incinerated documents, erased data disks and other traditional evidence of a hastily evacuated embassy. Most D.C. cops had seen that sort of thing before.

The senior Under Secretary was audibly surprised when Cavan answered his office phone at five. After he collected himself, he told Cavan that the gods' Mission had been set on fire twenty minutes before despite police efforts. He asked if Cavan knew anything that could help explain what was going on. The

National Security Council was meeting at ten, and briefing papers were required. The Secretary, said the voice at the other end of the line over the scrambler hiss, was still in intensive care at Bethesda and would not be able to contribute anything himself.

No one appeared to debrief or interrogate Cavan that morning. He was assumed to be too important for such things unless the situation was very grave indeed. The draft report he handed to the armed messenger two hours later said nothing about his son.

T HE NEXT FEW DAYS WERE EXTREMELY UNPLEASANT. Unrest increased rather than quieted after the departure of the gods' ship and the burning of their Washington Mission. The President and the new Acting Secretary of State communicated the nation's deepest regrets for what had happened to the gods. Special apologies, all drafted by Cavan, were sent to the Missions that remained open in New York, Toronto, Denver and San Francisco. These efforts at conciliation and understanding were not helped by the speeches given by some prominent individuals, Senator Dennis among them, that boiled down to "good-bye and good riddance."

An organized mob tried to ransack the National Gallery, which still contained the works that had made up the original exhibition as well as those brought from the ship before the explosion. They were stopped, but only after considerable violence and loss of life. The works were removed to the Gallery's deepest subbasement, and regular service personnel were assigned to guard them.

Cavan stayed at his office during the week after the gods left. Linda visited him twice, though travel into the city was difficult. They agreed she would not attempt it any more than necessary.

She was distraught but reassured when he lied that Timothy had only been hurt and taken to a military hospital in Virginia. Cavan had enlisted Wentworth and those colleagues who owed him a favor to produce documents, reports, and nursing notes, along with a remarkably convincing phone conversation Linda thought she had with her son. This was put together from archival tapes; everyone above GS–11 had tapes of themselves, their spouses and children on file so videos or conversations could be fabricated to suit any number of contingencies.

L INDA CAVAN'S GRANDFATHER HAD BEEN THE *CHARGÉ d'affaires* when Saigon fell. Her father was the First Secretary in Paris during the student riots in 1997 and when the real thing happened, five years later. She had grown up in the Foreign Service and harbored a genteel contempt for her second-generation Irish husband who could make such a point of being an exile in their own country. The "country" she always thought guardedly of whenever he talked about personal loneliness was always firmly located within embassy gates; it was constant, and microwave links always tied it to home and all its power.

The gods were obscure and condescending about their abilities, as if they had either acquired them by theft or, if legitimately, had been crippled by their use. There was nothing but obsessively refined vapidity in their paintings or sculptures. Still, she saw how Andrew gradually came to regard them. It was not her place to warn him, and impatience prevented logical argument when she tried.

He should not have dragged their child into this. *Not a child;* a young man the same age as the killers and killed in other cities. But still: he had been her child and her hope, whom she had even less success reaching than her husband.

She could not believe Andy's grotesque ruse about Timothy. Or that he thought she would have bought it for long. The phone call had been initially convincing, but its preparation had been a semi-major enterprise for some people at NSA, and he should have known that the word would get out and finally catch the ears of her father's old friends at State.

Why? She sat down in the one chair left in the living room and watched the men take the rest of the furniture out to the moving van. *There should have been affairs woven into all of this. Do people still indulge in that sort of thing now, when there isn't any more winter . . . and walks are taken in August fully clothed for fear of skin cancer? Who do I know who could answer these questions? Possibly the men my father once knew.*

The movers spoke to a woman who had exactly the same opinion of the gods they did. They exhanged racial slurs over coffee, although she knew she must not think like that. Real wives and mothers confronted with the destruction of their lives would not, but she would.

RANE BEGAN VISITING CAVAN AT HIS EMPTY HOUSE A month after the gods' ship left, at night and in secrecy. It was a wealthy neighborhood, with houses widely separated and protected by active security systems.

Cavan had brought a broad-spectrum noise generator from the office out of caution. He placed it on the living room floor, and they were careful to sit near it whenever Rane visited.

From the first, Rane expressed his own lack of rancor and his regrets for the suffering inflicted on members of both races. He also said he believed Timothy's recovery should be progressing, but slowly because the boy had been in terrible shape by the time the technicians reached him.

Once, nearly admitting his difficulty in remembering the appearance of his own child, Cavan asked Rane if he could draw a picture of the boy. He silently hoped this would miraculously release the memories he had inexplicably hidden from himself.

The god brought a rough sketch with him the next time he visited Cavan. It had none of the detail or delicacy of the one Rane had given him before, but the subject was entirely different. It depicted only a single, patched face that neither provoked any recollections nor healed or became younger as he looked at it.

Seeing Cavan's disappointment, Rane told him that the gods

had recognized the enormity of their error. He had been in desultory contact with Slate and flattered himself by thinking he could read between the lines of what he was told. "A miscalculation," he said abstractedly. "They should have listened to me."

Cavan looked at him. There was obviously more.

"The Washington Mission will not be rebuilt. The one in San Francisco will be closed this summer. The other stations, except for the scientific ones, will be cut back or closed."

Rane looked at the drink Cavan had given him. "After all, the careful thing for us to do is to reduce our presence on this world. They should have realized that, but Slate and his people thought a more substantial bond might have been fashioned between us." He sipped the scotch and water to be polite. "That is not feasible now. Not that it was ever necessary. They just wanted to watch from this place for what Blake's painting foretold."

Something occurred to Cavan, and he was surprised he had not thought of it before: "Do you . . . do any of you intend to stay here, even if you're ordered to leave?"

"As you think I have been? I do not, you know." That did not sound very definite, but his accent made it difficult to be sure.

"Have any of the other artists decided to stay?"

"A few of the others might have. But there will be a rush once they learn the race is evacuating the planet. That always happens, does it not?" He held his glass up to the window where the moon shone through the half-opened blinds; the scotch turned the satellite bronze. "How many of us are here, Andrew? I never asked."

"The best guess is eight or nine hundred. There might be more." Many more could have escaped counting, especially with cosmetic surgery.

"But I do not believe we would be really leaving," Rane said more earnestly. "We could not leave this . . . fascinating place. We must be only pulling back, to wait and see how things sort out between our races."

"That shouldn't . . ." A faraway explosion rattled the glass windows. "That shouldn't be very relevant to your purposes, looking for this threat Blake dreamed up."

Rane smiled for the first time that evening. "That was why most of us came. But I assure you that a number of us had more personal reasons, at least once the ships were committed and the government approved our passages."

He was dismayed for an instant. "The universe is immense and even our secrets . . . our 'miracles' have shrunk only a fraction of it to manageable dimensions. And even then, I wonder.

"The distances remain, as does the scarcity of life. We have discovered five other races, besides yours, but we . . . 'gods' . . . are the only ones to have been able to leave our home system. I often think how disheartening that must be to the others, Andrew. To bright, aggressive creatures like yourselves.

"There is evidence of other races, another score at least, but they are all extinct or devoured. That knowledge was exhilarating at first, just to think that *we* were the only ones who escaped, but we could not forget why it was being done, how morbid and suicidal it was." He braced himself to finish his drink. "Which is why I painted Blake's end and accompanied the triptych to Earth."

" 'Accompanied' the . . . ?"

"The one at the Gallery, Andrew. The copy. I told you that. We carry them everywhere to drive us on. I personally think the painting itself is the terror, even though I also believe in what it has told us."

Rane was sitting on Cavan's rented sofa, spilling his burdens into Cavan's ravenous Irish heart. As far as Andrew Cavan knew, Rane was the only god then speaking to a human being outside official channels.

"Andrew, was your son the only one to see anything in the triptych?" Rane straightened up. In the confluence of lamp and moonlight he looked like the first god who landed on Earth: serene, dignified, as unapproachable as the stars but not as

threatening. "The triptych was the first work . . . at least the
first one that survived its creator, that used the techniques of
perspective to create the illusion . . . no, the absolute, irrefutable *belief* in the observer of something more than depth."
Rane seemed to shrink from the unavoidable melodrama of
what he was explaining. "*I* can perform illusions. Blake was
different. I cannot believe anything else. He was the originator,
the inventor of a new organ of perception. He did not reveal
truth but *created* it.

"He addressed our minds directly and told us all about the
destruction of civilized life everywhere. I have to repeat this
so you can understand: destruction, absolute and complete,
everywhere. His triptych—the original, you understand—tells
the viewer all about the destruction of art, too." For a moment,
Rane looked perplexed with what he had just said, then ducked
his head once in confirmation. "Nothing less: an inescapable
entity or event stalks us to accomplish, first, containment, then
occupation, then enslavement and, finally, annihilation that
will be . . . evolutionary in its pace and thoroughness."

The words bounced off Cavan's intellect without inflicting
any comprehension. *How could they?* "Ah . . . what will cause
this disaster? Or who? We've always had a great apocalyptic
tradition, and . . ."

"It is not a work of art. It was a work of belief that transcended itself to become knowledge. The threat is out there
now. If you looked at it and *understood*, you would *know* this.
You saw how *The Death of Blake* affected your son, or how
the woman's portrait seduced that politician. We function so
differently from you. That is why the paintings were allowed
to come here. Slate thought it might be a way to open ourselves
to you without putting the blunt instruments of our technology
in your hands. After all, it might be your kind that will be the
agent of our destruction."

Cavan nearly laughed at that. "Really! But the picture
must've also told you it couldn't be us!"

"It does not speak in discrete words. No one has traced a
star map over the fear it has placed in the consciousness of

everyone who saw it. It is inarticulate, like the feeling you
have in dreams when you materialize in a deserted landscape.
Some of us react to the ocean like that. Your whole pseudo-
science of . . . psychoanalysis, is it not? . . . is devoted to re-
ducing such vast feelings to simple paragraphs. It cannot be
done.''

"Did he do anything else like that?''

Rane shook his head. "The fear he might exceed that work
has always been considered the most likely motive for his
assassination. But it does not matter if it was originally just
his personal nightmare. It is enduring. My *Blake* is a simple
illusion compared to it, though your son *believed* that, for as
long as he looked at it, a member of my race had just been
murdered. Well and good. The triptych demands the watcher
believe in a truth, directly, absolutely and without qualification,
forever. Its origin or original motive became irrelevant as soon
as it was finished.''

Timothy had spoken just as strangely about the paintings.

"We were considering a great effort to travel beyond our
home system when it was painted anyway, but science and
destiny were barely up to justifying the investment the voyages
required. Then the picture appeared and was seen by too many
of us. The timing was remarkable.

"The original always stays home. But each of our ships
carries a copy, precise to dimensions, brush strokes, the spectra
of the pigments, the placement of the molecules, as far as
uncertainty principles allow, I'm told. None of these copies,
however, duplicate the original's power, even though they are
the same in every physical respect.''

A hardness unexpectedly entered his voice. "I do not believe
such a thing is worthy of our race. After all, it was *made up*.
Just because it is unassailable does not make it true, does it?
Do you think the ability to create that sort of thing inside a
frame has corrupted us? And made us unable to realize it?''
He looked at Cavan with an unworldly vulnerability, foreign
to either humans or gods. "Do you think it has?'' Then he
closed up again. "An unfair question. I tell you about the

inadequacy of words, and then I bury you in them.''

It seemed intolerable that his son might have understood more of this than he did. Cavan forced himself to think more deeply, until he was finally able to say, ''I did understand something there. Was it like this?'' He began with a lie but kept talking, and when he was finished Rane pronounced that, at the most superficial level, it was.

CAVAN WAS PERCEIVED, WENTWORTH INFORMED HIM from the bureaucratic equivalent of Delphi, to have a unique tie with the aliens. He had dealt with them more closely than anyone else at State. It was known that they visited him, even after they had officially evacuated D.C.; State indulged this intimacy because it could be useful. He had been one of eight human beings, aside from the Secretary, invited to be under the ship during the landing on the Mall. He lost his son during that tragedy. Everything combined to enhance his credibility.

His records were combed for insights he might have unconsciously forgotten or obscured. He was given two bodyguards who were withdrawn only after much paperwork. That was the way importance worked. The noise generator in his living room showed evidence of tampering, and the discovery of bugs in his empty house lead him to converse with Rane through the old trick of children's magic slates. He felt confident enough of his position at State to believe that nothing overt would be done against him, but he would still be watched carefully.

The usual background for the god's infrequent visits was music from a portable player and the air conditioner turned up against local conversation ordinances to push air through ducts with microphones in them. Rane drew things with the child's stylus on the gray plastic pad to minimize conversation that might be picked up by undiscovered or inadequately masked bugs. The first picture was of a primitive ship, and Cavan was gratified at how easily he perceived its irrefutable antiquity.

Rane apologized over the noise. More of them were leaving; a few more individuals were summoned to the ferry ships each day. Soon, only the scientists would be left to keep searching for the promised doom.

At times, he whispered, he caught glimpses of the threat in Cavan's own words and gestures. He would then draw outlines that were immediately horrifying, despite their lack of definition. Cavan always grabbed the pad from the alien and erased it.

Rane said he did not want to continue drawing, but the pictures came more easily than speech for him and flowed onto the pad. There were drawings of his race's great leaders one night; they appeared on the pad, one after the other, until he had almost unconsciously narrated a simplified version of his race's ascent to Cavan.

Another night concerned Blake's visions. Cavan gave him an illustrated book of verse by the human poet of the same name, and Rane said he found it arresting, even considering its dimensional poverty.

"JOIN YOU FOR LUNCH?" NATE LANDER BLOCKED THE door of Cavan's office.

Cavan was getting his raincoat from the closet. "No. Sorry. I've already got an appointment."

"Too bad." Lander stepped into the room anyway and started looking around in his usual, proprietary way. "I thought we might discuss our section's prospects for the near term."

"Prospects?" Cavan tried to figure out a polite way to avoid talking to him. He had been after Cavan's desk ever since the latter's appointment.

"Yes. Now that they're leaving and all, it seems that our responsibilities will be rather diminished." He shrugged theatrically. "Might even vanish entirely."

"The gods aren't gone yet."

"They're on their way. Two years at this rate and all that'll be left will be some bad paintings in the Gallery basement and strange photos on has-beens' office walls, showing them shaking hands with a bunch of Greek statues." He shook his head at the transitory nature of fame—Cavan's in particular.

Lander drifted toward Cavan's desk despite the other's motions in the opposite direction. "Oh, you can't be reading *this* for fun, Andy. Where'd you ever get a copy, anyway?" He picked up the copy of Frank Snepp's *Decent Interval*. Cavan hadn't meant to leave it out.

"It's got some sickening gossip about Lin's grandfather when Saigon closed down. I had to get it to keep my sense of balance." The first part was true: his wife's grandfather had behaved terribly when the city was evacuated, but he had been ordered to. That was why Cavan had first read it, years before. Lately, however, he had been picking through it again out of a morbid fascination with the idea of a great power withdrawing from a provincial outpost that it had visited only to engage a mythic foe—and then left behind those such as Cavan feared he might turn out to be. He tried not to show Lander how anxious he was: "I really have to go, Nate."

The other man dropped the book abruptly. "Horrid story, I'm told. Mostly lies and scandals. But that's all in the distant past. The distant past. As it appears your gods soon will be themselves." He launched himself away from the desk and grabbed Cavan's elbow as the other preceded him through the door. "I'll walk you down."

The trip took longer than it used to because of all the additional security checkpoints. Lander remarked, as he always did these days, upon the wonder that *anyone* with business at Foggy Bottom could get from one office to the next. "I mean, Andy, even with the squatters and the rogue desks that none of *us* ever quite heard about—but which none of us ever have enough guts to call 'false' on—well, it's just impossible to get around and take care of the nation's business."

They showed their cards to a corridor patrol. Cavan felt his breath catch slightly at the thought of old professional obligations owed to the impeccably tailored men he sometimes met on dawn-lit piers or taxiways—"on the nation's business"; but that was years ago and easily set aside.

"You know, Andy," Lander continued, unasked, as they

got into the elevator and showed their cards again to the operator. "I can't help but think—and you *must* know that I'm saying this only because of how much I think of you—I can't help but think that you've staked a lot of your career on the wrong crowd. I mean, it seems like such a dead-end proposition."

Cavan looked at Lander, aching for the elevator to get to the garage. "How do you mean?"

"Well"—Lander sounded as if he thought Cavan were actually asking him for advice—"I can't argue that you've got an in that no one else has with those creatures. Lord knows that you paid for it! But you can't ignore the fact that they're leaving. They'll all be *gone* soon! Three years at the most, I'm told. And when that's done and finished, well, you might be left with something of an unmarketable skill. We can't follow them home or to wherever they're going next, you know. Not for a hundred . . . maybe not for a *thousand* years. Why, we can't even get the Mars project back on track since our yellow brothers turned off the yen spigot."

"I'll still have my traitors," Cavan said a little dreamily, thinking first of his son and then of Rane and the others he hoped the artist would still lead him to.

"That *will* be useful, Andy, but what happens when all the rest of them are gone and there's no one left to betray? See what I mean?"

Cavan was finding the man genuinely annoying. First, by bringing up his son, even indirectly. Then, secondly, he *knew* all these things; he thought about all of them constantly, from the moment he awakened in his empty house every morning. That was why he'd asked to meet the gods.

He stepped briskly from the elevator as soon as the doors opened. Lander tried to keep up for a few meters and then smiled again, satisfied that he had made his point: "Must be off, Andy," as if he were in the greater hurry. "Perhaps lunch next week?"

Cavan forced himself to look pleasant. The ass was right. *Oh Jesus! They are going, aren't they? Tim is still with them and I don't know if he's alive or dead or still something in between. And Rane's going to be as lonely and as useless as I'll be soon. Oh, why can't we get some good, useful technical people to start straggling behind? Just one! One!*

He passed through the final checkpoints, entered the garage and found his GSA Ford Fairlady. Identical blue autos, distinguishable only by the serial numbers on their doors and the color of the bell-shaped coffee cups on their dashboards, were parked on either side of his. He drove out of the garage, again showing his identity card to Department security personnel by the main gate pillbox.

The address he had wheedled out of Slate was in the northeast part of town, which in earlier days had been a good place to avoid. It had been the territory of the welfare masses and gangs for years. But he had not paid much attention to the city lately and perhaps things had changed. Cavan activated the sedan's security systems, anyway.

Miraculously, it began raining, and the streets were cleared of the usual encrustations of massed people. Buildings were actually visible through the gray downpour and the traffic seemed lighter than it should have been for a business day. Treason lingered around Cavan's thoughts, and he was thankful for the weather's slight concealment, even though he knew it would not matter if anyone was seriously watching him.

The quality of the neighborhoods steadily declined after crossing the Interstate, until he reached an area where there were almost no people, few vehicles, some pieces of derelict construction equipment and boarded, vacant tenements. Small fires burned in vacant lots, but the streets themselves were as empty of traffic as downtown had been. *Good.*

One block, however, showed signs of life with late model cars, quite a few of which were government issue, parked closely together. Some indicated considerably more exalted GS ratings than his own. Men and gods walked to and from a building on the east side of the street. Cavan drove past slowly and confirmed the address.

He found a parking space on the next block. It was pouring,

and he momentarily wished to stand on the sidewalk and re-member what that sort of thing felt like. He overcame this and almost ran from his car to the doorway. The rain obscured the features of the other figures hurrying past who did not have their umbrellas out or their trenchcoat collars turned up.

Cavan quickly stepped inside, and opulence poured over him with the same physical force of the rain outside. The gods had made the ground floor of the building into a single room, at least twenty meters wide and fifteen meters deep. The walls were paneled in rosewood and hung with dormant Earthly paintings of rustic hunts or pastoral dalliances in the manner of Watteau. *Even they have to escape from themselves occasionally.* The State Department had sometimes constructed rooms like this for treaty negotiations between bitter enemies, but never this beautifully.

Divans and settees upholstered in dark green brocade were clustered around low coffee tables with nothing visible on them. There were also several desks, done in a style reminiscent of early nineteenth century England, placed near the far wall on either side of a stone fireplace where an actual fire was burning. A god of the severely dignified type that seemed to comprise their entire diplomatic corps was seated behind one of the desks, looking politely at him. For a moment, Cavan thought it might be Slate.

The god, perhaps becoming impatient, stood up from the desk and waved at him. Cavan stepped ahead and promptly felt himself buffeted by random densities of air. "Excuse . . ." he muttered reflexively even though the only other figure in the room was the god.

"Please." The god walked toward him, indicating a carpeted runner for the human to walk on.

The quiet of the room undulated with barely perceptible tidal flows of sound and movement as he moved carefully toward the alien. When he was about three meters from the approach-ing god, something unseen struck him solidly on the left shoul-der and almost knocked him to the ground. "Excuse . . ." again. Then he understood that the room was built around holographic blinds and a sonic maze. It might be filled with people and gods, but he was allowed to see only the one in front of him. State and the Agency could do things like that too, though their capabilities were limited to smaller spaces. The effect was quite odd, almost a sort of reverse invisibility which imparted a conviction of secret insight based on the assumption that he should be as hidden to the other human beings presumably in the room as they were to him—if the gods were being democratic about this.

"Mr. Cavan?" The god offered his hand and sang his own name. "I am Day, Acting Chief of Mission for the Capital during this transitional period." Cavan shook his hand and smiled, distinguishing this creature from Slate only with some difficulty. The god then motioned back toward the desk and the chair placed in front of it. "You asked to speak to us?"

"Yes." Cavan's heart withered. *This isn't treason. Or even disloyalty.* "You're withdrawing," he said awkwardly.

"We are. That is common knowledge." The god looked around the room at things denied to Cavan. "Despite all of our best efforts, it has become painfully obvious that it is time for us to go home. It is now clear . . ." Then the god paused and his features unexpectedly fell into a nearly human simulation of melancholy bewilderment. "It has been clear for some time that whatever good we can accomplish here among you is more than offset by the damage that . . . has occurred and which shows no sign of lessening."

Day's aristocratic features lifted back into their usual racial serenity, and he took a visual data file from the desk and turned it on; columns of godly script swirled across its surface. "Regrettably, your son was one of those hurt during one of the, ah, disturbances that have attended our presence here." He ran his finger slowly along the file's scroll strip to bring more information up. "He will live, you know."

"I was told that."

"Were you also told that there was no assurance he will be someone recognizable to you? Were you told that?"

"No. But I would have assumed as much."

The god was relieved at Cavan's apparent calm. "Yes," referring again to the data sheet. "His condition was quite serious . . ."

"He was dead." Cavan said it to test himself as much as the god.

"Quite so. Extraordinary measures that were never intended for a member of your race had to be employed, and it is naturally impossible for our personnel to predict what the long-term effects might be."

"But . . ."

"He won't be a monster or externally deformed. According to this, his appearance and physical capabilities should be quite normal, though perhaps aged abnormally. He should adapt without great difficulty when he is returned."

"You're bringing him back?" The usual contradictory emotions struck Cavan. "When?"

"Considering the progress of the evacuation, it should not be too much longer." The god looked carefully at Cavan, now reminding the human of Rane rather than Slate. "That does not please you?"

"Of course it does. His mother will be delighted. Ecstatic!"

"As we will be too." Day looked down at the sheet. "To be truthful, Mr. Cavan, your son has been an irritation and a mystery to us. I suspect that several of my colleagues will be glad to give him up. Slate very much overstepped his authority when he ordered him saved."

"I know it was against all your policies to do that sort of thing. The Marquez girl caused the first big problem. . . ."

Day showed more ungodly impatience. "Yes. But you should understand that your son is, ah, particularly aggravating to some members of this mission."

"He's a kid! And he seemed to understand your art as well as anyone. Better than anyone," Cavan conceded a little desperately.

"That was the problem. He perceived a great deal more in those than any of us had ever anticipated a human being could, but he did not *understand* any of it. His perceptions were completely at odds with any rational appreciation of what the exhibition offered. For that matter, I think he dangerously *mis*understood almost everything of ours he looked at.''

''But Rane complimented him on how well he saw the meaning of his painting.''

''Rane is a self-absorbed, unreliable fool. We now appreciate that his talent is unrestrained by any sense of personal or racial responsibility. He and his work should never have been invited to come here. It is subversive, corrupt material, even if he does not realize that himself. He has ignored instructions to report for evacuation.'' Day raised both hands briefly in front of him in frustration, and then looked around the room again as if what he saw was merely the logical consequence of Rane's twisted abilities and the gods' strategic blunders. ''Forgive me, Mr. Cavan. I know that you have always acted in the best interests of interracial harmony, and I was unfair to be so critical of your son. It is probably something he cannot help anymore than Rane can.''

Cavan was dismayed as he realized he was more concerned that Tim had somehow offended the gods than he was about how Day spoke about him. That anxiety quickly obscured everything else. ''Will you take anyone with you when you leave?''

Day looked at Cavan for a moment without surprise and then placed another data sheet in front of him. He surveyed the room again, this time with more outward sympathy than before. Cavan closed his own eyes, trying to join the invisibility of the others who surely crowded the room, pleading as he was about to do. ''Quite a few have already asked to go with us,'' Day said at last.

''Why?'' *What are their reasons? Do they demean or ennoble mine by comparison?*

The god inclined his head. ''From fascination and fear. And thwarted ambition, I am sure. You can easily guess the sort of thing, Mr. Cavan. We are *leaving*, after all,'' the creature needlessly reminded him, ''and I, at least, believe that we are already taking along too much baggage from this world. But

I also understand you, Mr. Cavan. There will be . . . recriminations after all of us are gone. Scapegoats will be required,'' the god sighed. ''To stand in for all those vanished hopes. Dream piled up on top of dream until the whole structure would have collapsed under its own weight, even if we had stayed and shared everything with you.'' He looked at the man sharply. ''Cannot your own people protect you, Mr. Cavan?''

''They will for a while, assuming I and others like me stay in favor. But there's no assurance of that. Things will change drastically when you are all gone.''

''That has been predicted.''

''Especially because your departure will be more disruptive than your arrival.''

''That would also be consistent with our prior experiences.''

''What else do your specialists predict?''

Day placed another data sheet in front of him but did not bother to turn it on. ''No less than what I just said. Witch hunts, upheavals, disruptions, all kinds of unforeseen energies let loose. It will all be very regrettable, but we have no choice. Things will be worse if we stay.''

''Then I must ask to go with you.'' *There!* Cavan did not feel the shame he had expected; neither did he feel much exhilaration. The god put the second data sheet back in front of him. ''I believe that I might be in danger if I stay here.''

''You will.''

''But that is secondary.'' Cavan knew that he should speak as clearly and honestly as he could. ''I would suffocate here. You've made the world too small, and it was too crowded before anyone even conceived of a race such as yours. I can't imagine being confined like that again. I've tied myself very closely to your kind, Day, and discarded a great deal in the process. This isn't fear. But by now I don't know what I would do if I couldn't at least have the hope of seeing the stars.'' Then, quite without thinking, he added, ''Your stars.''

Day stared at Cavan for at least a minute, his face immobile, his thoughts fully contained and ageless. Cavan found some comfort in just sitting across the desk from him, despite the judgement that was being made upon him, for the god was obviously incapable of anything petty or mean. Day's presence elevated the betrayal of his son, his wife and his job, and excused his tentative desertion of Rane. The tumble of suppressed voices and indirectly observed shapes that filled the room drew away from them, leaving the two of them alone as if something had been visibly decided. "I understand," Day finally said.

RANE LEASED A SMALL APARTMENT IN DERWOOD, WHICH was within bicycling distance of Cavan's house. Cavan helped him with money, clothes and drawing supplies in exchange for more drawings of the gods' worlds, their heroes and achievements. Rane complied, though more and more impatiently; he purposely drained the genius from some of his sketches, even when he brought his pad to the house, so that Cavan could not share all the poignancy of the events he drew.

He watched the gods leave on television. There were also reports of assaults on their remaining stations: mobs confronting riot troops who sometimes did not seem overly concerned with protecting a Misson's grounds; irrational demands, first from self-appointed leaders of one crank group or another, than from more respectable groups like the Americans for Democratic Action or the British Labour Party for an "explanation" of why they were going and what they were "taking with them."

Rane watched the wall screen while drawing small experiments in chronic or emotional perspective, fixing a moment on the paper for no reason other than to see if he could do it, or drawing the faces of human beings he had observed on the street that afternoon.

He was getting better at that. At first, their faces and the times he tried to place them in were just slight variations of what he had done at home. Now the variety of their moods and situations were more familiar to him. He liked their unpredictable textures and how they were still unshadowed by a

mythic threat. He thought he should tell Cavan about this and
use the occasion to warn him, once again, against the morbid
romance the man was finding in his drawings and stories about
the gods.

One evening in late summer he pedaled out of town to
Cavan's house. The Earthly climate had been mismanaged,
but that was not unusual for an evolving race. Rane's had done
the same thing, and the stagnant air that evening reminded him
of home. *Not much of a god*, he thought, picturing himself in
his mind. It was good protection; the locals expected gods to
ride in luminous spaceships or in limousines with DPL license
plates like South African commissars.

A van was parked at the end of Cavan's street. It had been
there every night for a month, hidden behind a gentle curve
in the road and a thick stand of elms. There was a National
Guard armored car parked behind it.

Rane passed the gated driveways of walled estates. Some
were carefully tended and lights were shining through the surrounding trees. Others were overgrown with thorn bushes, their
asphalt drives imprinted by heavy vehicles. The crickets
sounded like the nachlins at home. A poignancy was almost
at hand, but it was too tenative for him to capture.

Rane liked the place. He had not wanted to come here, but
now he could barely imagine leaving. The triptych was here
with him. Even though there had been no thunderbolts of sudden understanding. there had been fragments of comprehension. *I've brought the edge of things to them*, he thought,
unexpectedly savoring the idea that they were not powerless
and might be the predicted agents of the gods' ruin after all.

There was a second armored car parked in front of Cavan's
house. An ambulance and three anonymous sedans were in the
driveway. The front of the house was illuminated by the vehicles' spinning riot lights.

Rane left his bike in the shrubs and walked toward the drive.
He reviewed his dress and judged it sufficiently conventional.
He should appear satisfactorily human under the circumstances,
but his heart rate was accelerating with anticipation. His eyes

noted the patterns the lights threw against the house and the surrounding trees. This might be a night worth capturing in a painting: this exact night, this precise time and this place.

Uniformed guards on the armored car watched him approach. *There is no need to be doing this!* a part of him pleaded. *Nothing requires this! If Cavan is gone I will be alone. That would be acceptable. I can pass if no one looks too closely. Surgical imperfections can be purchased, and I can always paint. I could give these . . . people paintings.* His concentration faltered with this last thought, and for a moment he could not remember how a human being walked.

A man in a dark civilian suit approached him. He was wearing light-intensification goggles that looked like heavy-framed sunglasses. Rane found the effect disquieting. There was too much earthly government here; too many of the sort of people Cavan had described to him.

He has gone to Slate or to one of the other official contacts. Treason oozed perceptibly from everything around him. Lines of perspective traced themselves in his head, and he felt his fingers tense and contract in readiness for the brushstrokes to capture it. *Good! Excellent!*

"Yes?" the man asked.

The van stationed at the end of the street must have recorded everyone who passed. Why else would it have been there? Rane stopped walking; there might be room enough to run if the soldiers on the armored car behind him were unprepared.

"Is Mr. Cavan all right?" he purposely mumbled; the music of his speech seemed to be deafening, but the man's reaction, if there was one, was impossible to read behind the glasses.

"Do you know him?" The voice was mannered.

Rane inclined his head in the local fashion. *Can the man really see the supposed "perfection" in my face, through the dark?*

"Do you know Mr. Cavan or any members of his family?" Evidently gestures were not enough.

"I . . . yes." Two more figures were coming up behind the government man. One was a muscular duplicate of the first, but the other was a woman. Rane squinted and recognized Linda Cavan in the pulsing lights.

"Hello, Rane," she said. "Why're you still here? Gone native?"

No need to maintain the pose now: "Mrs. Cavan. Is your husband all right? These men . . . ?"

"He's left." The man beside her jerked his head fractionally.

"Where has he gone?"

"I'd guess he's gone where most of your people have gone: home. Away." She shrugged with bitter indifference.

"He has left? Impossible." *This should have been expected. Idiot. Idiot!*

"All the diplomatic Missions are closed. All but a hundred or two of your kind were gone by last week. They also took Andy. He sent me a letter before he left and . . ."

The first government man interrupted her: "Mrs. Cavan, we don't know whether anyone went with them at all. That's what we're trying to find out." He stepped closer to Rane. "Most of you have left. Why're you still here?"

"I wasn't told about the departures. I have been keeping to myself lately. I am an artist." Rane winced as he listened to himself.

"I've told them that," Linda Cavan said coldly.

The second man laughed. "You the guy that got Senator Dennis to jerk off at the National Gallery?"

"No," Linda Cavan continued, "but he was the artist who showed my son what a murder victim looked like before he became one."

Rane did not try to explain what had actually happened: that information was no longer to be dispensed freely. Her son had been taken to, and perhaps remained in, a place she could not imagine.

The first agent removed his night glasses. His face was backlit from the vehicles' lights, but Rane assumed the man was looking deliberately into his eyes. "The past week's been pretty . . . violent, Mr. Rane. May I call you that? Mr. Rane, your people have skipped or shut yourselves up in secure positions. Now we've found that a bunch of our own people, good people, are suddenly gone, too. So we think . . .'' The man took a step nearer to Rane; he was within reach. ''. . . that when Mr. Cavan doesn't show up for work or answer the Secretary's calls, that he might be one of those that went away with the gods. Maybe you could help us understand what's going on.'' The man's voice was purposely vacant of emotion.

''You must understand what is happening,'' the first government man insisted, measuring anxiety into his voice.

''Do you?'' Linda Cavan added. ''Do you know where they've taken them?''

He thought it reasonable that Cavan might have gone over to the gods and even argued his way on board a departing ship. But the man's remark about ''hundreds'' of other people vanishing too was intriguing. He would have guessed that there were comparatively few of them as well placed as Andrew Cavan to appreciate the cultivatedly tragic glory of his race. But if they had been able to leave, what would have driven them away? The question was instantly absorbing. He envisioned misanthropes discovering the most extravagant betrayal history had ever been offered their kind. Some might have been seduced, as Andrew most probably had been. Others, the thought grandly came to him, might have understood the paintings as completely as any of his own race—the triptych especially—and forfeited their humanity on the spot. *That is possible—especially with the triptych.*

He was distracted by these people. He wanted to pry into their motivations as they crossed over the sacred line between the races. Then the first government man said, ''All right. I'd like you to come to Langley with us, sir.''

''Why?''

The man put his night glasses back on. ''We know that you're not authorized. The official ones still on Earth aren't telling us much. So, maybe, you, as a, ah, civilian . . . an artist, might be able to help us understand.'' The man could not rid his voice of its pleading note.

Rane stepped back to distance himself from the man and

study his gestures and how they fitted into the moment's net. The government agents, the soldiers deployed around the house and the half-devastated neighborhood, Cavan's wife and the weight of her personal sorrow, all fit within the outlines of a painting.

"Langley" did not sound inviting. The wish had grown in him to explain these humans to themselves. But all they would doubtlessly want from him at Langley would be explanations of the gods, the sort of things Cavan had wasted so much time on. Anyway, Rane had disclosed everything he knew about the gods in *The Death of Blake*. If they looked at it closely enough they would know as much about his world as he did.

What was needed now was knowledge of *this* world, what they possessed and what had been taken from them; and then a solitary place for however long was required to complete the painting he was now certain he could fashion.

"I doubt I would be helpful. I came here with the paintings because I was honored to be asked. I have not had contact with my countrymen since . . . since that affair on the Mall." Slate would have found the right blend of politeness and indignation to delay. Rane was not coming close to what was required.

"You don't understand the request, Mr. Rane," the man restored the flatness to his voice. He looked him up and down, signalling that he was physically superior and violence would be pointless.

Then Linda Cavan pushed forward until she was standing closer to Rane than the government man. "But you do know where my son is? You must know. Why won't you tell me? You must have told Andrew."

The anger in her voice stood out with geometric clarity. Rane knew this would have to be included in his painting, too. "I . . ." he began to lie, "do not know exactly. But I could guess."

The excitement of the risk he was taking eclipsed the new painting and his equally new, possibly imagined understanding of humankind. It exceeded anything he had dreamed of ex-

periencing at home. Did the man have a gun? Why even dwell
for a moment on that? *There is an armored vehicle behind me!*
The idea of its cannon trained on his back, ludicrous as the
visualization was, sent a sexual thrill across his belly.

The government man seemed to relax at Rane's vague hint
of cooperation, but this could just as easily have been distraction with the hysterical female disrupting his methodical im-
position of authority over the alien. "Then where would you
guess he is?"

"With the others."

"What others? Where?"

A voice called out from behind Rane, where the armored
car was. "Others were saved?"

"There were others," Rane continued apprehensively. He
heard someone jump down from the vehicle. A powerfully
built man in National Guard camouflage quickly appeared at
his side and started bellowing: "Then where? Where are they,
shithead?" He made a grab at the alien's arm, but the government agent batted him away. He must have hit a nerve
bundle because the soldier suppressed a yelp and grasped his
elbow.

"Please, Lieutenant. This is difficult enough."

The second government man walked up to them. "Problems?"

"Aren't they screening the morons we have to work with
anymore?" the first man hissed to the second through his teeth.

Before the other man could answer, the soldier came back
up to them. He had his hand on the butt of his holstered pistol.
"*Mister* Cochran," he began, his voice nearly being crushed
by the effort required to keep it civil. "This . . . man says he
knows where the dead were taken after the Mall."

Mr. Cochran turned his night goggles toward the soldier;
his colleague moved his right hand toward the bottom of a
clamshell holster on his belt. "No one said anything about
dead people."

The officer's self-control slipped away. "The shit he didn't!
He said it. *She* said it," pointing into the lights where Linda

Cavan was. "He could know where my boy is too, and his mother! What's with this Langley crap when we've got him here? Free information! More than all you Agency assholes've collected since the Mall! Jesus, Cochran, wake up!"

The first government man did not move. Then a comment drifted over from the armored car, as if someone was speaking against their better judgment:"Christ, sir.You saw the bodies. They died there and you buried them.We were all there. Don't you remember?"

"If they were dead," he said to no one in particular, "they may be with his kind. If that's true, they can be brought back to me."

Another voice emerged from the darkness, this time from where the government cars were parked in front of the house. "That's possible?" The voice was higher pitched and feminine, but the note of irrational hope was the same. Quickly paced footsteps on the asphalt drive approached them.

Cochran groaned and removed his glasses again, as if they were showing him too much of how the night was unraveling. "Elmore, *please* get back to the house, finish there, and keep the questions to yourself until . . ."

The woman was slender and of medium height; it was hard to tell anything else with the vehicles' lights behind her. "This's Rane? One of the artists?"

Rane tried to say he was, but was not sure if the words were intelligible. Things were moving at a terrifying pace, and he was still involuntarily thinking of ways to provoke them.

"My husband and children were at the Mall. They went to the Gallery before that. They thought your work was incredible," she said unaffectedly and proceeded to describe the portrait of the mad scholar—which Rane had not done. "I've been telling my people about your work. But it's so hard to get down in a memo. Especially the big painting. The one with the three panels. I . . ." she paused to gather her strength. "The gods know all about death. Don't you?"

Rane opened his mouth without any idea what he should say, but the soldier suddenly lunged forward and grabbed his left arm. "They do!" the officer shouted; this time the government man's blows failed to stop him. He had his pistol in his free hand.

"Lieutenant!" someone behind them cried. "Put it away, sir! They're gone! It's a goddamn scam! The weirdo doesn't know anything!"

Rane was indignant at the suggestion that he, personally, did not know the secrets of life and death. "I *know*," he said with suicidal malice. The humans were revealing so much to him. He could not let them stop.

"He does!"

Cavan's wife shoved her face up against his: "Then where is he?"

The two government men disappeared from in front of the vehicle lights. The soldier looked frantically around at where they had been, traversing an arc in front of him with his pistol. Shouts came from the automobiles and from inside Cavan's house; doors and trunks were opened and slammed shut; he heard devices being unholstered and frantically assembled. The armored car started its engine while the vehicle's searchlight played on them, then on the house and back again.

"Lieutenant? Would you please . . . ?"

The soldier could barely get the words out: "He *knows*, Cochran! He said so! So he's gotta tell us if his pals'll bring Jesse back." Rane felt the gun's muzzle at the base of his neck. "So why not him? Huh? One of their goddamn great artists! They'll give Jesse and Anne back for someone like him! Won't they? Right?" He pressed the gun harder.

The second government man's voice came from behind them: "One chance, asshole. Put the shooter down."

The searchlight wavered. "Leave'm alone. We'll take care of him. Jus' leave'm alone," came from the armored car.

The first government agent stepped from behind them on the other side. He had both his hands up in plain sight. "Enough! Please!" he shouted. "We have to . . ."

The soldier jerked the gun away from Rane's neck and shot at the man. He missed despite the range. The second agent was crouching on the other side and shot the officer at an ascendent angle, up through the bottom of his jaw, exploding the top of his head and showering Rane with cranial debris.

The grip on Rane's arm fell away. He brought his hand across his forehead and saw it was filled with gore and tissue that turned astonishing colors in the vehicles' lights. He must live to record this. His sense of time sharpened until it was at the peak of a sensory curve he had occupied only once before in his life, when everything moved in fractional units of time. Each one was tied to a vanishing point sunk into his heart.

His thoughts were broken when the second agent stumbled up to him. He was reaching out as if to grab him, but fell before he got within reach, jerking his hands back to his chest.

Automatic fire came from the armored car, answered by the weaker crack of pistols from the government agents beside the automobiles. The Elmore woman stepped toward Rane hesitantly, then changed her mind and began to run away; a stream of fléchettes from the armored car opened her back up, and she fell onto the driveway, out of the vehicles' illumination.

Rane wanted to stay and watch; the idea's delicious insanity fit perfectly with the violence. He dropped and spun around. The National Guard personnel were inside their vehicle. They would surely be determined to avenge the liquidation of their commander; they should have little to fear from the civilian agents scrambling for cover behind their cars or inside the house.

The vehicle crept toward the lieutenant's body. It stopped; a hatch opened, and the corpse was pulled up into the hull, a thin stream of blood and spinal fluid pouring from the hemisphere of the skull attached to it.

Rane finally began to inch backward. He was nearly back to the road when another agent stepped from behind the van parked there and shouldered a thin pipe. Its purpose was unmistakable, and Rane flattened onto the asphalt. He looked up long enough to see the rocket plume flash from both ends. The projectile struck the rear of the armored car, and a compressed blossom of jellied fire enclosed it.

The noise of the rocket's flight, the explosion and then the impact of the shock wave reached the alien sequentially, one after the other, without any perceptible interval between them.

Rane jumped up and began to trot away from the house, trying to keep his impressions under control. The risks would have been pointless if he could not assemble their components into a painting.

He paused at the end of the drive, looked down the road to where he had left his bicycle and then back at the burning armored car. The front of the house was blistering from its heat. A figure was in front of it, moving toward him.

"You don't know," Linda Cavan said conversationally when she was within three meters. "You don't know where Tim is any more than Andy did. He lied to me. So've you."

Events were no longer moving fast enough to provide Rane with a distraction. His hands jerked up in front of his face instinctively for protection. He observed Linda Cavan level the second government agent's pistol at him in a practiced motion, holding it with both hands. For a second, he thought he perceived the vanishing point from which her anger proceeded, but he had lost his genius and its location slipped away. He stepped back, but his heel struck something on the road behind him.

His hands overlapped at that moment; the right was opened with the palm toward the woman, while the left was drawn into a fist centered behind the intersection of the other's thumb and index finger.

He saw the piercingly bright muzzle flash, but the bullet's approach was screened by his hands. He felt the impact against the heel of his right one and perceived the shock wave radiating down the multangular and navicular bones, and from there into the radius, and then into the inferior and superior ulna. The bullet passed through that hand and traversed the distance to the left. It was spinning erratically when it tore into his bundled fingers along the knuckle-line, shattering the joints of the index, middle and ring fingers.

Warm ichor trickled down his forearms. The god searched,

but so long as he held his hands up in front of him he was unable to detect any pain. He postulated that the pain could not arrive at his consciousness until a more powerful thought had first been comprehended.

They came upon it simultaneously. Mrs. Cavan drew away in satisfied horror when she saw it. Rane dropped his arms and sang a shrill lament. He guessed, and then quickly believed, that his hands would be unable to fashion the great painting he had just begun forming in his mind. Its conception would not go away; it would continue to build on itself for as long as he stayed on this planet, accumulating details of time, history, distance and emotion until there was a finished composition that would never escape from his mind. His intellect would necessarily collapse under the truths it would continue to accumulate.

It would have been my gift to them! A masterwork to be fastened on their racial heart the same way the triptych was on ours! He stopped, horrified at the thought that he might inflict on the Earth what he had already risked everything to rid his own world of. *But mine would have been good!* he cried to himself. *A great and liberating work!*

Now this small, malicious woman had thwarted his beneficence. He recovered his balance, drew back and struck her in the face with his shattered right hand. She did not even raise the gun to protect herself. She staggered and fell to the ground.

He ran out of the driveway and down the road until he found his bicycle. He struggled with it, trying to pedal quickly but found it was impossible when he could not grasp the handlebars.

He slowed. The humid air drew away in contempt. His breathing was labored, and he wondered if he had sustained other wounds beside his hands. Ichor from superficial cuts on his forehead mixed with perspiration and dripped into his eyes, blurring his vision of the darkened road.

It was unlikely that there was another one of his countrymen within four hundred kilometers; the only possible medical help would be in New York, assuming the Mission there had not yet been abandoned. The immediate world was crowded with ignorant, brawling savages who would never be civilized by his masterwork. Their ennoblement would remain locked inside. The magnitude of his vision shriveled within him as a consequence, until he was left alone with his pain, trudging along the road under foreign stars.

"**Y**OU FED HIM INFORMATION. ANDY WAS YOUR FRIEND. So you might know where he went." Marinetti was a refined, educated man. Most of his government friends were with State or Defense, rather than the Agency. He and his wife attended the symphony, and he prided himself on the breadth of his historical reading. Still, Wentworth knew, as Marinetti's wife and grown children did not, that he had been in Direct Action for about fifteen years. Now he was asking him about their mutual friend, Andrew Cavan, and how he might fit into the larger questions raised by the gods' departure.

They were the old, nearly ritualized questions that had been asked since the arrival: *Why had they come? What had they hoped to accomplish here?*

The evacuations compelled variations: *Are the few of them left—if there are, indeed, only a "few"—in their Missions and redoubts still pursuing that original design, whatever it might have been? Why have all but those few left, and why have we felt this weight of . . . unease descend upon us since the day we looked at their art? Or was it shortly after the others left?*

After Andy Cavan's wife received the note he had left, this query joined the others: *Has he gone with them, as he said he would?*

"Look. Either he went over to the competition or he went with the gods like he said. Either way, he was highly placed enough for it to be trouble."

A good rule to follow, especially with one's own side, was not to look like one was playing games. But Wentworth really wanted to know. "Did they ask you to go with them, Tony?"

The man had obviously been thinking that all along. Every-one was these days. Marinetti shook his head.

"I think they may have asked me," Wentworth said, slightly amazed at his own willingness to speak. This was not the way NSA people acted. "It was quite roundabout. I thought it was buried in a transmission that was unusually easy to unravel. It came to my station, I picked at it, and the thing fell open like a sliced onion, just one discrete shell inside another. So there seemed to be . . . an invitation, and I assumed it was directed at me."

"Did you report this?" Marinetti looked genuinely anxious that the gods might have spoken to him.

"Report what? It was nothing direct. Even though the wire opened up for me more easily than anything I'd read before, it was still pretty obscure. But . . ."

Marinetti waited, ducking his head as if to urge Wentworth to complete the thought.

". . . I thought I should pursue it. This was just after the Mall riot and things were . . . indefinite about how we should continue to regard our betters from the stars. Well, I . . . look, I've at least got immunity for this, haven't I?"

The other man touched the papers with the Justice Department seal he had placed between them when the interview began.

"So I called up Andy, but it was as if the man never heard of me. Years working together, he gave me and Judy Ireland at DARPA the first crack at the fusion engine designs, and I just get a string of 'uh huh's' and 'oh's.' But I assumed that was because of what happened to his kid at the Mall. Terrible how that worked out. He was no help. So I waited . . ." He tried to estimate how badly the other man wanted his answer. Marinetti turned off the recorder beside his right hand. ". . . and eventually called up their UN Mission. This was after their D.C. Mission was burned and the rest of their local shops were shut down. And they knew me, Tony. They took the call and I found myself talking . . .

"I had the line rigged up to a phased digital reader, so I could see what I was hearing. And so help me, Tony, I start puffing myself up like a righteous Democrat on King Day. I knew how . . . incorrect it was, but it seemed so goddamn important to convince whatever I was speaking to that I was the greatest cryptanalyst since Herb Yardley." Wentworth glanced nervously at the recorder to make sure it was really off. "And all this time, I've got one part of my mind on the stuff I *really* can't talk about—the sanctions and the other wet stuff we helped your people with after the episode at the Mall—and another part on the 'scopes to dig into their speech. And the bit that's left over is asking the voice if I correctly understood their message to contain an invitation and, if it did, why I got it."

"And?" Marinetti asked dispiritedly, guessing the answer.

Wentworth shrugged. "So the god, the voice at the other end of the line, thanks me, asks for an address and, like a paranoid moron, I give him a standard-set phony one—and that was the end of it.

"That was a month ago and not a word since. They've almost all left by now. The UN Mission's shut down except for one observer who sits at the back of the General Assembly, all alone and not saying a thing. San Francisco's entirely closed—but you knew that before we did. I doubt there's any of them left on Earth to compromise me by now." He picked up the Justice Department's immunity agreement, folded it and put it in his jacket. "Which is good. A couple hundred unnaturals come down from the sky, and we all think it's the millennium. Call 'em 'gods,' even. And I can't even speak their lingo after nearly six years of trying. But they're still from heaven so we'd better keep listening. Right, Tony?"

"I called them myself," Marinetti said indirectly, as if Wentworth was seated at a distance from him instead of just across the table. "Like you. No, not exactly like you, because I hadn't found anything that looked like an invitation. But no one talks *to* the Agency. I called up the New York Mission, too, and after a while I thought I was talking to something fairly high up and telling him all these flattering things about myself. Just like you did. School record, combat, other government service, how much *I* knew about *them*. I didn't overstep any security limits. We're too old to do something that clearly stupid, aren't we?''

Marinetti would not have spoken as he had unless his recorder was really off. Oddly, the likelihood that no one would overhear their conversation was a little depressing to Wentworth, as if not only the gods but their own kind did not feel these affairs were of great concern.

"And I never heard from them again, either." Marinetti allowed himself a smile. "Both of us saved from treason by mediocrity. No reason to invite us along when they left . . .''

Wentworth raised his hand. "A million reasons, Tony! Age, uh, learning. And, come on, we've both got enough sensitive stuff between us to interest every nighttime operation on Earth. What made us so dull to the damned gods?''

"The question at hand is, what made Andy Cavan so interesting?''

Wentworth sighed in agreement. "And what made the others. . . . How many of them are your people tracking?''

"A little over six hundred, domestically. About the same number from the alliances. We're guessing at three hundred more from the closed parts of the world, but that's pretty vague. So, about fifteen hundred total is our best guess this morning. They already outnumber the gods that were on Earth.''

"Any common denominators? We haven't found any.'' He seldom told anyone what NSA found or did not find, though people like Andy Cavan sometimes thought he did.

"Just generally talented, important people—usually high up in things.'' Marinetti cleared his throat to signal a sensitive disclosure. "You know that our Assistant Director went with them. At least that's what his notes said. We don't think it was a cover for a local defection. If it was, a fellow with a profile like that couldn't have been kept undercover for this long.'' He glanced at the ceiling. "Imagine. Henry Thoreau Cabot III, of the silver hair and matching voice, skulking off to the stars with our visitors. Makes sense, I suppose. They were certainly well-mannered enough for Henry. Except for their peculiar ideas on art.'' Marinetti raised his eyebrows in disbelief at the picture he had drawn for himself.

"That's as high up as it's gone so far?"

The look of discomfort intensified. "That's getting more difficult to tell lately. Remember Koslinski?"

"My section intercepted the first word on his suicide from Vilnius. He *did* kill himself, didn't he?"

"He did. But the local agitprop also went out of its way to leak a bogus note saying he was leaving with the gods and he hoped the Motherland would forgive him. There was some god script in it. It looked pretty authentic at first.''

"Your people are keeping things from us." Wentworth was irritated with this. *Assholes in intelligence always think they can read the Rosetta stone better than the guys who do it for a living. What else have they kept from us?* Better stick to the subject at hand: "How many gods left on Earth?"

"No more than eighty, worldwide. Our shrinks think this is the worst thing they could've done. Apart from committing their miracles and all that bizarre stuff with their artwork. Now they're really going to be seen as semi-divine. As the distance between one god and another increases, the space available for rumors and lies increases geometrically. No matter how miraculous they were, you could *accommodate* them when they were out in the open and had offices in our cities, when you could *see* one of them or at least talk to someone who had. People will demand that people like you and me tell them what the gods still here are up to, and why the rest of them've taken some of our best people away to heaven. When we won't be able to tell them, they're going to start listening to their own worst feelings. Then we're going to have episodes like that awful business in Sierra Leone when they first landed, all over again.''

Marinetti's face reflected the glow of an incendiary thought. Wentworth had seen direct action people look that way before, even—especially, he believed—when the idea was something loathsome. *These guys love the apocalyptic. They can't sit down and just disassemble what fate and their listening posts gave them to work with.*

"So, the real problem for them now is how to get their remaining people out or keep them safe. If they don't, they're probably going to lose them one at a time, with each one who's left growing in imagined stature and powers in human eyes, becoming stronger magnets for hate and hope."

Wentworth had no trouble in following that reasoning: "Until they get down to one, and he will truly be a god to us."

"And he is going to be one sought-after gentleman. We should start looking for him now."

"As if you haven't been." Wentworth didn't bother to suppress his smirk.

Marinetti cleared his throat again, this time more officially than before. "The incident at Andy's house was entirely unexpected. If we *had* been looking for subjects . . . if that *had* been the operation's intent, then we would have been better prepared. At least it showed how little we can depend on Guard assistance these days."

"Another secret revealed." Wentworth knew he should not be sarcastic. Marinetti could *help* him. He could use some of these abandoned gods himself. No one especially talented, just a left-behind god able to speak the language and give him a better starting point than that ultimately disappointing book on the fusion engines. *That* would be the place to start, with the basics.

W ENTWORTH HAD NOT TURNED OFF HIS OWN BUTTON recorder, so he could do some stress analysis on Marinetti's speech if he wanted. But feeding his voice structures through the computers would probably ring up his file at NSA—and if CIA was listening in, at Langley, too. Then the poor, cultured thug would have to explain his weakness to others less compromised than Wentworth.

Too complicated! Wentworth manipulated the erase function on the button recorder.

Wentworth cursed to himself as he left the Agency parking garage. He was disturbed by a persistent sense of isolation. He was in his Buick, surrounded by hundreds of fellow intelligence professionals, in the shadow of the world's richest repository of secret knowledge. Despite this, he felt as he had when he was young and first became habituated to uniform distrust.

It was cool enough for the windows to be open. Thanksgiving was next week, and the leaves should start turning. Wentworth loved the promise of cooler weather, even though it was always delayed.

The access roads were no more than usually crowded with public and private transportation. The apartment blocks around the Agency's security perimeter were beginning to light up for the evening.

Had any of this been here ten years ago? he asked himself as he usually did when he drove this way.

Old farts always think like that, was his usual response to himself, as it had been for at least eight of the years in question. *There was one thing that was as it had been. The gods were gone. Only a couple of them left behind in remote places where they shouldn't bother anyone and a few more who may have gone native.*

But, essentially, they've gone. Wentworth braced himself against the thought. None of the speculations, paranoias or goofball contingency plans that their writers had always been so embarrassed to describe to the Joint Chiefs once a year had anticipated that the great day would come, that they would simply conclude the whole adventure was causing too much trouble and depart.

" 'Sorry, old shoe,' " Wentworth muttered to his car in an accent meant to parody Slate's, " 'but it was all a dreadful mistake. Typical Foreign Office fiasco. So we'll be off now. Sorry for the bother, old man, but *do* keep up the good work on the civilization and all that.' "

Wentworth became truly angry as he drove home. The whole episode was pointless at best. At worst, it was the same kind of horrid joke the rest of the world used to accuse America of always playing on it. Sheer, thoughtless arrogance permeated every act and gesture Wentworth could recall: their space flight, the revival of the dead, their goddamned art and their coy refusal to share their secrets with men. *Shit! They wouldn't even tell us if they could beat causality and outrun light. They acted like a bunch of society swells in the wrong neighborhood. Acted like they wanted to bare their bloody souls to us for a bit and then went right back up into the clouds.*

The paintings from the first show and the ones that had been unloaded from the ship before the explosion had been left at the National Gallery. Their UN observer, Slate, had demanded their return, though not very vigorously. The request was being "evaluated," a euphemism for no one wanting to do anything in particular for their departed majesties.

The Gallery basement where the gods' works were stored was guarded by regular Army people. But people with influence could visit, if they were discreet.

Wentworth wondered how much his connection with Andrew Cavan had diminished his professional status. Not much, he decided as he turned onto his off-ramp. Everyone in Washington knew someone who left with the gods, or said they were going to before secretly defecting or killing themselves.

Wentworth still lived in same house he and his wife had purchased when he was hired away from Middlebury College by NSA. During the succeeding years, the county had condemned the spaces between the federal-style homes and filled them with new houses. Municipal zoning tried to make the styles consistent and mandated the preservation of the old trees and front lawns. But the heat had killed the trees and grass years ago, and Wentworth always found the effect of driving down the corridor of nineteenth-century facades, unbroken on either side and running toward a point in the haze, intensely depressing.

The gods promised us something and then jerked it away

before they told us what it was. He parked, stepped out of the Buick Century and went through his ritual of careful breathing. Once the door was shut behind him, he knew it would be easier to defend his heart against these things.

R ANE HAD PREPARED HIMSELF TO HEAR THE ONLY THING that could realistically be expected from the doctor. He still handled it poorly. "The chances of restoring more than gross functions are minimal. I don't even know what your chances would be at a proper facility like Bethesda, but I'd recommend it. You need neurologists, automated microsurgeries, hand specialists. And a teaching hospital's pathology department to decide what specialties you need in the first place." The man kept his head bent over the small MRI screen, switching between the torus around Rane's left hand and the one enclosing his right as he was speaking.

"I do not believe that would be wise."

"Aren't you . . . any of your own kind still around? Can't they pick you up and fix things? They'd know what to do." There was envy and scorn in the physician's voice. Everyone had heard the bring-'em-back-from-the-dead stories and taken them the wrong way.

Rane had thought that such an ability would have elicited admiration instead of such pettiness. "I have lost contact with them. I am not even sure I can get in touch with the United Nations office." He looked at the doctor. "Is it still open?"

"The news says there's only one of you there, and he's lying low these days. That'd be reasonable. There were two murder attempts in San Francisco last week. I also heard the Kansas State Police found a body that's supposed to be one of yours outside of Wichita. So I guess I can see your concerns. Probably smart. You guys are *smart*, aren't you?"

The man then brightened a little. "All right. I won't do anything that Doctor Mudd wouldn't have."

"Excuse me?"

"Look. Do you want me to fix what I think I can, or do

you want to be patched up and try somewhere else?''

Rane considered the departing ships; a few of them might still be in orbit. A few Missions could still be open and, after them, there were the isolated observation posts and scientific stations that had been the point in coming to this world in the first place. But it was unlikely that any of them would be sympathetic to unreliable artists who had purposely wandered away from their designated evacuation sites. Disinterest would be the best he could expect; if his treason had been uncovered at home, he would be infinitely safer on Earth, no matter how crippled he might be.

Rane told the man to do his best. Then he asked, ''Can you change my appearance?''

The doctor nodded, having anticipated the question.

''Nothing drastic, and nothing that would affect my hands more than they already are. But just change enough to, ah, conform to the local environment.''

The doctor said that he thought that would be an intelligent move.

Rane put his head back on the pillow and considered the heroic appeal of mutilation. Anesthetic disks were pressed against his neck as the doctor looked for his neural analogue to the human medulla.

MARINETTI'S CLEARANCES ALLOWED HIM ACCESS TO THE basement where the gods' paintings were stored. People still talked primarily of the miracles they had withheld from humankind and the traitors that they had taken away with them. But the paintings that had actually precipitated the problems had been rapidly forgotten by the public.

He prided himself on his artistic sensitivities and had prepared himself for this visit by reading everything the critics had written about the doomed exhibition. There was remarkably little, considering the significance of the event. Most of the commentaries were printed in historical and anthropological journals instead of the artistic press.

The soldier pulled out one metal storage frame after another, so Marinetti could look at each of the paintings. The harsh fluorescent light did disagreeable things to the colors. He wondered if the impressions of time and place that some of the paintings were supposed to communicate were being jammed by that.

The soldier seemed familiar with the paintings, and often asked permission to speak, delivering an occasionally worthwhile observation about one or another. He seemed, in spite of himself, to be not at all impressed by the portrait of the godly female, although he had obviously heard the same vulgar story about Senator Dennis that the rest of Washington had. Instead, the landscapes had captured his interest. One suggested, he told Marinetti, not only a place but a specific day in his own youth, even though the world it depicted was not Earth. He shook his head at this and gently returned the picture to its place. Marinetti had seen only a distorted picture of a decaying, temple-like building with an alien sky behind it.

The soldier also liked a picture of what seemed to be a scholar. He said he not only understood the madness that had overtaken the alien, but felt certain he could unravel its psychological origin if he had enough time for contemplation.

Marinetti saw an elderly god surrounded by books, statuary and antique scientific instruments. The creature looked wild-eyed and anguished, but that was the extent of it.

As they walked down the rows of paintings, he became aware of several that had been too big to fit in the frames and were propped up against three of the basement walls. They were screened by the standing frames, and he saw them only in narrow strips that appeared between the other paintings as the soldier pulled them out.

Marinetti moved to the center of the room. He turned slowly on his heel, looking at each of the three paintings, one after the other. They appeared to define a night sky, though he could not recognize any of the constellations, nor was he even sure the patterns depicted stars at all.

A sense of externality, of looking down and of being placed

completely outside of all the normal physical confines communicated itself to him. And lying behind this exit door from the world of warmth and light there was, instead of routine liberation, the apprehension of a warning; and beyond that, the most indistinct outline of something terrible approaching.

"Sir? Sir?" The soldier might have been calling to him from a distance.

He knew without being told that the paintings were out of order; the central panel was on his right instead in the middle, and they were laid on end instead of with their long axis up.

The language that had informed their creator was expectedly foreign, but the informing concepts were comprehensible. These were shocking, not only because of what Marinetti thought he understood of them, but because he thought he could understand them at all. That should have been impossible. The articulate relationships of shapes and color that reached him were not like sensory homonyms, because they were not merely *like* previously experienced emotions; rather, they triggered immediate and literal understanding.

Marinetti whispered to himself and stepped to the side so the metal frameworks blocked his views of the paintings. The immediacy of their threat was transformed into the memory of something actually experienced, not just recently observed. He retreated from the basement as rapidly as the dignity of his security clearance allowed.

He wrote a draft request to move the collection from the National Gallery to Langley as soon as he got back to his office. He destroyed it the next day when he realized how much of himself it would reveal.

AFTER WEEKS OF HIDING, RANE DECIDED THAT HE WOULD have to chance contacting Slate. He had been reassigned to New York as the gods' UN observer and might have access to medical help that could restore the artist's hands.

His bus was inching through the center of Philadelphia, following a years-old detour required by the collapse of the

Memorial Bridge. The density of the crowds on the sidewalks was incredible; Rane was simultaneously repelled and attracted by it. At times he wished for a sketch pad, but faces and bodies appeared too briefly for him to capture, even if he had the facility of his hands back.

One figure on the opposite side of the street, however, distinguished herself from those around her by the way she walked. Surprisingly, the cadence of the crowd allowed him to watch her. He concentrated until he could trace the idealized features of his own kind and wondered frantically if it was someone he should have known.

She was dressed in the local style, but so self-consciously that Rane wanted to shout and warn her how conspicuous she was. She could not hope to escape notice in such a pathetic disguise.

There was no one seated next to him. He looked around, aware that he might be acting the same way the woman outside was. His own face was superimposed over the woman's image in the window glass. The doctor in Maryland had not been a cosmetic surgeon, and the procedure had been carried out in his office surgery. Rane's facial structure was unchanged but the texture of the skin had been coarsened by an acid mist; his eyes had been narrowed with slight epicanthic folds; his nose had been broken and reset so that it was flatter than before.

The doctor had expended more finesse on his hands; enough motor functions had been restored to allow casual sketching. But he had not attempted anything serious and believed nearly all of his original dexterity was gone. There were patches of numbness over the backs of both hands and, most distressingly, along the thumb and index finger on the right hand.

So, now he passed for an Earthman.

Why was the woman here? Why didn't she hide? She obviously wanted to. He could easily tell that from the way she kept looking around. So, presumably, could many of the humans around her on the street.

An odd, wave-like movement rippled down through the sidewalk crowd from the area of a disturbance, blocks away. Heads bowed and ducked as they received the rumor and then jerked around to pass it on.

Rane focused on the god. A fat man in a leather jacket emerged from the crowd and stood deliberately in front of her. He stared for a moment and then held a wallet up in his left hand and ostentatiously placed his right inside of his coat. He started talking, his eyes widening in recognition as he looked at her.

She did exactly the wrong thing by turning around and trying to walk away. Rane half rose in his seat to follow her, then caught himself and carefully placed his scarred right hand against the side of his face to display his imperfection to any passenger who might have been looking.

The man said something after her and then to the crowd around him. Three other men, younger and more athletic that the first but similarly dressed, appeared. People on the sidewalk began to notice the confrontation and cautiously backed away.

The fat man then presumed to touch her, and she gestured toward him imperiously. Anger veiled her face, and Rane was as arrested by its appearance as the crowd. Gods did not often react in such a way at home and had never done so on Earth. Even when their Chief of Mission in Washington, some of their finest artists and most treasured artworks were assaulted by a madman, they had reacted with calm civility.

Rane watched his own expression change in the window glass. It was filled with morbid wonderment at how such emotion might have been finally provoked from one of his imperturbable race. The repulsive and endlessly tantalizing thought that violence might recall the designs he had first grasped at Cavan's house came to him. He tried to check himself, but he found he could not dismiss the wish for suffering.

One of the thinner men walked up behind the woman and thrust his hands forward to attach a neural lock between her shoulder blades. She spun to face him, brought both hands up and then across her chest in a cutting motion. The man opened his mouth and jerked his arms back with both fists crushed.

Rane involuntarily compared what he saw to his own

wounded hands, and then quickly looked back again. The woman must have been with the military to have learned such techniques; that would also mean that armaments were woven into her limbs. *Miracle*, he thought; the irrational assumption was shared by the crowd which arrested its flight.

The man fell to the pavement, howling loudly enough to be heard inside the bus; then he rose and pointed the stumps of his hands at her, screaming constantly. A third man came up behind him, motioned toward the woman, and found his right hand instantly crippled, but still managed to bring the truncheon in his other hand down against the side of her jaw.

The blow staggered her, disrupting her concentration so her next counterstroke only glanced off the man's upraised forearm. The man hit her again with his good hand. The fat man was trying to motion his subordinates back, but the two who could still function were not listening to him.

A woman came out of the crowd and tenatively stabbed at the god from behind with a piece of scrap metal. The young men shouted encouragement and she hit her again, where the kidneys would have been on a human being. The god's back arched upward, and then she fell in a twisting motion.

The crowd moved in around her. At first, only a few of them dared to kick or reach down toward her with their fists. The fat man stepped back, apparently bewildered at what was happening. He finally took his hand from his coat pocket, but it was holding a radio instead of the gun Rane had expected. He began yelling into it, pleading for some kind of assistance.

The men who had been with him were suddenly hurled backward, out of the crowd; one's features had been smeared into a bloody oval, and the other's left arm had been chopped off at the elbow. The third man tried to run away but his eyes were either gone or disabled, and he kept running into other people who recoiled in shock from him or into the buildings fronting the sidewalk.

The man without an arm looked as if all awareness of his surroundings had been driven from his mind. In utter contrast to the blinded one, he strode unsteadily away from the crowd for about ten meters, stopped and looked around as if he had just arrived at the street corner, took off his belt and wrapped it around the stump of his arm for a tourniquet, then continued briskly north where the smoke was coming from. He seemed embarrassed by his loss and thoroughly perplexed about how it might have happened.

The crowd drew back from the female god. Her right leg was unnaturally bent halfway between the knee and ankle, and her earthly clothes were shredded from the assault. She glistened in the smoky afternoon light from facial wounds and a deep gash that started on her bared right shoulder and descended into the folds of her jacket.

She regarded the human begins surrounding her. There was nothing to be read on her face except rudimentary fear and pain. The inflexible martial discipline made necessary by her self-defense remained only as a rime of emotion.

Is that what happens when you are alone here? he thought. *Or a reflection of Blake's prophecy?* He reviewed the most likely responses and found none of them within himself: he was not terrified, although he felt sickened by what he was watching; he did not feel any necessity to try and rescue her, after all, he did not know her and she must have chosen to stay on this world as he did; no one had helped him but a ham-fisted doctor, and even that was after it was too late. And beyond all that, there was still the possibility that this might open the door to his genius.

All the passengers were by now on the side facing the battle, but no one was saying a word. Police sirens could be heard rising in the quiet.

The god faltered as she tried to stand on her left leg. The people to whom her back was turned edged closer when they were sure she could not see and then drew back again, though not as far as they had been when her eyes came back around to them. The circle they formed was therefore spiraling shut.

Her clothes were soaked with ichor, but none of the humans watching understood this in terms of pain or imminent death. She was not bleeding as they would. The color and viscosity were wrong; it was more like a machine losing hydraulic fluid. The female became less and less godlike, and once that was lost, less humanlike too; the things that held the mob back were gradually lost to its attention.

Rane recalled what the government man at Cavan's house had told him about people leaving with the gods. He had read stories about them in the newspapers later; they were supposed to be very good people, often from the highest levels of society. The billions left behind resented them terribly. Now he might be seeing the reverse: the *god* who was left behind, who suffered an even more devastating judgment than that borne by the humans deserted on this world. At least this had always been their home.

Was that what was fatally undermining her invincibility? Rane surveyed the mob. He believed he could identify at least five humans who had seen the triptych and understood it, whether they had known it or not. Their sensibilities flared up visibly in reaction to the god's cornered emotions.

The fat man who had started it all was still shouting into his radio, powerless to do anything to stop or even understand what was happening in front of him.

There were more sirens now, strongly doppler-shifted toward him. He rose in his seat to keep the spot where the female alien had been in sight. A National Guard armored personnel carrier with riot lights on its top deck was plowing along the sidewalk, forcing people into the street. It stopped in back of the man with the radio, pointed its turret at him inquisitively for a second, then raised its gun until it was aimed at the spot where the god had been enclosed by the crowd. That was enough. The bodies immediately started untangling themselves, regaining their feet and fleeing down the sidewalk or through the gridlocked traffic, away from the vehicle.

The carrier's rear doors opened and a squad in battle dress tumbled out. An officer followed and rushed to confer with the man with the radio. The soldiers began dispersing the few people who remained on the sidewalk and motioning the cars and trucks in the street to move away.

Rane's bus moved forward in response, but he could still
see the fat man and the Guard officer walking toward the
glistening, pummeled mass that had been the female god. The
fat man kept gesturing down at her, looking at the officer and
then up toward heaven, which he obviously thought had inflicted a personal tragedy on him. The officer looked crestfallen
enough for Rane to conclude that the fat man was, in some
manner, his superior.

There were light tanks in each of the first three side streets
they passed. Each had a soldier in front of it, motioning the
traffic on, away from the area. He fell back against the seat,
breathing heavily. *They are looking for us*, he thought. If only
he had known as many humans as Slate had. But he had
foolishly confided only in Andrew Cavan, and he was gone.

T IMOTHY CAVAN BELIEVED HE WAS ASLEEP, EVEN THOUGH
he could perceive his immediate environment. He was naked
and lying on the wooden floor of his own living room. Dust
and plaster had shaken loose from the ceiling; although he had
not moved yet, he could feel its texture under the back of his
right fist as blood pulsed slowly through it.

He unfolded that hand and then followed with the rest of
the arm, the other arm and his legs until he was stretched out
straight on the floor. His heartbeat accelerated; a sense of the
world's oppressive heat displaced his initial coldness. He had
the impression of a series of small penetrations abruptly withdrawing from the base of his skull, his spine and from below
his groin where the right and left femoral arteries were close
to the surface. These intricate, metallic presences coiled briefly
against his skin and then propelled themselves away.

The dimensions of the room were familiar, but there were
no rugs, books or furniture to confirm that it was truly his own
home. He sat up unsteadily, wondering if there should be any
pain.

A few books were scattered around, along with a beat-up
sofa, two coffee cups and some beer cans against the walls.

An enigmatic box was plugged into a floor socket; there were anechoic baffles over its exterior surfaces, so he supposed that it was some kind of auditory masking device. The windows were blown in; there were carpets of glass splinters under each of them.

The only object in the room that belonged there was the bust the gods gave his father. Timothy stood up when he saw this, made sure he could walk and tottered over to the bookshelf where the tiny sculpture was. He looked down at himself as he did this and found scars, more hair than he last remembered, a pervasive coarseness and an unfamiliar lack of surprise with his body.

He stared into the sculpture's eye, finding it a useful focus for memory. It assisted him in recalling a light, the panicked singing of gods and an onrushing constellation of shrapnel. A blank space followed, which was implicitly occupied by pain and confusion. Then, the beginning of tranquil coldness, during which the penetrations he felt withdrawing had been fastened on him.

He peered out the living room window. The gutted hulk of a tank or large armored car was in the driveway; the turret was pointed away from the house and the tube weapon drooped toward the scorched lawn. A similarly ruined car was between it and the house, the four doors open and all the window glass shattered. Both vehicles were beginning to rust.

This was enough to feed an adolescent imagination for months. Timothy considered this, but emerged with only a contradictory sense of relief. He felt as if he had actually escaped from something. He suppressed a grin as he walked around the room, unconcerned with nakedness for the first time since the sixth grade, melodramatically inhaling the air and swinging his arms.

He was convinced that he had been *gone*, though he had no idea where he had been or how much time had elapsed during his absence. That idea made it easier to believe that his parents were gone too, along with substantial fragments of their world and the little stability it offered.

SLATE HAD DONE EVERYTHING CORRECTLY, JUST AS DIP-
lomats on all worlds did when things were slipping out of
control. The encoding chips were first ground to powder and
the debris flushed down the toilet. Next, the communications
gear was disassembled and loaded into the security furnace for
incineration. Books and other sensitive documents written on
flash paper that instantly reduced itself to molecular ash followed. The Mission's security and defensive systems were left
intact.

He had to do all of this work alone, but it was absolutely necessary. The locals were clever, and becoming more so with
each additional month they were allowed to observe his kind.
He suspected they might be on the verge of unraveling the gods'
elementary grammar. A gentleman named Wentworth, he had
been informed shortly after the evacuations began, had been especially successful in deciphering bits and pieces of unsecured
radio traffic. He was supposed to have been the fellow who de-
duced the presence of the home-ship behind the fifth planet
months before the CIA astronomers had any suspicions.

And he had misguidedly tried to advance their education!
He had actually thought he would engage the indigenous population on something like a common ground without giving
away a single secret of genuine significance except for those
inconsequential fusion engines. The aesthetes of his race would
be satisfied, the xenophobes would be placated and the generals
and scientists would have their observation post, farther out
along this arm of the galaxy than ever before.

Slate cursed himself as he walked down the stairway. He
had fabricated a plan that he disliked and which, for that very
reason, he believed would be accepted by his superiors. If art
was supposed to be at the core of their souls, and if the threat
it had revealed to them was the secret of their travels and
inescapable sense of tragedy, then the inhabitants of the world
should be gently introduced to it so they would begin to understand.

All that was supposed to have occurred subconsciously, of course. No one, not even the artists, expected the locals to instinctively grasp the literal messages their art communicated—especially old Blake's morbid triptych. Their childish sense of awe was supposed to have been chilled and brought under control as they realized the mortality the gods shared with humanity, albeit, on a much higher plane.

Therefore, his reasoning had ultimately run, they might eventually be trusted if the gods stayed and if more immediately practical secrets were disclosed to them.

Slate had never felt more than a tremor of anticipation from any painting or sculpture—or even from the best copies of the allegedly sacred triptych the navy was obliged to carry on each of its ships like stellar anchors. He had thought it unlikely that the most sensitive of the humans would be more deeply touched than he, a god, had been.

The Mission's copy of the triptych was hung in the cavernous stairwell, its impact muted by the placement of the left and center panels on the walls with the right-hand panel suspended above the stairs. Slate glanced at it as he descended but, as usual, found only dark smudges interspersed with bright dots.

Now, he *had* sensed something profound when he had seen the original at home. That one had seemed different, but had become so only after hours of concentrated study, so that he was never sure how much of his feelings he had forced upon himself.

He never shared these doubts. The triptych was too central to society to admit disbelief. Certainly, as announced by his colleagues at every conceivable opportunity, it transcended all science and philosophy.

So he had foolishly underestimated the locals' reaction to the first exhibition, even though some of the artists had *told* him what would happen. Then he had come up with the final, fatal inspiration that they should be exposed to more of this great art, when less or none at all would have been the best course. Even Rane had warned him against that.

Slate winced as he listed his errors for the hundredth time. The Chief of Mission in Washington had called it an "inspiration," a "career-maker" the morning before the Mall riot. Slate had thought of that remark every day since the riot, as his influence and prestige evaporated until he was left with a one-room office at the United Nations Secretariat, the New York Mission, a First Secretary and a Puerto Rican housekeeper.

Then the Secretary vanished and the Puerto Rican quit. His communications with the departing fleet were inconclusive. Requests for evacuation were "directed to diplomatic cadres at home-ship for consideration."

His self-recrimination intensified as he neared the front door. He should have kept his home's teleological art away from this backwater world, no matter how that ass, Cavan, had pleaded with him and his superiors. That would have been safest.

We should have stuck with their idea of our divinity. Nothing wrong with that. It was convenient, useful at times, and much more easily managed than this artistic "truth" I thought we should share with them. He said their name, "the gods," to himself over and over again until all meaning had been shaken from it.

Shadows from the traffic outside passed the bulletproof stained glass door. His current situation was insupportable. Nearly all the human beings he regarded as trustworthy had left with his own countrymen. The maid had called them "the gifted," and Slate supposed this was the popular name assigned to those fortunate people.

He had not been told why they had been allowed to go. At least he was spared the agony of not knowing why he had been left behind. He envisioned a memo on some superior's desk, doubtlessly written by a bright clone of his younger self: Slate should simply be left behind as our last ambassador, as it were, to temporize, apologize, explain in the vaguest terms, and then merge into the crowded Earthly landscape and, hopefully, never be heard from again.

He rolled his eyes in amazement as he rounded the banister and continued down the stairs to the basement. After throwing their history into an uproar, showing them sciences and art with the impact of addictive drugs, igniting riots, raising the dead, promising unlimited power, they apologize for the fuss and exit—leaving only a few fellows behind—and think, really think, that no one would bother them while they watched for the end of creation.

Random assaults had been common since the incident at the Mall. But now there were reports of government-sponsored sweeps, obviously aimed at capturing stragglers. Slate tried to keep his unease at a distance. He had felt this way once before, but then there had been an evacuation ship kept in orbit especially for him. Now he had only the tatters of his diplomatic immunity to protect him. It was time to leave.

The Mission's contingency plan postulated a standard scenario: the long-awaited threat had actually appeared and the orbiting fleet and home-ship had to withdraw before effectuating a full evacuation. The plan identified safe houses and the routes between them and the permanent observation stations; these, in theory, would not be evacuated under any circumstances but would remain staffed until the threat either destroyed them or passed by in pursuit of the fleet and after it, of their homes.

He had memorized the plan, packed some things in a Mission automobile and resigned himself to driving to Kansas, where one of the nearest permanent observation posts had been established.

A tunnel in the Mission basement descended into the bedrock and surfaced in the basement of an apartment building on East 57th Street. Building it in secret had been difficult, but construction lasers and the city's own noise and constant shuddering made it feasible. It had been valuable during the evacuations, when public assaults on gods were common. Conversely, some of the traitorous gifted had used it to enter the Mission surreptitiously.

Slate entered the tunnel and waited until the basement wall

slid shut behind him. He adjusted his clothing till it appeared as conventional as possible. He had thought cosmetic surgery was beneath his dignity, but now regretted not having it done.

Gods were as varied in their appearance as humans, but the things that distinguished one from another were much subtler than the gross deviations between human beings. It took more than a casual glance to tell a god from a human, even to other gods. *Even to ourselves,* he marvelled hopelessly.

The tunnel was lined with seamless white ceramic; fluorescent globes at ten-meter intervals provided illumination. To minimize the chances of detection, the ventilation system ran only when the tunnel was in actual use, so the air was nearly unbreathable.

Slate reached the barrier at the other end. Warning lights cautioned him that the basement on the other side was occupied, and he had to wait ten minutes in the stagnant air for an all-clear.

He activated the wall and stepped into the apartment building's cluttered basement. Once it closed, he set a security lock that would weld itself permanently shut in twenty-four hours.

The building's freight elevator took him from the basement to the parking garage. The Mission car with his supplies, clothing and a radio was where he had left it. There was no sign of tampering, so Slate allowed himself a last look at the city. He followed the exit ramp onto the street.

The traffic was heavier and the air denser than at Sutton Place even though he was only about six blocks away. Push-carts lined the curb. Human beings from all class levels packed the sidewalks, shouting at each other for no apparent purpose. Slate felt himself contradictorily at ease; there were places somewhat like this at home, although none of the paintings that had been brought here hinted at such a thing.

Then a small and finely proportioned young man pushed by him, almost knocking him back against the garage entrance barrier. Slate suppressed his usual displeasure at being touched and gazed after the fellow. There was an uncommon grace about him, even though his features were stretched against his skull in fear.

A loose crowd charged past a minute later, pursuing the man. They were yelling and carrying clubs. Slate flattened out against the building to let them pass, but the mob's periphery caught him and dragged him along for a few yards until the vanguard caught up with the man.

They converged on the victim at the edge of the sidewalk, so the density of the crowd lessened if Slate moved forward but stayed against the buildings. He also wanted to see the man again. He reminded him of one of the Mission staff members who vanished during the evacuations and not been accounted for.

Slate saw the man backed up against a pushcart. There was a National Guard armored car on the other side of the street, but the soldiers standing beside it were only casually interested in what was going on.

Ours? Who? The young man might have been one of his own sons. He remembered each one with a piercing intensity that traversed the distances separating them.

Everything was there and correctly placed: the strong, fine features, the compact body hinting at extravagant musculature under the clothing, the refinement of gesture defying the man's own obvious panic.

Thoughtlessly, Slate half-sang something in his own speech and gasped when the creature glanced toward him. At that instant a nightstick rose behind the creature's head and came down heavily. The victim's eyes rolled back, and he staggered under the blow.

Slate remembered himself and hurriedly searched the crowd for government operatives. He thought he spotted two men who stood out from the mob by their self-containment and the quality of their clothes.

He tried to step back toward the garage entrance, but an indescribably filthy woman, dressed in moth-eaten furs in spite of the heat, grabbed his shirt and began yelling at him: "They's crazy, man! Stay 'way from 'm! Crazy shit, man!''

Slate realized that was her normal tone of voice. He looked at her for a moment against his will, as if she could tell him more. When she did not, he looked back to where the man had been and found only the crowd thickened into a tangle of struggling limbs and heads.

The Guards across the street at last showed some interest. They slowly took their helmets and body armor off the car's hatchback and put them on. Then one strolled across the street, holding up a gauntlet against the traffic. The other got into the armored car, started it and followed his comrade toward the crowd.

When the soldier was in the center of 57th Street, he took a concussion grenade from his flak vest and casually withdrew the pin. Slate could see the man's mouth moving through the count to "three." Then he tossed it into the gutter, just ahead of most of the people.

Slate immediately crouched down with his face toward the building, opened his mouth and put his hands over his ears.

The grenade went off with an enormous crash, spinning the derelict away from Slate. He waited for a moment and then stood up. Most of the crowd was staggering off, down the street and away from the explosion. Nearly every one of them had thin lines of blood descending from their ears and nostrils; a few had their hands over their eyes, and blood was seeping from there, too.

Slate pushed stunned human beings away as they tried to flee. He found the original victim's body, crushed into the gutter by the weight of the mob. Slate searched for emotion inside of him, as he always felt obligated to do, and found something that appeared authentic. He reached down to the body, as the emotion instructed.

He drew his hand back in revulsion before touching the corpse. Even for a countryman, the toe of his shoe seemed more appropriate. He hooked his heel around the shoulder of the creature and turned it over.

"Friend of yours?" the soldier asked. He had come up while Slate was concentrating on his revulsion. The man's English was barely understandable through the ringing in his ears.

The back of Slate's shoe was smeared with red blood. He refocused on the ruined face. Everything was soaked in redness. Although he could feel sickness rising from his stomach, he looked carefully enough to make sure that there was no clean, godly ichor effusing from the creature's massive injuries.

"God, huh?" the soldier asked.

The man did not know the difference. No god had been hurt on Earth before the incident at the Mall, and only a few had been wounded in public after that. There was no reason for them to know about the ichor yet. If they kept on killing humans in the belief they were gods, they might never realize this difference. "You think so?" Slate said carefully; he limited his words though his accent was flawless.

"Yeah. Righteous sonofabitch. Weird to end up like this, though. All this way from home and none of his pals to bring him back to life. Maybe they'll be along inna minute." The soldier spoke something into a microphone clipped to his shoulder.

"I doubt it," Slate replied and backed away.

WENTWORTH SLAPPED THE NEWSPAPER. "JUST LOOK AT what they've left behind! Things were in less of an uproar when they first landed. Now, we *know* that most of them have skipped, but everyone's still acting like there's one under every bed." He held up a sheaf of blue internal briefing memos. "And for once the press is understating things. Can you believe that? Why, that business at New London yesterday when someone got the bright idea some gods were hidden out in the sub pens! Morons! No one's got any idea how long it's going to take to clean that one up, and while we're doing it, half the NorLant fleet's out of action and there's a plume of radioactivity bright enough to read by at night going fifteen kilometers out into the Sound."

Marinetti shrugged. These present troubles did not upset him greatly. Chaos was an accustomed environment; if he was not provoking it, then he was shaping its course to serve the national interest. "Our departments have credible information that a number of them remain. Some've obviously been abandoned. Others've gotten the idea they like it here and want to stay. There're others that we have no ideas on or location for, but they're here. We were never sure why they arrived, except for that 'mutual instruction and protection' and search for the stellar bogeyman crap they gave us, so a certain amount of paranoia about what those left behind are up to seems understandable. Possibly even a healthy way to look at it." He politely sipped his coffee. "Tell me. Do you still have those feelings of loss over their departure? Wish you and your associates at National Security could find one, if only just to talk to him?"

Wentworth answered with his customary unease. "Sure. I'm still steamed they were invited along, or kidnapped or whatever, and I wasn't. Aren't you?"

"Not at all."

Wentworth raised his eyes. "Have you heard what the news is calling the people who've left?"

Marinetti had. The people down in Mass Psychology had announced it a week ago: "The gifted."

Wentworth could not help smiling at the name. He repeated it with too much sympathy: "Right. 'The gifted.' I'm sure your people have been plotting the demographics of those who left."

Marinetti leaned back in his chair. "The 'gifted.' Pretty exalted name for traitors and deserters."

"You're too harsh. Some very important people . . ."

"Some *extremely* important people," Marinetti corrected. He was allowing Wentworth to control the conversation, but this did not displease him.

Wentworth nodded in agreement. "As you say. And we both know that a good number of them really went away with the gods. They didn't kill themselves. Direct Action didn't disappear them. A lot of them truly left. Fascinating."

"We should have anticipated that." Marinetti envisioned the triptych in the National Gallery basement. He wanted to talk about the opportunities for exploitation created by the departures of gods and men alike. Capturing disaffected stragglers and the painting were subsidiary issues. Still, they might invite analysis if the funding became available. Marinetti changed the subject: "Are you making any progress with their transmissions?"

Wentworth was prepared for that. "Less and less, now that the traffic is declining and the fleet's getting farther away. They don't have much contact with the ones left behind. There've been some burst transmissions to the active stations, but there aren't many of them."

"Well, at least we've got some dissection subjects now. The doctors at Atlanta are delighted, but I'm not sure they're on the track of anything usable yet. Just a number of perfect, idealized alien corpses, all perforated or mashed to a pulp. And not one of them uttering a word of god-speak for you fellows to work on. Pity."

Wentworth ignored the needling. "Right. More 'opportunities'? I know social weaknesses show up where the mobs are thickest, but the morons just end up killing people most of the time. They're surely after gods, but they've hardly seen one in person before, don't have the slightest notion about the difference between blood and ichor yet, and even when they do, they still have to cut their target to tell. This is becoming a real witch hunt in places. Return to the darkness."

Marinetti was smiling; the dark sounded appealing, the Agency's natural environment. Really, he should tell Wentworth to give up these pathetic efforts to round up a god to talk to. They were out there, but he wanted ones who meant something. Ones who could not only talk but had something to tell him. Their efforts were getting in the way, driving the ones who were really worthwhile further underground. At this, Marinetti found the triptych shouldering its way back into his consciousness, chilling him deliciously.

Both men stared across the desk for a minute. Professionally,

Marinetti thought Wentworth was an ineffectual snob, even though his organization sometimes provided useful information. Wentworth, in his turn, considered the other man a cultured thug whose integrity became intolerably convoluted the moment it descended from the light of day.

R ANE TRIED TO TELEPHONE THE MISSION AT EVERY STOP his bus made. He would have tried again from the Port Authority Terminal on 43rd Street, but the cavernous building was overrun by wretches living in territorial corners and stairwells fortified with particle-board and plastic scraps. Those who were not obviously residents were in constant, brawling motion either going to or coming from the bus and mag-lev train gates that circled the building's fifteen levels. Rane could not imagine where they were all going.

He had been in New York once before, when he was brought down to work on the proposals for the National Gallery exhibition. He had disliked the place, but at least then it had meant he nearly finished his task of getting the triptych to where it could be hidden in plain sight. Now that the gods were gone and his part in the insurrection at home was finished, he was physically and emotionally unprotected from the city's natural aggressions.

He shouldered his way through crowds of stinking, diseased humans until he was out of the Terminal. But he remained in the grip of tidal masses of human beings on the street. Waves of them would carry him forward and then back across the walkways. At times, he felt himself stepping on something irregularly soft and was sickened at the thought of what it might be.

The crowds thinned out as he moved east toward the Mission. There were more police and National Guards in this part of the city, and things were correspondingly more orderly. But there were still columns of smoke at the far ends of some north-running streets. Sterile office towers and apartment buildings alternated with vacant lots or decaying structures left over from the last century. Some of the empty spaces were cratered as if they had been hit by bombs, and the interior walls of the bordering structures were often charred.

The effect should have been unsettling, but Rane found himself as intrigued as he had been months before, when he was entering Cavan's driveway. He knew that he was forcing the emotion, and it may have been that there was nothing more than fear or common disgust at the bottom of it. But clues to his great, unrealized painting were nevertheless surfacing in his mind, trying to work their way down to his hands.

They were still stiff and responded imprecisely to his commands. He had sheafs of grotesque, childish sketches in his bag as evidence of this. Only some of them contained fragments of accidental power.

There were puddles of blood in the gutter, although they might have been from animals. These alternated with slick pools of clear fluid, but he doubted that these could have come from a god; he had not seen another one of his kind since the woman in Philadelphia.

The place is coming apart, he thought. Shop windows were either empty, piled with jumbles of used or stolen goods, or barred and filled with clothing and luxury appliances of the highest quality. There seemed to be nothing in between.

He asked for Sutton Place once, but his accent was faulty enough to cause the civil police officer to look at him inquisitively for a moment. He dared not ask anyone else, but came upon the Mission by accident when he turned a corner to get a better look at a disturbance on a side street.

He walked up the marble steps and knocked. No answer. A National Guard armored car was parked at the end of the block. A soldier was sitting on the turret, holding a pair of binoculars in his lap but not watching at anything in particular.

There was no response to the bell. Rane tested the door and jerked his hand away from the security shock. He stepped back and looked up at the windows. Everything was locked and secured.

The outline of his next great painting receded in the realization that the place was deserted. His breathing became rushed and shallow.

He impulsively struck the door with his right hand. The house increased the voltage, and a small blue spark stuck to the flat of his palm as he pulled it away from the glass. Rane yelled something against his will; he could not afford to attract attention.

The Guard jumped down from his vehicle and walked toward him. There was another armored car at the other end of the street, so running was out of the question. The soldier was unarmed, but he picked up some passersby as he approached Rane. There were six or seven other humans with him by the time they reached him.

The soldier asked if there was any problem. Rane was unable to answer until he forced himself to remember how he looked and how unlikely it would be for anyone to mistake him for a god. "This is the embassy of the . . . ah, people from space?" Rane cringed at this artifice. "Of the gods," he quickly added, nearly stumbling over the name.

"It still should be," the soldier replied. He was a dark man whose expression was unreadable. He looked up at the facade, as if examining it for the first time. "Locked?"

"It seems so." Rane stepped down to the sidewalk and tried to share the human's mystification.

"Sound's like you expected someone to be home. You here to meet one of 'em?"

Rane's heart accelerated as it had at Cavan's house. *If only it was night.*

"You're here to meet 'em?" the soldier asked again. The humans bunched up behind him.

Rane said he was. Obviously, he was. Anything else would have been a transparent lie, but the people looked at each other as if he had said something unexpected. "Do you know where they might have gone?" That sounded harmless enough, but the crowd mumbled again and pressed up against the soldier's back.

"No," shouted a man. "You know?"

"I . . ."

Another human repeated the question: "Well. Do ya, man? Ya know where the bastards went?"

Rane wondered frantically how a human would answer. He unquestionably appeared human. Why couldn't he at least speak like one? But all that came to him were the usual vague intimations of an immortal work of art and a droning panic that he might die at this place. At last he found himself saying, "Christ! I should know? Gone back to the stars where they came from, I guess." He prayed that it sounded authentically indignant.

The humans quieted for a moment. Then a feminine voice asked with a note of sudden discovery, "Wish you'd gone with them?"

He must answer like a human: "Who wouldn't?"

"And they were supposed to be here. To meet you?" The soldier confided something into his shoulder microphone. Rane heard the armored car's turbine start up at the end of the street. The soldier then pointed at his bag. "What's in that?"

"Drawings."

"Of what?"

"People. Buildings. The world." Rane began edging to one side of the crowd, toward the approaching armored car. He had lost control of the situation but he could not understand why.

Another voice came from behind the soldier: "Man thinks he's gifted." Murmurs of agreement followed.

The soldier looked at his audience and then made sure the armored car was near enough. He resumed his questioning in a louder voice. "You say you were going to meet 'em here, but because they're gone you wish they'd taken you along? Do I have that right, sir?"

It would be stupid to argue with the man. Rane nodded dumbly and continued to edge away from the people.

"Then may I goddamn ask, sir—and *please* stay where you are while I'm talkin' to you—why this place isn't good enough for you to stay, and why you've brought drawings of this world to show 'em?'' He glanced over his shoulder to see how this went over with his companions.

They approved. "He wants to leave . . ."

"We ought'a help'm on his way . . ."

". . . but that'd mean he's takin' something with 'im. They didn't take just anyone, man. Only the best. Just the gifted guys who've got somethin' they needed. Stuff we need more."

"Yeah, shithead! What's your prize?"

The soldier was pushed ahead by the last speaker's hostility. Rane thought he whispered something like, "Careful. Back me up," into his shoulder microphone, and then louder and directly to him: "Okay. Good point. Open the bag, sir."

Rane used his fumbling with the clasp to move another half meter down the sidewalk. Now the armored car was behind him and most of the crowd directly in front.

"What'cha got?"

"Drawings. As I said." Rane was momentarily embarrassed by the quality of what he had to show them. If anything, these should convince them that he was not, in any sense, "gifted." He picked one he thought was not too inept. But some among the group of humans gasped with shock when he spread it out on the sidewalk.

Rane saw nothing more than a sketch of a city skyline with patterns of constellations rising behind it. He thought he had done the sky from memories of his home, but the city was Washington, D.C., seen from the Virginia side of the Potomac. He could not believe there was anything of importance in it.

The soldier bent over the drawing. He raised his right hand to the side of his face; it was half-opened and the index finger was directed to a point in space halfway between the drawing and Rane. "Ah . . ." He was truly wrestling with the picture. "Ah. There's a . . . thing in this, man. Real sharp, and cold. Di' you put it there?"

Epithets spilled from others in the group as they either saw something unexpected in the drawing or felt compelled to act as if they did. "Oh, shit and Jesus! I *knew* that was on its way. How'd this asshole *do* this? It's like a picture, a photo, but it's not. Like he *knew* . . . !'' Then more dithering, until the same voice rose in sudden realization and said: *"That's* why they're going. There! *That's* why the gifted're going with 'em.''

Rane began to shake with apprehension. His audience had found more than he had conscious knowledge of. It had just been practice and had nothing to do with the great work forming in his mind.

This was unfolding like the episode at Cavan's house had: there was the crowd of menacing humans, the mystery and even one of the ubiquitous Guard's armored units grinding toward him. But there was none of that evening's intoxication. All the humans' emotional violence was now directed at him and his works instead of being shared among themselves.

He finally detected the smallest confluence of chronic perspective in the painting, located above the city's skyline. It was so inconsequential that he momentarily wondered if he had even put it there at all. But who else could have? As he moved his head, the spot seemed to move in relation to the drawing, creating the impression that it was actually hovering above the surface of the paper. Something must reside there. He could not imagine how he had missed it before.

Rane impulsively shoved the drawing toward the crowd with his foot. When they jerked away as if they had touched a charged field, he spun around and ran toward the armored car, ducking under its machine-gun turret.

The soldiers in the car had not expected this. Someone inside hit the trigger and sent a burst toward where Rane had been standing the second before. The bullets tore into one of the people in the crowd, opening his head and left shoulder so quickly that the rest of the body actually remained standing for a moment before it crumpled and fell, gushing blood.

The other bullets hit the Mission stairway and front door. Unlike Cavan's home, it defended itself accordingly. Plasma jets ignited along the stoop and walls facing the sidewalk. The human beings nearest the mansion had their legs severed at the ankles, and they toppled over into the sheet of blue luminescence, sinking into it as if into a pond as the charged particles disassociated their molecular structures.

One edge of the beam sliced through the armored car's front tires and dropped the vehicle's nose to the asphalt. The charge was not powerful enough to burn through the ceramic armor before it automatically shut down. The rear wheels were still operational, and the crew dragged the vehicle backwards, away from the building while raking the facade with machine-gun fire.

Rane sprinted down the sidewalk, his presence completely forgotten by the crowd and the men in both armored cars. He turned around long enough to see the other vehicle moving cautiously from the far end of the block toward the Mission. It held its fire, but the crippled unit continued shooting, blasting out the windows on each floor until a bolt of plasma spun back along the bullet stream; it enshrouded the the hull with pulsating brightness. The guns stopped, and everyone who was still alive on the street instinctively inhaled, crouched and braced themselves.

The armored car exploded spectacularly. Rane could not believe that anything used for domestic police work could carry enough fuel or munitions to cause such a blast. The shock wave threw him down to the sidewalk even though he had been able to run almost to the middle of the next block. A second, equally violent explosion buffeted him, but he had his head buried under his arms and could not see what had caused it.

Rane waited until the shower of granulated stone and glass ended and then stood up unsteadily. Much of his view was blocked by billows of smoke, but he could see the gutted remains of the other armored vehicle, lying on its side at the far end of the street. The first unit had disappeared; there was the lip of a shallow crater, at least five meters in diameter, where it had been when the plasma bolt struck.

The breeze cleared away the smoke for a moment. Astonishingly, the blasts had also leveled all of the buildings on the east side of the street except the Mission. It stood among the new ruins, blackened and with all its windows blown out, pulsating from the energies of its defensive systems.

Then the Mission methodically spewed its luminous fire up and down the street, even though there was nothing now to threaten it. It varied the emission spectra, shifting the light-fans from blue through a pure white to a purple that became a darkness of its own, playing up and down the smoldering street, re-churning the rubble on the east side and randomly cutting into the buildings on the west.

The inevitable sirens began, probably coming from the garrison at Bellevue or the 11th Street Armory. He tried not to look back as he trotted away. The mob saw something in his drawing powerful enough to stop them from advancing on him. They had all died because of it, and he experienced an unexpected rush of sympathy for them.

People began running past him toward the Mission. He wanted to warn them away but said nothing. *That should be saved for the picture*, he thought and was appalled at the perversity of his talent. *What do I need these creatures for?*

S LATE'S DEPARTURE FROM NEW YORK WAS A NIGHTMARE. He had almost no experience driving; there had always been Earthly chauffeurs to take him around the city or out to the landing field at Flushing Meadows. He made one wrong turn after another after leaving the garage. He was supposed to go south, to the Holland Tunnel, but the streets were either one way in the wrong direction or blocked by construction, police checkpoints or, the further north he went, by populist barricades of rubbish and gutted cars.

He did not escape until after dark, and then only to Queens, in the opposite direction from where he wanted to go. His maps identified one of the five safe apartments that the gods had established before the evacuations.

He unloaded his car, set the alarms and walked up to the sixth floor, dreading the thought of facing any more human beings. He had no confidence in his fluency by now and wondered if he was singing audibly to himself in his native speech as he climbed the stairs. Rats waited on each landing and moved aside only if he kicked at them.

The door was steel with a cheap wooden veneer. A thick layer of dust covered everything in the sparsely furnished apartment. That was reassuring, as were the ceramic armor plates on the walls, the ceiling and floor. A low-frequency jammer was installed in the kitchen, but there was no reason to turn it on.

Slate left the lights off. He unpacked a bottle of Black Label, filled a glass with ice and sat down on the living room sofa, looking out the window at a narrow view of midtown Manhatten. It seemed as it always had to him: a trivial city, concerned with enormities he found boring. But he often thought of the cities at home that way.

He poured a second glass and felt the liquor gently pry his heart away from his habitual self-willfulness. He had once endured the psychological torture of riding a ship solo through interplanetary space. But that remembered loneliness was not so deep as the one which fell over him as he stared at the city. For the first time in ages, he indulged in extravagant self-pity. He tried to force tears into his eyes but they would not flow.

After an hour of this, Slate thought he could see the sunrise reflected in the glass of the United Nations Secretariat and the office slabs behind it. His watch showed only 11:00 P.M. Half the bottle was finished by now, and he wondered if his vision was going.

The light reflected on the buildings' facades brightened and then began to flicker erratically, the way sunlight did around a starship's field generators.

Sirens drifted across the river and penetrated the neighborhood's monotone of ventilators and traffic noise. He switched on the apartment's television. The news stations were only reporting some general disturbances on the Upper East Side, but the radio from the embassy tapped into the police and National Guard channels. These were seething with official traffic: the middle part of the island had become the territory of mobs which threatened the rich neighborhoods along the

East River. The lights he had seen reflected in the building facades were from fires in the streets. The local garrison at Bellevue was pleading for more men, fire equipment and armor.

Fireballs roiled up between the skyscrapers, backlighting the buildings and illuminating formations of helicopters gathering over the area. Slate began to find it beautiful, especially with the confused torrent of radio traffic pouring out of the tiny monitor as a backdrop.

It seemed unreasonable to suppose that the plague of his race's art figured into the violence across the river, but the idea became more plausible as he progressed into the bottle. His own kind had been decisively affected by the paintings. They had appeared one at a time at home; the first one, the triptych, was reportedly the greatest, but it was held almost in secrecy while near geniuses approached Blake's inspiration and inured the race to the idea of created, rather than revealed, truth. Too many of these works had been abruptly unveiled on Earth instead of the slow unfolding of appreciation that allowed the gods' racial history to be bent but not broken.

The scotch had blunted things too much to connect one speculation with another by early morning. But the sense of the paintings stayed with him. Some of them fit like a backdrop against the burning city, and, against his will, he felt his eyes looking up into the thickening haze, to where Blake's hated stars would be.

Slate WATCHED THE FIRES ALL THROUGH THE NIGHT AND into the next morning. Seven blocks were involved at one time. The military and commercial radio channels were saying that the small firestorms over the gods' Mission on Sutton Place were the work of anarchist mobs.

Clandestine radio and television channels appeared after midnight, probably operating from trucks or from boats on the East River, broadcasting incendiary gibberish. Slate heard transmissions "from the front," from the financial district, from the West Side and from the perpetual powder keg of the Bronx, which now seemed determined to set itself off, once and for all. The blacks' rantings against the whites and whites' against the yellows included futile swipes at the departing gods and declarations that the humans who went with them were the ultimate traitors to their race. The gifted were singled out as creatures possessed of the vilest, most loathsome passions, who demeaned the gods by clinging to them as they did ". . . and taking all the treasure we possessed with them," as one hysterical voice screamed over the radio where WNBC should have been.

The gifted had gone and taken something valuable . . . something that they should have known was not theirs but *ours*. How dare they! How dare they pass such a judgment on the proud, imprisoned peoples of Earth who were left behind!

Then a station that suddenly appeared on the FM band in the middle of a dolorous Schubert symphony began reading off the names of those who the announcer said were among the gifted. Slate had never heard of most of them or knew that others were either dead or still on Earth as of a week ago. But some names, like Cavan's, were true. After each name, the radio gave a brief, vague description of either the person or the gift he had wrongfully taken from this world: "Adrian McCulloch: healer; a physician devoted to the welfare of his fellow humans and possessing irreplaceable knowledge of our genetic imperfections. H. K. Osuthlue: leader of his people and brightest hope to those oppressed by the very tyranny that seduced him and took him away from us. Henri Boumediene: lately of 147th St. and our only true poet; our only voice heard above the sound of our oppressors' march before the greater noise of the gods' ships overwhelmed him . . ." And so on past noon until the pirate station was silenced along with the others by the authorities.

Slate wished for something more to drink, but he did not want to leave the apartment to get it. The impression of a race that suddenly imagined the loss of any number of valuable things, some of which had been its own forever and others that were only new promises, was unutterably depressing. He wondered if he actually felt something for the wretched breed.

How could *his* race have permitted all of this to happen? How . . . *why* should people, good, though flawed and deficient people like Andrew Cavan, have decided to leave their own world and take their chances aboard the ships? Slate moaned as the thought of space travel penetrated his ripening hangover.

S HE HAD RETURNED TO THE STATE DEPARTMENT JUST IN time, Linda Cavan told herself, to participate in all the chaos her father had predicted before he died. Rather than simplify things, the gods' departure had created a vast emptiness, as if they had occupied a vitally important place in human society for centuries rather than a few years.

She noticed that everyday conversation, even at the Department, usually twisted itself around to include the gods. They emerged naturally as the beginning and end of every problem that the Department had to address, no matter how old and Earthbound its origins.

People who did not know about her husband cited the gifted almost as frequently as they did the gods as explanations for the latest upheavals. There was a famine in Senegal because a brilliant agronomist had left with the gifted; the Mexican elections, which everyone had so hoped would put a genuine democracy in place, lapsed into traditional fraud and corruption when Iberra Diaz vanished and presumably left with the gods; the Upper West Side of Manhattan had become a battleground now that Henri Boumediene was no longer walking its scorched streets telling the oppressed about invented times and places so much better than their own.

She had asked to work with the group charged with reestablishing contact with the gods still on Earth. The Secretary of State had recovered from the wounds suffered during the incident on the Mall and was convinced that the gods maintained some sort of shadow diplomatic presence, even though there was not a shred of objective evidence to support this.

Mrs. Cavan's request was politely turned down when it was pointed out that her last contact with a god had ended with her attempting to kill him. Her actions were "understandable," but she obviously lacked the "cool objectivity" necessary for such a sensitive task.

Instead, she was allowed to work on the withdrawal of the legations and consulates from around the world as unrest spread. It was substantial work, but would not cause any great national damage in the long run if it was badly done. So she watched many of her father's old friends emerge from the tropical rot of what they thought would be their last posting into the relatively cooler environments of Washington or Paris, talking in the amazed voices of people suddenly awakened to how much time they had unintentionally squandered. They invariably talked about her father as if he were still alive.

"We can't do anything more here," was the endlessly repeated substance of the cables. It was always followed by formal requests in plain language to the Secretary to close the consulate or embassy and withdraw the personnel. The gods' own evacuation may have helped establish this predisposition toward retreat and consolidation. For the first time since her father told her about the late '30s, it seemed like the right thing to do.

Many good local people followed the withdrawals, as if they believed that this was different from earlier fits of American isolationism. The professionals with their competence and money left after the diplomatic people, just as did the geniuses and weirdos with all *their* inspirations and self-reproach at not having been among the gifted.

WENTWORTH SET THINGS UP SO HE WOULD BE LEFT alone. His initial success at unraveling the gods' language and codes had brought him too much attention. Then there had been that bungled attempt to capture a god in Philadelphia. He still felt his jaw tense when his mind forced him to replay the whole stupid episode. He had squandered too much information locating the female and then, like an utter fool, had thought he could bring her in himself.

At least the cover-up appeared successful. She had killed his four security men, and the National Guards who rescued him had been too preoccupied to look past his phony identification.

But Tony Marinetti knew about it. He was sure of that from the way the man had spoken to him: *as if he thought the failure amusing, like he had more important things in mind! If only he'd play that card instead of just pestering me about their transmissions! He knows how awkward it is to share this stuff with him outside of channels!*

He still had the assignment of deciphering the fragmentary traffic that found its way to Earth, either directly or by relay from the string of trans-Uranian satellites the Japanese had put up twenty years before. Someone had to listen, even though the finality of the gods' departure was so crushingly obvious. *That's what Tony is always too careful to tell me. Bastard.*

So many things promised and lost in such a short time. The shock became institutionalized as the months progressed and the signals weakened.

He patiently ran the fusion engine drawings and book which accompanied them through his computers, cross-referencing their texts to the isolated words and phrases that were picked up from the gods' traffic, assembling fragments of operational conversation which heartbreakingly confirmed that the story of the gifted was not a fabrication.

Transmissions from the home-ship behind Jupiter were incomprehensible. The planet's bow-shock distorted direct reception. Presumably, receivers of unknown design were required by the gods' active stations.

But the trans-Uranian satellites behind the planet occasionally picked up useful fragments which Wentworth kept to himself. Surely there were other people at NASA and EuroSpace who were aware of the signals; there was no need to bother them with this small opening. They also kept Marinetti pleased and always turned the conversation away from the murders in Philadelphia.

The first bit of interest came in the spring, after the rains ended and the grass was browning on the Mall. Minute red shifts inferred that at least one of the ships was slowing before the half-way point to Jupiter.

"There," Wentworth said to himself; his Agency keeper was not in the room. He pointed to the place amid the gibberish on the print-out where it said: " ' . . . at home. Sanctioned copy. . . . Enhanced . . . detection until this date. Recovery imperative. Imperative.' "

"Sounds heated," he mumbled, cautioning himself against being so casual. The laboratory was wired, even if his keeper was not present. There was nothing to hint at why the gods were so upset—it was uncertain if they were upset at all—but there was a panicked ring to the comprehensible parts of the transmission. He thought he could fool himself into picking out other comprehensible parts by staring at the rest of the print-out until he nearly fell into a trance. Most of the things he half believed he saw evaporated when he shook himself awake. The good parts remained, however: ". . . Recovery imperative . . . ," and the possibility that they might be coming back.

T IMOTHY CAVAN ACCEPTED THE FACT OF HIS DEATH, RESurrection and return to Earth as he did the massive plate of scar tissue across his chest. The adolescent mind is naturally inclined toward such theatrical notions, particularly if one is returned to a point of beginning strengthened by sad and terrible knowledge denied to everyone else. He wondered if Susan Marquez had felt the same way when she had been awakened at the Mission's infirmary.

A spike of intractable belief anchored these thoughts to his consciousness. It was driven down into his mind, letting a shaft of darkness fall across everything he felt. It was not the usual sort of youthful despair, which only serves self-absorption.

This was colder and more substantial than articulated thought; no matter what he said to himself about it, it remained in place with the same shape, ringing like a tuning fork whenever he tried to bend it with logical analysis.

He stayed in his old house for two days. There were some clothes and shoes in the upstairs guest room, but no food. Then he left, walking down the street lined with abandoned and burned-out residences. The hulks of expensive cars were rusting in some of the driveways. All the deserted houses had been looted, but he was able to find enough preserved food to sustain himself.

There were occupied houses at infrequent intervals, perfectly normal in every outward respect except that their owners, when they were in sight, were always accompanied by armed men.

Timothy was working in a garage in Rockville when he found out about his father. He had picked another's name, and his face and body had aged sufficiently since the incident on the Mall to prevent anyone from connecting the grainy newspaper photographs of this Cavan and his family with him.

Being among the gifted elevated Andrew Cavan. The gifted had pronounced the judgment of a strong, reserved son, the kind who concealed large portions of himself from everyone around him and who, on an appointed morning, would pack and depart before anyone else in the house was awake. He would leave a note, as most of the gifted did, which would speak in general terms of an existence that would remain unknown to those left behind, to be read with shock and amazement by brothers and parents, because they would know that the note was correct and that it would stay that way forever.

Timothy also felt the helplessness and rage of the people he talked to, but from a comfortable distance. The gods had set him apart from both Earthly mankind and the gifted. He listened to people in a way that he had not imagined before the incident on the Mall. The adults no longer possessed special knowledge; he was able to see around their ragings, toward a sinister strength that might survive their present despair.

That was the way he felt in the good times. During the bad

times, when he was alone in a rented apartment, he sometimes
held a calendar in his hands and stared at it, trying to force
himself to be as young as it said he was, trying to force the
dark out of him so he could agonize over his parents' departure.
Then he could cry only by making the conscious decision that
it must be done.

MARINETTI OSTENTATIOUSLY DISMISSED THE CONVICTION
that he might be too old for this sort of thing. He straightened
himself, although he habitually stood with a military posture,
and unobtrusively checked the tautness of his biceps through
his summer suit.

Marinetti looked around. Instead of finding confidence in
his forces, he was appalled at the insecurity that had driven
him to request them in the first place. He had asked for people
with Direct Action or combat experience, even though there
were supposed to be only three gods in the cluster of farm
buildings below them. Four helicopter gunships were parked
in the burned grass, half a kilometer behind him, their engines
on "silent." Six M-2E tanks were arrayed in front of the
choppers, their shoulder-high silhouettes hidden from the farm
by the intervening ridgeline. Three more tanks were positioned
on the opposite side of the farm. Two jeep-mounted TOW
batteries were dug in at right angles to the axis of attack. Two
companies of airborne infantry would make the actual entry.

Everyone but the eight Agency men with him were regular
service. *This is not going to be an amateur operation like our
friends at NSA try when they don't want to share their secrets
with the people who know how to use them.*

"Jesus," he whispered to himself. "Was it ever like this?"
All he could remember from the times before the gods came
were slick, wondrously professional operations that attained
their goals with the minimum expenditure of resources and
violence.

Marinetti looked at his watch, then at the horizon, and
pointed to the man with the radio. The soldier, in turn, touched

a key on the side of his transmitter. Everyone watched as one gunship silently drifted up from the ground. It hovered at thirty meters, scanned the farm buildings with radar and FLIR, and then came back down.

"Quiet."

Marinetti walked over the crest of the ridge and down toward the farm. Four infantrymen with adaptive camouflage sprinted ahead of him and vanished. Marinetti could track them only by looking at the field indirectly and then picking up some movement of the long, dry grass.

The sun began to warm the back of his neck. Today would be warmer than yesterday; it might be unbearable by afternoon. Another reason to get it over with.

There were four two-story houses, a long dormitory, equipment sheds, three silos and a barn. The place had originally been a Mennonite cooperative farm, but had been abandoned ten years before the gods arrived. They restored the buildings, installed elaborate antenna arrays and, if the briefing papers were accurate, had discreetly fortified everything.

Three mobile, twenty-five-meter dish antennas were clustered together on the open commons between the residential buildings. Rail tracks ran out for about a kilometer in three directions to allow them to increase the effective aperture when they were operated as a single unit. There was also an older wire-mesh antenna one kilometer square strung from metal tripods north of the buildings.

All the antennas and associated sensors had operated in an essentially passive mode since the gods had built them. It was impossible to tell what they were listening to or for. The inferred power drain indicated the antenna arrays operated around the clock, even when the planet was facing away from the departing fleet. However, the dish antennas were lately beaming discrete burst transmissions to the ships.

Marinetti had reviewed the engineering autopsy of the New York Mission and it justified his caution. Neutralizing that building had required the destruction of seven blocks of the Upper East Side, and that was when it did not have a single god inside to direct its actions. Impressive stuff. All their arts and manners had lulled people into thinking they were just a bunch of decadent sailors, questing about the galaxy in search of the ineffable.

The radio operator gave a thumbs-up. The advance team had reached the silos. They turned off their camouflage suits and became visible again. Marinetti and the Agency men trotted down to join them. The infantry followed, spreading out in a half-circle around the complex. *All right. Still under control. No need to bring up the heavy stuff.*

Marinetti re-checked his deployments and sprinted from the silo to the nearest house. He almost tripped over one of the antenna rail tracks as he ran.

"Heartland, shit," he heard someone behind him whisper viciously. "Grant Wood, asshole," hissed another. Marinetti's eye caught the incongruity of the austere farmhouses with careful gingerbread trim under the porch eves and the glint of ceramic armor butting up against the inside of the window frames.

The house was deserted, as promised. He glanced inside: empty rooms, some with random bits of old Earthly furniture scattered around, but each one with the white plates fixed to the walls, the script of the gods pooling like Arabic in the corners of certain panels.

The antennas were around the other side of the house. There were no crickets, birds, whirring alien machinery or other sounds except the muffled rattle that heavily equipped soldiers make no matter how carefully they move.

The radio operator pointed to the dish antennas. "Down," he said, then looked around at the rest of the compound. "Everything's down." Marinetti wondered if there were any gods there at all; his last intelligence was two days old.

They were supposed to be living in the bunkhouse, two buildings to his right. He waited while the infantrymen secured each of the other buildings in the complex. They would all be checked before the bunkhouse.

One by one, they signaled all-clears. Two soldiers and one

Agency man, the latter theatrically dressed in a white tropical
suit, then crept toward the equipment shed that was farthest
from the point at which they had entered the farm. Any big
technology would probably be kept there.

The sun was above the horizon now, but the humans still
cast long shadows as they dodged around the dish antennas'
frameworks. They reached the front of the shed, one soldier
pausing on each side of the door. There were no windows in
the structure and the ventilators on the roof had been covered
with fifty-five-gallon drums. The agent seemed to lean forward
for a moment, as if he heard something inside. Then he stepped
forward, grasped the handle and slid the door back along its
overhead track.

Marinetti's breath caught; he forced himself to breathe again
when nothing roared out of the interior darkness. "Go in," he
said, feeling that the agent should not. "Tell them to go in."
The radio operator spoke into his microphone.

Across the yard, partially hidden by the dish antenna frameworks, the Agency man pressed his earphone to hear better.
He checked the action on his machine pistol and slipped into
the shed. One of the soldiers followed while the other waited
outside.

Marinetti kept shifting his eyes from the equipment shed to
the dormitory to his right. That would be the last objective; he
would not move on it until everything else was under control.

A minute passed. Marinetti could see the soldier left outside
nervously looking at his watch instead of into the building.
"Ask 'em what's in there."

After a moment the radio operator reported back: "Equipment . . . Supplies . . . Paintings. That's basically all he can see
with the lights. He says the place's a lot bigger than it looks.
Gods've dug out the floor or something."

"What kind of paintings?"

Another moment: "Mr. Atkinson reports the same kind of
stuff they showed off in D.C. The weird stuff, he says, sir,
but most of it's messed up."

"Are there any in three sections that look like they should, ah, go together? Ask him that."

"He says it's hard to tell, but there could be a couple like that. He says they look pretty beat up. Lot of 'em are full of stars, he says, and, uh, clouds. Mr. Atkinson says, 'clouds,' sir."

Marinetti was about to grab the soldier's headphone, but the man kept talking, stolidly repeating the agent's description of the shed's interior. "He reports 'clouds' and . . . I think the word is 'threat' or 'thread,' sir. I can't tell. The transmission's partly blocked by the building. It also sounds like there's some active interference going on. Real hard to understand."

Marinetti could not see the lights the men inside were using. Also, the building's alignment should have let the new sun shine into the entrance, but the interior was incomprehensibly dark.

"Sir," the radio man said softly. "Mr. Atkinson says there's a god in the building, and it wants to talk to us. He says the guy's acting so happy to see us he can hardly talk English." The man put his hand over his microphone. "Weird shit. Sir."

Marinetti asked the radio operator to check if either Atkinson or the soldier with him had sniffers. The man reported they had and that the shed and the god had been checked for explosives. There could still be something surgically implanted, but there was no easy way to check for that. "Ask Mr. Atkinson to bring his god out."

Marinetti motioned the squad next to him to take up a position in front of the equipment shed, so they could cover both it and the bunkhouse. He and three other Agency men followed the soldiers across the open ground.

They reached the door as Atkinson emerged, smiling at his accomplishment. He and the soldier held the god between them. Marinetti had not seen one of them for more than a year, and he could not stop from gaping at the creature's perfection. Its skin was fair and drawn over such a wondrously imagined frame that it was impossible to tell whether it was male or female. It was idealized to the point of unreality, and only its smaller stature kept Marinetti from feeling humiliated in its presence.

It opened its mouth and music poured out. The soldiers all turned to look at it, momentarily forgetting that they should be watching the bunkhouse.

Marinetti listened, almost unwilling to ask it to stop and speak English, if it could. But the inherent melodies of godly speech were slightly off key. He tried to remember if he had ever heard one of them speaking like this, but nothing came to mind. Perhaps he should have paid closer attention to them before the evacuations. "Please," he asked at last, assured that his own voice was controlled. "Do you have any companions?"

The god stopped in mid-chorus and looked inquiringly at Marinetti and then at the armed men around him. Atkinson and the soldier released their grips without being instructed to.

"My name would be Kord," it began. "I cannot express the gratitude your arrival inspires."

Marinetti guessed it was a male. "Why should that be? Kord?"

The alien looked around at the farm buildings and the desiccated prairie encircling it. "Why, so that now I can stay here. In all this peace and beauty. It is safe here, is it not?

"I have ruined this station's copy of the paintings. The great one in three parts, especially. Your companions saw that I did." He pointed back into the shed. "I do not believe that the painting—perhaps even the original, though I never saw it—had any power of its own. But it was still necessary to rid ourselves of all that . . . that oppressiveness."

The sun was shinning directly into the shed now, forcing enough of the darkness away to reveal the lower half of one framed painting and the corner of another. The canvases had been slashed, the frames broken, and dirt and motor oil smeared over them. Marinetti still recognized them and found an unexpected reassurance with that as if, in some way, he had attained a superiority over the god. "Now . . . ?" He let the god finish the question.

"Now I want to stay here. I have secrets to disclose, so I would not be a burden."

Marinetti's hopes soared. *A collaborator. No. Better yet. The guy wants to join us. A defector! The first one. Ever!* The fact that he was at the station at all meant he was scientifically literate. It was too much to hope for. Marinetti forced himself to speak cautiously. He must not forget the house behind him. "But you'd be staying anyway, wouldn't you? Your ships have left. There is nothing in orbit. Your countrymen are going home."

"But they *are* coming back for us. At least one ship will return."

Marinetti inhaled sharply, irritated that he had not known this. "Why?" He would have to bring this up with Wentworth.

The god evidenced as much surprise as his natural serenity allowed. "Why, for the painting, of course. The very thing that *I* have to be free of. The very thing that must not poison your race as it did mine with its knowledge..." His right hand spiraled up languidly toward the sky. "...of our night-mares' never-never land."

The god reviewed the terrain around the farm again, as if he now sensed the tanks and helicopters behind the hills. "...Of our nightmares," he repeated distractedly.

He spun on his heel and took a step back toward the shed. He remained that way for a moment and then turned to face Marinetti. As he did so, Marinetti felt a line of heat trace against the right side of his face; it resolved itself into a thread of blue light drilled into the center of the god's forehead.

With the same sense of comprehension and powerlessness one experiences when unexpectedly falling a short distance, Marinetti watched the god's head blur and then abruptly diffuse into a globe of silvery mist. The electric sound of the plasma jet became understandable a moment later.

Marinetti, Atkinson and the two soldiers stared at the head-less corpse which remained standing between them. The image had been conjured up too suddenly to be accepted immediately. Then one knee folded up, and the rest of the body fell in a gentle twisting motion to the ground. Clear ichor spilled from the seared stump of its neck.

"Sir!" someone bellowed behind Marinetti. "That's from the objective. Permission to fire?" Then, more urgently: "The goddamn house, sir! Can I fire?"

Marinetti heard this distantly, his attention still fixed on the corpse of *his* defector, Kord. "No. Wait."

There were supposed to be three of them. The others were obviously not so anxious to cooperate, but they would be better than nothing. That was all he had been expecting anyway.

He instructed the tanks and helicopters to stay where they were and confirm that the bunkhouse had been fully acquired by their targeting computers. The TOW missiles were line-of-sight weapons, so he ordered them onto the ridgeline to do the same.

One of the Agency men tapped Marinetti on the shoulder and pointed to the bunkhouse porch. Another god had appeared and was walking uncertainly down the steps. It looked much like Kord. However, its racial serenity vanished as it approached them. Its movements became those of a crippled old man. Its lips moved but emitted no music. Its eyes wandered distractedly from Marinetti to his men to the buildings and dish antennas and then back to the bunkhouse it had just left, as if it were afraid it could become lost while traversing the short distance between them.

The soldiers and Agency men looked to Marinetti for instructions. The creature probably observed this, and steered for him as the apparent leader. It stopped a meter away, trembling and trying to form some words in English. At last it stated that it had to ". . . apologize for these deaths. I believed they were necessary."

"You did that to Kord?" Atkinson seethed. *His defector!*

The alien raised its fingertips to his forehead, as if it were unsure of the answer, then nodded affirmatively.

Atkinson's voice rose in frustration. "May I then ask why the shit you . . . ?"

Marinetti cut him off with a gesture. "We believe there's a third member or your race here. Is there?" He had quickly shovelled all his disappointment and anger into the restricted parts of his intellect. He had been able to do that in the old days and now found the exercise calming.

"There was. She would have been identified as Tahl, if I am rendering it into your language closely. I am Cast, this station's supervisor." The alien inhaled deeply. "I had previously liquidated her. Her remains are in our residence building." He looked to Marinetti for approval. "It was my decision. I thought the integrity of our project depended on it. It was after that that Kord fled to the building you found him in."

"You killed this Tahl too?"

"Yes. She wanted to leave. At every opportunity, she shifted the antennas from the correct, passive search mode to attempt active communication with our departing ships. The integrity of our project was being seriously compromised." Cast looked sadly at the dish antennas in the center of the yard. "Now that is necessarily over." He shrugged and returned to his original subject: "Her unguarded speech would have been of assistance to your race."

Marinetti was surprised by the god's frankness. It was looking for absolution instead of approval. "Just as you thought Kord might assist us?"

"Kord would have been a deeper problem. He wanted to stay as much as Tahl wanted to leave. He wanted to join your race and tell you everything he knew." Cast said this wistfully, as if the killing had been an act of destiny in which he had been only collaterally involved. "He would have taught you only enough to make you appear to be a threat in time. I thought it best if that risk was not taken."

Marinetti had trouble following the god. "In time for what?"

"For my kind's return. One of the ships is returning now. Their suspicions are aroused. We try so hard to *respect* others. We have, so far, although it has been a trial for us on this world. You and the other races are not burdened with our knowledge and the responsibility that comes with it.''

He looked at Marinetti with an expression that presumed complete sympathy by the human beings with what he was patiently explaining to them. ''But now, some of my country-men are distracted by . . . events at home and are confused. They were not here long enough to see how harmless things are and have drawn the wrong conclusions. I am sure of this, but to argue with them would have taken valuable time away from our task of searching for the true threat. They now wonder if they may have overlooked something while they were here.''

Cast faltered. ''I am not sure. The messages are unclear. Densely coded and very weak. They were never directed to this station.''

''But they . . . some of you are coming back?'' Marinetti's pulse quickened with irrational expectations. ''And you're afraid we might seem, somehow, threatening to your fellows?''

''It might seem that way if Kord or someone like him had given you things that would appear . . . inappropriate.''

''Like?'' Atkinson growled.

''Understanding of how this works.'' Cast gestured at the three dish antennas in the yard, and lines of blue illumination suddenly connected their bases to a window in the bunkhouse. As they watched, each of the dishes gently collapsed, their structures smoking and crumbling into a white paste.

Cast continued before anyone could react. ''Or the infor-mation in our residence.'' At his words, the light again emerged from the window, extended outward a meter, then snapped back and wove itself around the outside of the building, until it was encased in a luminous chrysalis. Cumulatively, the threads were too bright too look at.

The light hesitated around the building, which then shud-dered and rushed in upon itself so violently that the sound of its destruction was sucked away from mortal hearing. Dirt and debris followed lines of force, into a miniature sun at the center of the vacuum. This hovered in the air for a moment and then spilled itself onto the ground and vanished.

''I had wished to continue the search,'' Cast murmured,

detached from events that he was orchestrating. "It is the obligation of my race. It is required if its extinction is to be made honorable. There are a few other stations which will continue. For the moment, it is better that this station was kept out of your possession. You understand, don't you?"

Atkinson beat his fists against his thighs in fustration, but Marinetti could not summon any more anger from these losses. He improvised a question: "You're more concerned about us than about your search for whatever threatens you?"

Cast shifted uncomfortably on his feet. "I would say that my station has been compromised. The mission was impeded by my own inadequacies for months before this morning. I am now only trying to minimize the damage."

"You're concerned that *we* might be perceived as the threat, if we were suddenly wielding things we should not?"

"Not *the* threat. Your kind *cannot* be the threat. You could only be a simulation of the threat, at worst. Anything more would be preposterous." Cast allowed himself a self-satisified smile.

Marinetti persisted: "It is possible, however, that we could become the threat? The one, ah, foretold." Then he stared at the alien, sensing equivocation.

Cast looked back into the shed. Then he leaned close to the agent and lowered his voice. "No. No. I do not believe that you are or could be. But Tahl did. That was the greater part of her problem. Her fear grew to horrible dimensions before she died."

"What did Kord believe?"

"Why, he believed the same preposterous thing: that your race is *the* threat. That was why he wanted to stay. That made him equally intolerable.

"I have no wish to fall victim to either fantasy," Cast whispered as the blue light that Marinetti was subconsciously expecting from the house instead welled out of a surgically implanted generator at the base of the skull, folded back around his head and then draped over his body like a cloak. He was destroyed in the same manner as the house. Marinetti was close enough to be nearly blinded by the plasma combustion and hear the air rush into the space the alien's physical presence had just occupied.

"THIS IS MARVELOUS!" WENTWORTH COULD BARELY contain himself as he read the print-outs. He had not felt such fascination since he had penetrated the Peoples' Republic's so-called New Triad and its ghastly aftermath. This was much less clear, but infinitely more exotic. "Trouble at home, Benton. Trouble of the worst sort for them, though I can't understand much of what that may be." His superiors—and probably Marinetti too—had placed the stolid, reliable Benton in his office to monitor his revelations.

Benton never evinced excitement over anything, so he helped keep things in perspective, not only intellectually but also in terms of intramural politics.

Wentworth therefore insisted on showing Benton the computers' most intriguing distillations from the intercepted signals: "'...conspiracy unmasked.... Penetrated to the highest levels of the... administration before discovery. Immediate review and... reevaluation of loyalty of all, repeat, *all* personnel, whether currently embarked, in place or abandoned.... Original lost... Destruction unthinkable but... such... course must be considered....'" *That* was sure to get back to Marinetti; perhaps it would make up for Philadelphia or not having told him immediately about the returning ship.

"They could be talking about the food supply for the trip home," Benton responded, making notes on Wentworth's behavior and making sure all the data was double-banked, no matter how incorrect the interpretation might be.

"Whose 'destruction'?" Benton asked after the printer stopped. "Ours?" making another precise notation.

Wentworth's enthusiasm was untouched by the suggestion. "No. Doubtful. Well, impossible to say, Benton. The approaching ship hasn't transmitted a thing since it started retrograde. And the rest of the fleet and the home-ship have been nearly as quiet. Most of this stuff is from the trans-Uranian satellites and most probably comes from the gods' home, or at least from the next outpost down the line."

"If they haven't forgiven us for not appreciating them and their sacred mission, one might imagine that they left something or someone behind."

"Could be they've gotten sick of their gifted already," Wentworth suggested, then recalled Andy Cavan and felt embarrassed over the remark.

"There must be something here. Something more important than whatever brought them to this world in the first place." The man sounded positively dreamy; completely out of character.

"*Very* good, Benton," Wentworth remarked patronizingly, reaching up to pat the other man's massive shoulder. His keeper had put it nicely, though.

T HE KANSAS STATION HAD BEEN ESTABLISHED A MONTH after the first landings and was not nearly so well hidden as the newer ones. Slate was therefore unsurprised to find it in ruins.

He had driven up from Garden City in the early morning, and wandered across the grid of section line roads for most of the day before finding it. There was evidence of considerable violence, such as the crumbled framework of the three primary dish antennas and the shallow crater where one of the staff residence buildings should have been. Miscellaneous bits of clothing and discarded equipment were scattered around, and beyond the cluster of buildings there were the imprints of tracked vehicles. Large disks of flattened grass indicated that helicopters had been there too.

There was no trace of the gods who were supposed to have been at the station, nor any hint of where they might have gone or if they had been taken forcibly away. He was remarkably uninterested in who they might have been.

Slate decided to spend the night in one of the deserted houses still furnished with its original Earthly furniture. He had gotten accustomed to that and now preferred it.

The main antennas were useless, but the ground array was untouched, probably because it was away from the main buildings and nearly hidden in weeds and sunflowers. Its power leads were still connected to the farm circuits; the auxiliary monitoring station attached to it had been only slightly damaged by whatever had happened at the farm.

There were instructions in his Mission radio on how to use it in conjunction with such installations. It still took him more than an hour to find the right combination of jacks and switch throws.

Then he stretched out on the grass, cooling at last in the early morning darkness, and looked up at the sky, wondering if this part of the Earth was even pointed toward the departing fleet.

At four o'clock in the morning he heard the distinctive music of a transmission from either the home-ship or home itself. Transit-ships were incapable of generating enough power to force such resonances past the causality barrier and make themselves instantaneously understood, no matter how small the intervening space.

First, there were snatches of a panic song, full of terror and political collapse. The intensity of the the feelings it conveyed forced his fingers into the dry Kansas earth, and he actually found solace there.

The next song followed ten minutes later. It was in code, but the Mission radio deciphered it. It was repeated several times, and, after a while, Slate understood that the great triptych had disappeared from home. A copy had been put in its place, and the deception had only lately been uncovered.

Every godly ship and every one of their stations had a copy of the triptych. The most important stations, like the New York Mission, had copies of such fidelity that they duplicated the

original down to the very shape of its brush strokes and placement of constituent molecules. One like that had been displayed
at the National Gallery. But these were only echoes. Blake's
genius never inhabited them.

But someone, Slate overheard, had painted an inspired copy,
a demi-masterpiece that did *not* precisely duplicate the original
and therefore expressed a new and subtly different truth about
what was hunting the godly race. One's conviction in the threat
and the consequent necessity to expand the race's vigilance
throughout the universe was refreshed, but only so long as one
studied it with reverent consideration. Doubt intruded as soon
as one looked away. Violent confrontations had erupted, but
it was only after things had gotten out of hand that the deception
was unmasked.

He was as unmoved by this news as he had been by the
absence of any gods and the destruction of their station. *So
it's gone,* he thought. *Grand. Rane or one of his pals could
surely paint us another curse if we need one so much.*

Then the radio picked up a solemn wish that the triptych
had not been destroyed. The "provisional government" now
suspected that it had been substituted for a ship's copy and
spirited away to a remote province of the universe.

Slate raised his eyebrows. "Provisional government": the
term was perversely exciting. Just as was the idea that the
painting might be in a "remote province of the universe"—
such as the one to which he was now exiled. The masterwork
had been removed from the center of its power; the center was
therefore directionless.

Impossible. The painting must have been chopped up or
hurled into a star or, more likely, was being held in some
irrelevant place for ransom.

Still . . . He had intended to continue west, to a station in
the mountains above Grand Junction, Colorado. It was new,
having been completed just before the evacuations, and thus
heavily fortified, well concealed, and possibly still unnoticed
by the government. Direct contact with it was naturally in-

advisable, but if it was still functioning, the gods there might . . .

Might what? Slate was disgraced and abandoned. The station would be staffed with soldiers who would have little sympathy for defrocked members of the diplomatic corps.

A plain language song awakened Slate as the sun was coming up: one of the evacuation ships was heading back to the planet. His first guess was that they intended to evacuate the remaining stations. Then he made the association between the disappearance of the triptych and the ship's return.

Impossible, he thought again, now fully awake. Such a thing could not unfold in a time and place accessible to him, but the mere possibility that it might was enough to determine his course.

M ARINETTI FELT THE SAME EXHILARATING DREAD HE HAD at the farm when he read the copies of Wentworth's latest reports. The transmissions from outside of the solar system, which were assumed to be from the gods' home, were highly agitated—at least in Wentworth's translation. The loss of this seminal painting appeared to have thrown their society into an uproar. It was hard to get any specifics because of the difficulties in rendering the nuances of godly speech into English, but a general sense of the upheaval still came through.

Marinetti considered the old problem of the speed of light and whether the gods really solved it, as everything suggested they had but which nothing explained. *But we don't know.* If they hadn't, this apparent simultaneity could have just been an illusion fostered by their own foreign conception of time and causation. If so, all this panic might have occurred a millennia ago. *Christ! We can't even guess at that because we don't even know where they live!*

The transmissions from the returning ship were less encumbered by such esoteric considerations. Those intercepted as the ship began retrograde and left the evacuation fleet were restrained enough; the gods' polite formalism fit Wentworth's algorithms. But as it approached Earth, the signals became careless and more emotional. Implied threats and irrational vows of decisive action intruded into its messages to the evacuation fleet or to their Earth stations as it passed inside the orbit of Mars.

Marinetti saw that briefing memos with his initials on them obliquely discussing these interceptions were leaked to the right National Security Council people. His stature rose accordingly.

He visited the triptych as often as discretion allowed. Its darkness penetrated more deeply each time, especially now that he knew the outlines of its power. By the tenth visit, it explained to him, directly, how the universe concealed something of infinite terror, and that this *quality* was approaching the *place* where it resided. The belief became firmly enough set in Marinetti's thoughts to masquerade as knowledge.

The regular Army security detail at the National Gallery informed Marinetti that the basement was becoming increasingly popular with senior administration and DOD people. The diplomatic community, or at least those of it who could wrangle clearance, were also showing up. They all made quite a show, the soldiers told Marinetti over cards and the best scotch in the world, of coming down to look at one neglected Earthly masterpiece or another or to look at the portraits and landscapes the gods left behind. But most of the stuffed shirts were really after the triptych, and the soldiers and the curatorial staff made a game of rearranging and reorienting its three panels or putting other works in front of them to see how much hemming and hawing they would try before either ordering the works out into plain sight or departing in embarrassment.

The soldiers shared their excitement and fear with Marinetti. Most of them, including the officers, were not educated, and the possibility that a mere painting should affect them at all was unnerving enough; that it should so strongly evoke actual dread made it a virtual test of courage.

Marinetti assured them that steps were being taken to understand what was going on. He had the soldiers remotely monitored to assure himself of the authenticity of their feelings.

Wentworth was, by turns, ecstatic and then speechless with frustration. The returning ship had begun regular active transmissions aimed at Earth. They were being easily intercepted at Green Bank and Woomera, but the only computers that could render the signals into intelligible English were functioning erratically. Of the anointed geniuses who could understand a battery of linked Cray 9 computers, three had inadequate security clearances even to enter the building he worked in; two were on Defense Intelligence's payroll; one was committed to the machines directing the NORAD/NATO Shield System. Three were listed as suicides during the past year, but that term was lately being used to identify people who had left with the gods, too.

A month of tinkering by his own people and the fortuitous availability of one of the DIA geniuses seemed to get Wentworth's system back on line, but the translations did not ring true. He did not want to flatter himself by thinking he had acquired any personal understanding of godly speech, but the print-outs seemed incomplete and unbalanced, even considering their increasingly hysterical tone.

Frequent, though minor, instances of decay and unreliability now joined his homeland to the deteriorating present world, rather than to the future as it had previously been. That seemed especially so on summer nights when the temperature never dropped below thirty degrees Celsius. It was silent then, the air conditioning usually shutting down along with the street lights. The heat had killed most of the songbirds and crickets. There were no more fireflies.

He considered trying to find some school friends, but felt himself hopelessly removed from them even as he went through the telephone directories at the Post Office. His father had vanished, either by suicide, government removal, or treasonous departure with the gifted. His mother was probably still around.

He called the State Department switchboard on impulse one day but hung up when the operator said her extension was busy.

He believed he needed to speak to the gods, or at least to someone who had been among them. But the gods were either gone or in hiding and none of the gifted had returned. He then remembered Susan Marquez, the young girl who had been trampled at the National Gallery and inadvisedly restored to life. His father and Rane had discussed that blunder in his own living room, some weeks before Slate compounded that mistake with his own fabulous miscalculation over the second art exhibition.

The magazines were carrying articles on her again. She was thirteen years old that summer and had been set up by unidentified interests as a semi-religious figure in a large, secure estate in the New Jersey pine barrens east of Hammonton. He did not believe she would have anything to say to him that would be enlightening. Even if she had endured the same experience as he, it was unlikely she still had any revelations that had not already been squandered on the crowds that petitioned her or sold to the check-out-counter press.

Most of the thick groves of fir trees were gone, as were many of the towns that had been among them. The sand dunes were moving inland from the coast where they had already filled in the old Intracoastal Waterway, but they had not reached the central part of the state. That was mostly charred scrub pine, weed fields and dirt that spiraled up with the wind in the late afternoon.

He entered the state at Collins Park and followed State Route 40. That road was in fair condition, but the next highway, State Route 54, was a dirt track with slabs of asphalt appearing at half-kilometer intervals to remind the driver it had once been paved.

Timothy became locked into a crawling procession of automobiles and trucks, although he could not imagine where they would be going to or coming from in this backwater country. He was still south of Hammonton when he pulled off the road, as everyone else seemed to be doing at dusk. He walked around a bit before trying to sleep, watching people set up camp beside their vehicles as if this were the most natural way in the world to travel through a civilized country.

Lines of cookfires marked the trace of the ancient road after sunset. There was laughter and fighting, cooking sounds and drinking and a high, singing hopefulness all around that repelled him. Timothy stepped aside for the few vehicles that chanced proceeding through the potholes and debris in the dark, listening, politely refusing offerings of drinks, drugs or food.

Most of the people along the road were uneducated or poor, usually both. Their grammar was deficient, though that could not obscure their sincerity; cars and trucks old and worn, children unkempt though generally laughing. No one Timothy passed was reading anything other than a tabloid sheet, their slack features illuminated by the phosphorescent glow of the animated pictures with the story line running underneath, illustrating the news in two-minute stories that repeated themselves as long as the newsprint batteries lasted.

Some of the groups were clustered around pirated National Guard trucks or tracked carriers. None of these vehicles had any armaments on board, but they still loomed menacingly over the people and the junkers parked carelessly next to them. The people on them were the same as everyone else along the road that evening, rough but generally in high spirits. Timothy thought they should not be using Guard equipment; there should be soldiers or people with some pretense of discipline on the carriers, or with some better purpose than wandering down a dustbowl road toward a thirteen-year-old girl with nothing more to offer than tales of her own death and resurrection.

They were all going to see her, Timothy gathered from the few conversations he was able to sustain before well-bred impatience caused him to walk away. She would *reveal* things, tell why the gods had left, or at least why people should not be concerned that they did; why the gifted joined them and why the works they performed before leaving should be reviled.

Timothy returned to his car, too tired to care about the food he had refused. He locked the doors and looked down the road, seeing the camp lights flicker as cars or people passed in front of them, casting long shadows through the mob's dust.

The smell of morning defecations woke Timothy before sunrise. No one along the road could have slept much. Cooking continued just as it had that night; there were still men sitting on car fenders, swapping bottles and howling at jokes. The same children were playing on the same truck flatbeds.

Camp stoves were put away as the morning advanced, clothing and food bundles put back into trunks, and the whole shambling convoy lurched back onto the trace of Route 54. Timothy stayed with them, hoping that his rented Toyota would not shake itself to pieces on the dirt and rubble roadbed.

Signs and sweating marshals dressed in luminous plastic vests appeared in the roadside dust clouds around noon. Timothy was waved into a line of parked vehicles and stopped beside a National Guard armored car; the turret had been removed and the hole covered by a canvas parasol. A dairy van packed with a large extended family parked on the other side of his car.

He was reassured to see some kind of organization and walked in the direction the marshals indicated. A grove of pine trees materialized out of the haze, and he could see the sun again. There were a great many people walking through the woods with him.

He passed clusters of buildings; some were occupied while others had been deserted for some time. Asphalt fragments underfoot showed that he was walking on what had been a paved street. A small town had probably been there once, but its abandonment may have predated the arrival of the gods on Earth.

After a few minutes the trees thinned out and he came upon an open field, half a kilometer across. A crowd occupied the middle of it, clustered around a raised platform about twenty meters square. Droning music, punctuated by unintelligible speeches apparently being delivered by figures on the platform, issued from loudspeakers suspended from telephone poles.

Timothy Cavan was amused by the idea that this might be America. It seemed more like the stories his father brought back from India and Meunas Guerias when the gods landed there. At least there was no terrible ship hovering above this filthy crowd, bending heaven's light in sickening ways.

Timothy heard the girl's name shouted or muttered or whispered by nearly every person he passed: "Susan" or "the Marquez girl."

"She'll tell us about the gods," a fat woman at his elbow shouted when he bumped into her. "*They* confided in her, you know! They made her promise to keep their secrets while they were gone. But she won't, you know! She'll *share*'m!" Timothy politely stepped away.

"Look!" A man was pointing excitedly toward the platform. "She's here!"

Someone pushed Timothy into the crowd. He found the stench appalling, but it was unlikely he smelled much better after two days on the road. He worked his way forward, conscious both of the depth of his contempt for the people around him and of his own strength. There was a sense of fragility about most of them, as if he could press his hand through their bodies if he wished.

A blast of off-key horns spilled from the speakers. Timothy saw a collection of adults in ludicrous costumes climbing onto the platform, some in formal wear, sweating buckets, others in parodies of clerical vestments, and even one fool in a toga being roughly ushered back down into the mob.

One of the priestly types said something into a microphone, but it was lost in the crowd's noise. As he was speaking, a small girl was led to the front of the platform by an extravagantly dressed woman and turned by the shoulders to face the crowd. The people quieted at this.

The priest bent down to place his ear next to her mouth. She spoke to him for a moment. Then the man straightened, cocked his head as if considering something profound and said, "She sings in the way the gods did. They taught her to do that, after she had lost her life and they gave her a new one of their own to use.''

There were sounds of astonishment, as if some among the crowd had actually expected something less.

"She says you have not been forsaken by them." Cheers of relief. "They have left, Susan tells me, because they were not certain we were worthy of their beneficence. But she assures me that they continue to watch and weigh our virtue against the evil they also found here.''

The man bent down to the girl again. . . . Intrigued, Timothy began gently shouldering his way nearer to the platform. The man kept talking: ''. . . There were some who were found especially worthy, and they were taken away as the gifted. There were others, however, who were found to be especially evil. They too were taken away, but for different reasons.'' Timothy thought that was a nice twist to the usual agonizing over the gifted.

The man kept replenishing his wisdom from the child's lips. "They *have* saved us in a way, even as they have carried their promise of grace back to the stars for a while! They have taken the worst of humankind away with them, along with some of the very best, all under the name of the gifted, and left behind the purified essence of ordinary humanity to prove ourselves worthy of their return!''

Her apparent youth conflicted with the agelessness that invested her expression when the man stood up to resume speaking to the crowd. There were plates of scar tissue over the right side of her head; her hair was carefully arranged to exaggerate how deeply they penetrated her scalp.

Then she looked at Timothy, and he had to forcibly repress the sense of recognition: *Eyes are not luminous; they are wholly passive. She cannot imply the same things I perceive in my own face because, alive or dead, we are different people. The gods could not have made us alike.* Timothy nevertheless inclined his head in answer, as if she had actually picked him out from among the hundreds around the platform.

"They've harvested the superhuman and the subhuman!''

the priest bellowed. "We, *we* are left to wait with Susan for their return! We must prove that we . . ." He bent down again. "That we understand them." The last words were oddly phrased, as if he realized he was not following what the girl was saying.

She suddenly stepped up to the microphone, almost pushing the startled man aside despite his greater size. "We must understand them," she said; her voice was controlled and deeper than it should have been.

"I've seen . . ." she searched for words a child would not naturally use, ". . . seen their *works* and I believe that they, the gods, have *revealed* themselves to us in ways they had never intended." She was looking directly, pointedly at Timothy. "They have revealed *ourselves* to us."

Then, with a contemptousness that caused most of the crowd to shift and murmur uneasily: "They have revealed a destiny which is beneath *us*, but which we should help them find, if we ever get another chance." The girl's words were unnervingly sinister and presumptuous.

She had died at the National Gallery of Art. She had seen the portraits of the courtesan, the scholar, Blake and the triptych just as he had, but he could not believe that her understanding now compared with his own. But then, she had died before he did and, more important, had returned to life while the gods were still on Earth. She had awakened in their company, instead of alone, as Timothy had. She could have gone back to the Gallery and seen the exhibition again or been watching at the Mall when the ship landed. The timing of her death and resurrection could have taught her something that had been denied him, even though he had surely been taken up bodily into their ship, while the miracles had been performed on her in the basement of the gods' Washington Mission.

"I've *seen* their fear!" Her voice was rising to a higher pitch better suited to her age. "I *know* that they came here because they were afraid of something in the stars, something strong that was hunting them." The adults on the platform were now looking as uncomfortable as the crowd; they took turns gesturing at the ranting girl as if one of them was supposed to know how to deal with this. For a moment, a man in a cutaway seemed ready to step forward and take bodily control of her, but the priest put his hand on the man's shoulder, restraining him while fearfully looking at the girl and then at the crowd.

She was sounding progressively younger and more irrational. "They didn't come to help us! They didn't care about us! So long as everything was okay and we didn't get in the way of their watching too much. They only wanted to watch from here! They're watching from a hundred planets, more than that, for this thing they think is on its way! *We* don't have a thing to do with that fear. I know this! They . . . I could *see* it and understand it."

Then, with a guileless look directed to everyone in the crowd at once: "Can't *you* understand it? Am I the only one who . . . ?" Her voice trailed away for a moment, and the man in the suit used the suspended moment to slip away from the priest. He reached the girl in two steps and grabbed her arm.

The crowd around Timothy surged, not knowing what to do or which way they should move. Their bodies were intolerable.

The priest moved up, but the man pushed him away. He persisted and received a kick to the groin that sent him spinning off the platform and into the crowd. Other people rushed toward the girl, some trying to grab her or put their arms around her waist, while others began shrieking, warning them of the sacrilege of touching her. There may have been some figures with pistols in their hands standing uncertainly at the rear of the platform, but Timothy could not be sure amid the crush.

Susan Marquez began crying and screaming hysterically, tears running down her face as the adults shoved and punched either to get her away or to make sure she would stay where she was.

The fighting spread into the crowd as realization of the girl's danger swirled through it, igniting anger or despair in people who had been looking only for brainless hope.

The first shots came from the perimeter of the crowd, moving randomly behind him as they approached, until they were were very near, and then on the platform itself.

The man in the formal suit flung the girl away and clutched his shoulder, There were so many other adults falling over themselves that none of them could get a strong hold on her. Her glistening eyes were open wide, and Timothy recalled the Gallery's portrait of the insane scholar. Then she found him again, looking directly at him, pleading.

The man in the suit could not find where the wounding shot had come from. He looked back at the girl, unwilling to move his good hand away from his shoulder, but following her gaze to Timothy. Then another shot hit him on the same shoulder, and the arm was blasted free by the impact, pinwheeling away over the heads of the crowd. He caught a third shot in the chest, the back of his cutaway erupting from pressure waves generated by the bullet in the thoracic cavity. He fell back toward the edge of the platform, rolling as if there were still life in him until he dropped over the edge.

Timothy had watched carefully and was certain that the clear, secret ichor of the gods had sprayed out of the man when the bullets struck.

The Marquez girl was now at the edge of the platform, still looking at him and seeming calmer although ten or more adults were battling over her. The bitter serenity she used when she first spoke returned as she continued to look at Timothy. Then she simply shook off the few hands wrapped around her neck and arms.

Timothy shouldered his way to her. There was some resistance. He pushed tentatively at first, then dug in the toe of one shoe and deliberately drove his fists and elbows into the surrounding bodies. Amazingly, they fell away before him. *They are not like us. Not like me.*

He picked her up from the edge of the platform and was surprised at how easy it was. "I've seen you," she said as if it was she who had to justify herself to him. "In the magazines.

You were taken away after you died, and your dad went away with them for good. Help me." Then she hid her face in his shoulder so no one could see who she was.

The crowd was too absorbed in its own confusion and violence to bother with them now. Young men scrambled onto the platform, grappling with the costumed adults and armed marshals at the rear. They were followed by more people until it collapsed, and the crowd overran it.

He heard automatic weapon fire as he reached the edge of the mob. Marshals, some armed and some holding only batons, were emerging from the woods, half of them assessing the chaos on the field in front of them and turning back the way they had come, the other half plunging mindlessly ahead.

She murmured to him as he walked. Most of it was unintelligible over the noise of the crowd, but she could be understood once they reached the woods. She was cursing the gods and all the gifted who went with them.

"Why?" he asked, keeping his eyes straight and one hand protectively over her head.

"Because they left. They left me behind, but they took others who didn't deserve to go." She lifted her head briefly to look at him. "You must know more about that than I do. Your dad went. Mine . . . wanted to go. More than he wanted to stay here with me." She put her head down again.

They emerged from the pine grove into the vehicle park. People ran past them, trying to find their own cars or hot-wire someone else's. One of the stolen National Guard armored cars was taking the most direct escape route by crushing the autos that were in its way; a crowd of maniacs, visibly drunk even at that distance, hung on to its flanks, cheering as each Chevrolet and Hyundai was flattened.

"So he stayed?"

"I guess," she said at last after he had put her down and they were running toward where he had left the Toyota. "But it was too hard for him. Then I was taken and they brought me back, and he tried to thank them for that. He's around somewhere. Either that or he's dead. It doesn't matter much. The gods never noticed him.''

Timothy noted how her voice hardened when she talked about something she valued. She would begin coolly, become progressively more upset as she placed the idea out in the open, and then, having measured its true dimensions in the light of her special reason, would regain her composure and consign the former object of her anxiety to an inferior station. Timothy heard her pass judgment on her father and appreciated its finality.

He found his car, quickly unlocked it and shoved her inside. She hid in the passenger's footwell without being told to. Timothy dove in and relocked the doors. He started driving slowly out the way he thought he had come. Other cars and trucks careened in front of him. One clipped the Toyota's right front fender but kept going. He saw burning vehicles through the dust clouds that had been stirred up again. People, some wild with panic or holding wads of clothing against wounds, staggered in front of him.

Against every self-conceived shred of personal decency, he turned on the air conditioner and instructed the radio to find classical music. The machine selected a Baltimore station playing Carl Nielsen's Fifth Symphony. Its polished brutality suited him.

"**M**RS. CAVAN?'' THE VOICE WAS CULTURED, ALMOST up to the American conception of British English.

"Yes. Who is this?''

A pause. "I knew your husband.''

"Many people did. He's gone if you had business with him.'' That was a poor way to begin. She was being rude for no reason, and there was always the possibility that the caller might have something serious to discuss. "I'm sorry. What can I do for you?''

The other end of the line was silent again, as if the caller was watching something that had to be completed before he would feel confident enough to speak. "I met you too, once. I was the artist: Rane. Do you remember?"

The artist. The weakling who had visited her home when that poor young girl had been brought back to life. She touched the "priority trace" button on her telephone. "Yes, Mr. Rane. I remember you."

"Are you well?"

Right. Right. Gods are like that. But I tried to shoot this guy! This is impossible! "I am. You're still, ah, here, on Earth. Has there been a problem?" *Jesus! I'm talking like an idiot! I don't need any more of this spaceman shit!* "I . . ." She could not think of anything but his nearly perfect face, flawed to the precise extent necessary to imply artistic sensitivity, illuminated by the floodlights in front of *her* home, as all the governmental lunatics tried to find some trace of *her* husband. She wondered if she had enough hate or irrationality to try and kill him again. "I'm well, thank you. Where are you? Are you well yourself?"

"Not entirely. I have been spending the time since those of my race left trying to understand your kind."

The silence again. He was waiting for her question. "Do you? Now?"

"In some ways. Yes."

She knew that she must not interrupt when he was speaking, but she could not help herself: "Was your *Blake* worth the trouble?"

Gratification welled up unexpectedly in the caller's voice, and he seemed pleased with the observation. "Why, yes. How remarkable that you should mention that. It might have been worth being killed over, after all." Rane's hesitation was displaced by something like enthusiasm. "It is difficult for me. I no longer feel like one of my race, and I certainly would not pretend to be one of yours. But I feel things inside of me. I . . . *see* them as I used to when I was doing good work, and I need help to get these things down."

"To paint?"

"Yes! Exactly."

"Then why don't you?" she asked, even as the answer uncovered itself.

"I cannot. I have been hurt. My hands were hurt, and I have difficulty holding a brush. They will not respond as they used to. I cannot begin the sort of work I now have in mind, although I have done some sketches and oils which have . . . shown promise."

Rane was on the Department's Blue List. Not important enough to make the Red List, like that Slate everyone had been looking for since their embassy in New York went berserk and took out half the Upper East Side, but still significant enough to try and bring in.

"You aren't with any of your kind?"

"No. I am alone." That was a disappointment. He named some small towns along the Chesapeake where he was selling his paintings, but said he wanted to get back to the Capital. He missed its "intensity." The alien seemed to put great emphasis on that word, drawing the "s" out into a hiss.

"Could I help you?" He would not be a great catch; a diplomat or scientist would have been much more useful. But most of those left on Earth had either been killed or were sitting in secret detention cells, purposely sinking their consciousnesses so deeply into their psyches as to be beyond recall. So much fury and frustration was stirred up wherever these monsters went. *Why'd they ever come?*

"I would like a place to work. In the city, or at least near to it, with good light and supplies. And the help of technical people, if they could render it, to help me overcome my disabilities."

The creature's presumption caught her off balance. "Do you think I owe you something? You . . . your kind took a lot from me."

"*I* took nothing." The voice became impassioned. "*I* stayed! But I do not wish to talk about that, Mrs. Cavan. I have . . . needs and, I think, worthy ambitions. I may have something to give your kind, if I am allowed."

"Like what?"

"It remains indefinite. I have accomplished nothing yet. That is what I need to attempt."

The trace was finally completed to a pay phone at Broome's Island. A regular forces detachment was automatically requested from Patuxent River Naval Air Station to pick up the god. Linda Cavan assumed that he would not be hard to spot in such a small town.

Keep him on the line. "That sounds reasonable. We could help you with that. Would you consider requesting political asylum?"

"Whatever for?"

"You don't know?"

"About what? I am here, on Earth. What could I require asylum from?"

"One of your ships is coming back. That's already in the rumor mill, and the papers should be getting the story any day now. Your friends are coming back. For you, Rane?"

The alien hung up as she was talking.

MARINETTI PUT A PHOTOGRAPH OF THE TRIPTYCH IN HIS office, but was dissatisfied with it. He replaced it with a holographic print that conveyed more warning.

He had primary control over the search for "cooperative" gods who might be turned to the cause of mankind. To date, he had only come up with two corpses to be dissected at Bethesda. But he kept listening, and lately there had been some vague, tenative leads.

Cavan's wife, for instance. She had first tried to interest her pompous colleagues at State in this Rane but gave up after they had made it clear that they had no use for abandoned artists from outer space. Then she had called Wentworth because he had known Andy and seemed fairly harmless. He, in turn, had at last had the good sense to call Marinetti.

Marinetti returned the favor by giving Wentworth the tape he had actually made of their meeting when the latter confessed how he had asked the gods to take him with them. Now, all

Wentworth wanted was the chance to listen to Rane if he was brought in, and that did not seem too unreasonable.

But this Slate is a refreshingly arctic personality, Marinetti thought. He never pretended to much believe in the wonders their works of art could inflict on the viewer. He was not exactly like us, but neither was he much like most of his fellows. Slate might be accessible, and the fact that he had been abandoned made him the best bet Marinetti had so far.

And if I snare him, what will I use him for? Marinetti stared ruefully at the holograph of the triptych. *Bring him back to this artifact of his own world, thrust him into the center of it and ask him to explain it?*

Marinetti checked his watch, turned on the scrambler and waited. The phone rang two minutes after the agreed time. After some pleasantries, he broached the subject of an "accommodation."

"Betrayal, you mean?" Slate sounded amused.

"Not at all. You're the one who's been betrayed."

The following silence was too long to be unintended. "That came about as much through an error in my own judgment as from any decision by my superiors. My usefulness was, ah, diminished, so it was only reasonable that I should stay behind. Others chose to stay behind, you know."

"Yes. I think I saw some of them at a station in Kansas," he said pointedly. Surveillance cameras had watched Slate camped out in the ruins; the ground array antenna had been tapped and Wentworth had deciphered most, but not all, of the messages that came through Slate's Mission radio. A great many things seemed to be unfolding around Marinetti.

"Our remaining operations are not running very smoothly, are they? But this 'accommodation' of yours sounds much more, ah, affirmative than what I was trying to promote with my misguided ideas about art and all." The voice remained pleasant: it made Marinetti realize how heavy-handed he might have been during their previous conversations. "I'm getting along well enough without anyone's assistance. That may not last . . ."

"And the local populations now treat gods roughly when they discover them."

"Of course . . ."

"That hostility will only increase when they find out about the returning ship."

"Ah. You've spotted it, then? Everyone will know about that soon, won't they?"

Marinetti had promised he would not trace any of Slate's calls, but certain passive measures could be invoked to give a general idea of where the god was calling from. "But, for all we know, the effect might be just the opposite. Many people still regard my kind as saviors who would grant all sorts of wondrous favors to them, if only they could discover what pleases us."

Marinetti liked the alien. There was no bitterness or pleading, just a fatalistic gentleman adjusting to disagreeable circumstances. Time to press him, then. "What do you think will happen when they find out why the ship is coming back?"

Carefully: "What, I should ask first, will they 'find out'?"

"They'll find out about the painting."

"They know all about the paintings. Largely thanks to me, I'm afraid."

"They don't really know how important one of them is to your race. That it may be the reason for your flights through the galaxy, and that its disappearance has thrown your worlds into disarray." Marinetti could not imagine where he came up with these turns of phrase. He had been staring at the holograph when he uttered them.

"You have been listening carefully. Reading the signs very well."

"I and some others."

He heard Slate inhale deeply at the other end of the line. "Do you believe in that painting?"

"I believe in what I've learned about it." Marinetti was surprised how he emphasized his own words. "Where is it, Slate?"

"You know as well as I do."

"Do your friends?"

"The ones who are coming back? Almost certainly. There were only three full-sized copies on this world: the one at your National Gallery, one at the New York Mission and one more at a station in Kenya."

"I was unaware of that one."

"That was the idea. The original could not have been secreted there. That operation is entirely automated. Its machineries would not betray their leaders. The one in New York was not very well done. Even *I* could see that. Therefore, the painting in question must be the one at the Gallery exhibition." There was a snatch of musical laughter over the line. "So it seems I was used even more than I thought. And by Rane, too! Appalling."

Slate waited a moment. "You've looked at it quite a bit, Mr. Marinetti . . ."

He interrupted: "As you say you have."

"I never talked about it like the others did. Like you're doing now. Doesn't that give you some pause, Mr. Marinetti?" He kept the faintly mocking tone of voice, as if they were discussing errors in political theory.

Marinetti tried to recover his balance. He continued to stare at the holograph, feeling it push the gods aside so it could communicate directly with him. "If there's no danger, there's usually nothing to exploit."

"You seem intent on making things more dangerous than they have to be, Marinetti. I'm not sure I need to be associated with this." The voice became tired, as if Slate were suddenly losing interest in the conversation.

Marinetti applied himself to his script, dropping any reference to the painting. He promised Slate understanding, protection, cosmetic surgery, whatever he wanted.

"Which would help, I suppose, until I happen to bleed," the god said after Marinetti finished. "I can't tell you what I should do now. I'll call you later."

"Can I help at all?" Marinetti was both disappointed that

the god had not consented to join him and relieved that he was not breaking off contact entirely.

"No. Nothing's required right now, But I might be able to help you. I'll mail you my Mission radio along with some instructions I've tried to translate. I'm sure it can do many more things that I'm capable of understanding, and might help you track the incoming ship and understand its intentions."

Marinetti was silent. The history of Ultra, Magic, Purple, and the Black Room at State came to mind: *Wentworth will be blind with envy! Furious!* The fiasco with Kord might be overcome after all. "That will be extremely useful," he said mildly.

"Quite. Promise me that you will keep me advised of what you learn. I'm finding some measure of peace where I am. I do not want to abandon it without a good reason."

Marinetti promised he would. They arranged for another phone call in a week.

L INDA CAVAN DID NOT RECOGNIZE RANE. SHE HAD TO ask him who he was.

"Why, I am the painter, Mrs. Cavan." He sounded hurt that she might have forgotten.

She reviewed her memories of the alien: him seated with her husband in her living room, spinning all kinds of repulsive stories about his exalted art and the error of saving childrens' lives, drawing her husband further and further away from her and dragging her son along with him. Then the insane evening at her house, after everything she believed Rane threatened had actually occurred: her husband a traitor and Timothy dead. The alien was not personally responsible for any of that, but he was the one who had trespassed into her sight, and trying to kill him was the only thing she could do then.

"I must apologize. I was not thinking very well when I . . . when that happened." She looked at his hands.

"I was not thinking clearly myself. Obviously. I chose to stay."

"Andy chose to leave," she said, trying to sound sympathetic.

Rane cleared his throat and changed the subject. "But now you've given me this." He waved his crippled hands around the room. The north wall overlooking the Potomac River was glass; the hazy light suffused the room softly enough to eliminate shadows. A conventional easel, fitted with sliding tracks that could hold panels up to two meters on a side, was in the middle of the room. There was a wheeled stand with hinged trays beside it, holding every kind of pigment from microencapsulants to gold leaf and preserved albumen for tempera.

"Will your people be watching?" Rane asked, looking at the room's blank walls.

"*Mine* won't," she said too harshly and then brought her voice down. "I'm afraid there'll be others keeping track of things. They really have to." There was no point in lying; he would figure things out soon enough, if he hadn't already.

"I may want to move around quite a bit or leave the house and go into the city. I have found it helps to be out watching your kind."

"I'm sure there'll be no problem if you want to. Just let the people stationed next door know your plans."

"That would be necessary?"

Linda Cavan smiled indulgently at the alien, surprised at how difficult it was to place him in her memory. *They all really do look alike.* But the sense of divinity that she remembered the gods all possessed was absent. Rane had consciously allowed his miraculous racial identity to slip away, perhaps just to see what would be left over when it was gone.

"This is courageous of you," she said, when she had just meant to say good day and leave.

It WAS THE SAME EVERYWHERE SLATE STOPPED AFTER KANsas. The stations were either deserted, burnt to the ground, or the gods on duty had committed the least disagreeable suicide possible or just wandered away, sometimes leaving their equipment out in plain sight and operational.

Once, Slate was shown ruins which he was told had been a station that had been "cleansed" of the gods' presence. In actuality, it was three doors down from the real station; the human mobs had only killed their own kind, while the gods cowered in fear, waited until the storm had passed and then drove away in leased Buicks, abandoning devices of astonishing perceptivity behind unlocked screen doors.

He met creatures who looked like him, skin taut over idealized bone structures, but unshaven and crusted with filth, sitting in front of Earthly televisions, often watching documentaries of the ongoing collapse of the environment or alleged miracles portending an escape from these terrible problems: faith healing of epidemic melanomas from ozone depletion; synthogenesis of Antarctic krill; psychic contact with the gods' fleet and their anguished apologies for having left humankind too soon.

The ship was less than two light-minutes distant. None of the gods he found still at their stations knew or felt like revealing anything about its intentions. The ones who would speak to him were aware of the disappearance of the triptych from their home, but none of them believed the suggestions that it might be on Earth. That would be inconceivable.

He was aware how equivocal his thinking had become. Sometimes, he set fire to the abandoned stations so they would not fall into Earthly hands. At other times, he left them as he found them. He even told Marinetti about one and felt genuinely pleased with himself afterward, as he had when he sent him the Mission radio.

He found comfort in the absence of countrymen who could put a coherent paragraph together, in Johnnie Walker Black Label and in his telephone conversations with Marinetti.

There were roughly compatible women, too. That was easy enough after some initial, fumbling practice. Although he was many times the age of the ones he met, they seldom guessed that there was anything more to his bodily perfection than exercise and their own good fortune. They were different from his wives at home and not in an unexciting way. He was reassured when they felt as remote as his wives had, as if they were only pictured on panes of glass lying next to him.

"Our friends are almost in orbit around your world," he said to Marinetti during a conversation in early summer. The weather was comfortably warm for Slate, but the human population was beginning to suffer.

"Everyone knows that. Any more insight on what they've got in mind?" It was difficult to hear over the background noise; he thought the quality of the signal had declined noticeably over the past months.

Slate chuckled. "You have the radio now. You should know better than I. And you've got hostages now, too. Is Rane of much help to you?"

"We haven't imposed on him much. There's some difference of opinion over what should be done with him. For the moment, he's being left alone."

"And painting?"

A pause. "Yes." Marinetti used to think his voice was unreadable, at least over the telephone.

"You realize he was considered a has-been long before we came here. He did his best work at the beginning of his career."

"He seems confident now."

"Is he doing some of that, ah, time and place magic for you?"

"I think you should come in now, Slate, and see for yourself. We could use you."

Slate said that he would consider it seriously this time.

"**A**ND WHY THE SHIT CAN'T I TALK TO HIM?" MS. IRE-land was a large woman, habituated to bellowing. "Why *can't* we even be told where he is? You finally come up with one breathing, certified god who wants to join us and you rent the sonofabitch a *studio*, for Christ's sake, and let him *paint?* Jesus H. Christ! We've got these monsters coming back on us with enough power to wipe us out—Christ knows why they didn't do it the first time they were here—and this time without a shred of explanation, and Marinetti tucks this Rane twink away in a soft little place with the goddamn requisite northern light pouring through the windows so he can *paint!*''

She stamped around the table to address Wentworth directly: ''We've finally got an *asset*, and all we're doing is indulging his hobby when there's a million things even a technological dunce like him could help us with!''

A two-meter-square display screen at one end of the room showed a stroke-by-stroke analysis of the painting that Rane was working on. The holographic effect was startling, as the scale of resolution made individual layers of pigment seem five or six centimeters high.

Hazy quanta filled the screen as the computers completed an analytical cycle that started with a full-life view of Rane's back, then moved through successive stages to his scarred brush hand with the electro-hydraulic prosthetic brace Marinetti's people built for the artist, continuing down to the brush tip and then to a systematic review of the canvas in square centimeter sections. The computers went down past the molecular level only where Rane's brush strokes were building the picture. The screen went dark for a moment, and then the picture returned with two quanta noticeably moved from their position in the preceding depiction. Ireland squirmed at this, as if it were indiscreet to show such things in literal terms.

''Look at this shit!'' She was speaking more softly; the trace of fear put unexpected femininity into her voice. ''Seem cold to you in here?''

''No. I haven't been cold anywhere in years. No one's cold these days.''

''This is getting bad, Wentworth. Look.'' Judy Ireland pointed to a line of wildly fluctuating data projected along the bottom of the screen. ''Oh, Christ. He's doing that temporal perspective trick again.''

''Does it make any sense yet?''

Ireland sighed and sank into her chair. ''No. I can't . . .

Here. Le' me stop it for a second.'' She used a hand controller, and the figures froze into columns of four-dimensional coordinates. "Doesn't make much sense." She shrugged. "Spatial and chronic coordinates don't locate anything more specific than this galaxy and this millennium. Big deal."

"But he's just starting, after all."

She used his first name, which she had never done during the fifteen years they had known each other. "Marty, the important thing is that our *machines* are picking up that kind of information directly from the painting. This is all new, so the sensors are responding to patterns we can't appreciate yet. But the *machines*, for Chrissake, are reading this stuff from a two-dimensional painting and making enough sense out of it to write dimensional coordinate catagories, even if they don't match any real space-time yet!"

Wentworth waited before speaking. "Then he's not doing illusions. This's real, isn't it?" He reached over for the controller and brought the screen back up through stages to full scale. "Equipment anomaly?"

Ireland shook her head. "We don't need this, Marty. We should stop it, at least until we can get a better handle on it, with better oversight authority than Tony Marinetti."

"Tony's not so bad. He's had more experience in this sort of thing than either of us. Anyway, I'd have thought you—especially after all your DARPA black magic—would be all for seeing how Rane's picture turns out. After all, I'm the one who could use him immediately, not you, and I'm not completely upset by this. It's, ah, intriguing.

"Marinetti's also got Slate on his line. He's already sent him that trick radio of his. It's likely that he can fill in for Rane after Tony brings him in. How's that sound?" Wentworth knew his voice was wandering all over the place; he was still unable to keep his feelings about Marinetti's project straight. *One misstep and he's going to push us all over the edge.* Wentworth did not intend to be dragged along.

Ireland might not have been listening to him. "The feed, sensors and primary analysis are all going through Langley.

The security people in the studio and in the townhouses on either side are Marinetti's.'' She touched her fingertips to her forehead and then continued miserably: ''Christ, we don't even know where this studio *is*! Can you believe that? All the sensors are shielded and too short-ranged to see out the windows. It's sound- and vibration-proofed, so we can't use seismic trucks to let us know where he's stashed. Just that it's either in or somewhere near D.C. The Secretary's on Marinetti's side. You know that? We can't do anything operationally ourselves. There used to be plenty of people at Defense I could count on, but not any more. Things've changed so much since the damned gods came and left.''

''Great,'' Wentworth said acidly, despite the thrill he felt at her suggestion. Treason and civil war were something to be provoked and studied in other places. There was no reason to practice such nastiness at home. ''Where're you get ideas like that?'' His sympathy now turned away from Ireland and toward Marinetti.

HE WOULD NOT LEAVE A MESSAGE, BUT CALLED HER OF-fice at hourly intervals until she returned. She was not as upset as he had expected. He pointed that out to fill in the awkward spaces in their exchange.

She speculated that the departure of his father and, strangely to a greater degree, the reappearance of Rane had drawn all the shock out of her. ''You went away, like he did. Now you've come back, too. Just like your god, Rane,'' she said in her old, bitter way. ''Did you join them when you died?''

He said it had not been like that at all.

''Did they give you something? Have you acquired second sight? Some of the knowledge they kept from us? Are you immortal, Tim?''

He nearly hung up on her. ''I have Susan Marquez with me,'' he said after his voice steadied.

''The prophet. I read about her revival meetings in New Jersey.''

"She's a kid. She didn't have any more choice about what happened to her than I did."

There was a thoughful silence. "Of course. I'm sorry. There seem to be so many other people crashing around these days who did have choices. I shouldn't . . ."

Timothy said he understood, although he was not sure if he did. Underneath the hurt she had just inflicted was the contempt and impatience he lately felt toward everyone.

Linda Cavan cleared her throat. "Do you want to tell me where you are? Can I help you?"

He gave her an address they occupied a week ago. "There's a lot of people on the road now, Mom."

"I know," she said, her voice falling away into unaffected sadness. "It's like that everywhere. Everyone trying to find some place to go. The weather doesn't help much, either, but it hasn't for years. I can help you a little. I have a place in the city with good security. The Marquez girl's pretty famous but I haven't seen anything in the public press about you, Tim. You could come back to me."

Timothy thanked her, testing his reactions against himself. "I want to talk to some gods. This is important. I think Susan wants to do this too."

She sighed as if he had missed her intent and there had been no point in her letting her guard down with him after all. "They used to be all over, Tim. Couldn't you find one on your own?"

"There weren't that many. And the one I've seen lately are either crazy or on their way to being killed. You know the one I mean, Mom. I need to talk to the ones who might explain what happened to me and Susan. I . . ."

"We're looking for them ourselves. We need explanations as much as you. Especially with that ship. . . ."

"You can see it in the northeast when it's clear."

". . . coming back. Some people act like they know what's up, but that's how the fools at NSA and the Agency always act. Oh, Tim, if we had any gods who knew anything talking to us now, we wouldn't be acting like a bunch of scared rabbits."

"I want to know if the ship's coming back for me," he continued against the course of her conversation. He had not intended to say anything so pretentious, but as he did he realized the question was an honest one. He also recognized the joy that inhabited any suggestion of meeting the gods again. "Aren't there any gods talking to us, at all?"

"I know some," she said at last, dispiritedly. "I'll have to check with them before I can get back to you on that." Neither said anything for a full minute, just listening to each other's breathing, trying to read it as they had been able to do once. "Please be careful, Tim," she told him at last and hung up before she could say anything else.

"IS THE SHIP AS NEAR AS IT SEEMS?" SLATE ASKED. "THE newspapers say it will outshine Venus this week."

"The news is correct." Marinetti paced his words, allowing enough time to weigh each one. "It's a week's coasting away."

Slate smiled. "That should be three minutes' powered flight, even with braking."

"Your kind can go faster than light, can't they?"

"I'm told we can. We must." He smiled with his usual casual elegance. "But we accomplish such feats only because of our fear, Anthony. It'a shameful that we would spend such time and energy in the service of one artist's paranoia—however brilliantly he communicated it." Slate sipped his scotch and water. "Things might be different if I *believed* what I saw as deeply as everyone else, if I *knew* it like the others did. A failing on my part, I suppose, not the painting's."

"But now we've got a shipload of believers coming back. Do you think they'll be as civil as they were when they first landed?"

"Unlikely. You've heard the traffic over the Mission radio, and your Wentworth'a doing a fair job of rendering some of it into your language. But there are nuances of tone and melody that your kind can't fathom. I can. They're panicked, Tony. Totally unhinged by the thought of losing that hideous painting.

And then there's the reason why the original was taken from home and hidden here in the first place. Domestic politics! I never could understand them.

"I think our ship just wants to recover it and leave. Though they're not going to let manners slow things down as much as they did on the first visit." He swirled his drink, appreciating the pale bronze color. "This isn't such a bad place. It could do with a few less people. And some direction. Direction is necessary. But not like the royal fear we've had in our backsides forever. A noble race like yours deserves something, umm, something more vigorous."

Marinetti searched the creature's voice for special irony, but that was his normal tone anyway. "Our history's been a constant search for such . . ."

"No, no, no," Slate said impatiently. "Something deeper than anything I've seen here is required. All the 'isms' are just so much dust. None of them can sustain a racial fury for more than a generation or two. Religions are good. There are some I've read about here, but it's usually the same story: the savior leaves, his disciples die, revelations become doctrines and everything gets stale."

"So what's required is something that will remain directly accessible to the race. Something like a painting."

Slate's reserve broke down at last; he rolled his eyes and held up his free hand imploringly. "Please! The universe already has that curse. Another one's not needed even if it could be done." Then he paused and looked shrewdly at Marinetti. "All right. You've got Rane?"

Marinetti nodded. He could not conceal his smile.

"You're becoming very popular with, ah, the expatriate community, Anthony. Perhaps you understand us better than I thought. So you have Rane, and you're hoping he's going to recapture his genius?" For the first time Slate looked at Marinetti with genuine wonderment. "The original's never been equaled. No one, not even Rane, has ever approached its *truth*."

He tossed down the rest of drink and immediately made

himself another from the bar at the side of the office. "Is he working?"

"Yes."

"Does it, ah, show promise? Can you tell if it does yet?"

Marinetti leaned forward, placing his elbows on his knees and holding his drink in front of him with both hands. "We believe he's creating something of great potential. There's nothing I understand yet, but he's creating temporal and spatial information clearly enough for our computers to pick up."

"You want to encourage this?"

"I do."

"Without knowing what he's creating?"

Marinetti felt the same unease he had been stricken with every morning since Rane started painting. "That's an acceptable risk. I doubt he knows himself. He's done a ton of sketches and studies, and we've analyzed all of them. Some of them are pretty powerful, but none of them relate to what he's putting on canvas now."

Slate saw Marinetti's discomfort and was predictably amused by it. "What if, say, Rane paints something that tells your racc they should have surrendered to us, to the 'gods,' but now you can't do that because we've gone? Or what if his truth is racial suicide or universal war? That would be awkward, wouldn't it?"

"He's working under tightly controlled conditions, whether he knows it or not. Whatever he produces will be thoroughly screened before anyone outside the current management group sees it."

Slate sighed again. "But that was the very problem with the triptych: if one of my kind, only one, saw it, he *knew* it was right. He would never . . . could never order its destruction, or even its concealment after that."

Marinetti sat up against the back of his chair. "That is all tentative now. For the moment, he's working and seems to think he is more of this world than of his home . . ."

"Ah . . . treason," Slate interjected quietly.

"Not at all."

"Why not?"

Marinetti had rehearsed his approach. "Because it all revolves around a truth. Either the one you could never grasp and that the ship's coming back for, or the one that Rane's convinced he can reveal."

Slate accepted this thoughtfully. "Then everything seems to be in place."

Marinetti forced himself to move ahead. "Not entirely. I'm concerned the ship will not only be looking for the triptych but also for artists like Rane."

Slate looked surprised. "There are others?"

"None that we know of. But if Wentworth is reading the intercepts correctly, such a thing has been mentioned with considerable emphasis. They may also spend some time looking for others."

"Still thinking of 'treason'? I don't think so. Remember, I was left behind. I remained at my post."

"I'm just repeating what Wentworth's told me. But, as you said, there are still nuances to the language we don't understand. Their arrival presents too many variables. It even rules out just giving the painting to them. We'd still have the arrival, press coverage, all the old hysterias being stirred up again. I don't know. Maybe even getting it back won't appease them."

Slate resumed his ironic pose. "How many people know about the triptych?"

"Quite a few. There's been a real parade through the Gallery basement lately."

"But how many of these people know that the ship is coming back for *that* painting? How many of them know that there was a revolt or some kind of upheaval at home and that its disappearance was part of it?" He looked suddenly distracted for a moment. "Things are happening at home and I know nothing about it. My friends and colleagues, my old opponents could be dying, and I don't know why. I approve of removing that terrible picture from the sight of my race, but it hurts not to know why it was done." He shrugged, trying to distance himself from fantasies of civil war at home. "Ah, but as you said, Anthony, it was they who left me here. If their struggles can still affect my interests, I'll find out about it in good time. So, as I asked, how many people know the triptych here is the original?"

Marinetti had resolved to be as honest with the god as circumstances allowed. "That information has not been widely circulated. Even if it is true . . ."

"What else could it be? I heard the transmissions myself."

"You have to remember that your, ah, reliability may appear rather ambiguous to some people in the government."

Slate shrugged. "But outside of the occasional crazy, Rane and I are the only ones who're talking to you. Correct?"

"As far as I know," Marinetti lied. There were dozens of other competing, secret and semi-secret projects going on around Washington and at least as many more at bases all over the country. Some of them were almost feudal baronies of their commanders or Under Secretaries. The Defense Intelligence Agency was supposed to have a star-pilot, of all things, under lock and key at Edwards Air Force Base. The FBI said it had indications of godly "cells" located in the autonomous regions of the Pacific Northwest, but local conditions made this impossible to confirm.

The Russians had confided they had a whole colony of abandoned gods, happily working for them in the Urals. The Germans carefully leaked the supposed defection of their former Chief of Mission at Brussels, and the Indians implied that all the mass sacrifices committed during their first landings had actually induced two gods to come over to them years before the evacuations began. And so on. It was more trouble then when they first arrived.

Anything could be going on, Marinetti thought, recovering the excitement of this moment on Earth. "I need your help."

"How?"

Slate was warming to him. Marinetti wondered how many of his allegiances he had jettisoned. "I want you to talk to them, to the approaching ship, and try and convince them that the true painting is in New York.'' His heartbeat accelerated; this was surely treason, if it had not been committed before.

"Why?" Slate asked mildly. "If we want to keep them away as long as possible, why not try and lead them to the Kenya station first? New York is so near. So many people would be in the way."

We. Marinetti relaxed. "You told me yourself: the Kenyan station's automated and they could check the copy there through the machines. New York's the best we can do."

"But the people, Anthony. I don't . . ."

"There's too many people here, too. But the painting's here and so is Rane . . ."

"And so are we," Slate put in.

Good. He's trading treason for cowardice and thinking that's even. Fair enough.

"We can't stop the ship. But anything that might slow it down, even for an hour or two, could be helpful. Anything to make them give us a hint of their intentions will help. Don't you see?"

Slate went to the bar again. His walk was less steady than it had been. There were no studies on how alcohol affected the gods. Knowing little of their normal, logical processes made anticipating their drunken logic impossible. The god said that he did see and that he would help.

Marinetti then allowed the conversation to shift to his own work on Earth. He felt an unexpected release in purposely revealing to Slate the most highly classified information about Agency activities before the gods arrived. It was a gesture of trust as much as triumph, and Marinetti believed the alien understood it as such, He permitted himself a few real drinks before he took Slate down to the garage. An armored limousine drove the alien to a secure estate near Makley's Corner.

T HE RETURNING SHIP WAS THE LARGEST OBSERVED IN THE gods' fleet. It had never descended to earth during the first visit, but remained in polar orbit, five times more luminous in the night sky than Sirius. It inserted into the same orbit in late July, when the northern hemisphere was turning brown with the seasonal heat and high tides washed up the Potomac to flood Washington's esplanades.

There were none of the effusively polite broadcasts to the "honored races of Earth" as had preceded the first arrival. It was quiet except for brief, directional broadcasts toward the home-ship or to some of their Earth stations.

"Everyone's becoming nicely polarized, Tony," the director told him after one Monday briefing. "The smart ones, you and I and the rest of the community, are doing everything we can to get an insight of our own and play it for whatever it's worth." The director had been around Langley quite a while and had long ago given up trying to police his major subordinates; it only bred unnecessary suspicion—as if there wasn't already enough of that to go around.

"Some others are getting ready to kill them the first chance they get. The Air Force's dusting off the old ASAT Theseus missiles that've been moldering away at Davis-Monthan since the Shield System went up. Others're thinking the gods are coming back for them, to apologize, to make things better, to take them away from this great goddamned threat that's supposed to be behind everything they've done. Did you hear the rioting is starting again in Bengal and Amazonas? Pretty small so far, but enough to get the tenured faggots down in Mass Psychology all atwitter.

"And the guys that aren't obsessed with the gods are obsessed with taking out the ones who are. Christ, the FBI's loving this. They've finally got enough local conspiracies cooking to justify their existence. Have you seen their budget request for next year? Their black items alone're half of what the whole Army wants. The goddamn regular Army! Can you believe that?"

"Presumptuous of them," Marinetti ventured. The Agency's budget had remained constant. The environment it operated in remained essentially stable, even with the arrival and departure of an entire race from the stars.

"I know you're a careful person, Tony. I assume you'll stay that way. I may be obliged to lean on you. Let's try to avoid that. Other people may already be after you and your pets. Be as careful as you can."

T RUSTED PEOPLE WATCHED OVER SLATE AT THE COUNTRY home and over Rane in his studio on the Virginia side of the river. Marinetti controlled enough funds to maintain three decoy studios, complete with sensor-feed simulations of the signals that were coming from the real location.

The signals showed a canvas half-filled with the outlines of human or godly figures against a starry background. The picture lacked *The Death of Blake*'s clinical illumination, but when Marinetti looked away from the monitor in his office an incredible volume of images crowded into his immediate memory. The remembered figures were of men and not gods; the stars and constellations were those seen from Earth before the atmosphere's present opacity; there were the outlines of fabulous cities, dense mixtures of daVincian fantasy and Japanese asceticism; the particular time of the painting was not yet as definite as *next year*.

Rane had demanded that his prosthetic frame-glove be refined for more control. The visions flowing through the sensors to Marinetti's office strengthened and clarified themselves after this was done. The space-time readouts at the bottom of the screen became more exact, confining themselves to a period of a thousand years and a spherical volume of the galaxy that included the Earth.

Marinetti's people went back over the shielding for the cables while a National Guard patrol ransacked one of the decoy studios and made sure that all the bugs and taps and parallel induction leeches were gone.

There was the predictable howl from Ireland and those who had joined her. She put the Guard thugs she could count on back on the street, looking for Rane's studio. The private corps of some Under Secretaries of Commerce and Treasury occasionally joined her people in the search, but they usually had their own agendas for the capital after dark.

The regular services tried to stay aloof from this unseemly intrigue, mostly because they were outnumbered and outgunned locally.

This, Marinetti and his colleagues often reflected over morning coffee, was the kind of environment Direct Action had often cultivated in other countries. At least now their people did not have to worry about phony accents or forged papers.

"**I**T ISN'T ROUTINE ORBITAL DECAY. THEY'VE DROPPED the last two hundred kilometers in discrete stages. It has to be a powered descent." Marinetti spread a global projection on the table in front of them. "Here's the predicted track. They'll have to be in fully sustained flight within the month."

"They won't stop at the Kenyan station," Slate said. "I've listened to the tapes you got from Mr. Wentworth's office, and that's been ruled out. Wentworth missed that entirely. I think they're coming directly here."

"Can you do anything about that?" Marinetti avoided looking at the alien.

Slate inclined his head as if he were listening to something outside the room. He had begun looking more human to Marinetti lately; imperfections and asymmetries had infiltrated his features. "There's no reason they should listen to me."

"We've secured some of the stations. Perhaps you could use one to suggest that the true painting is buried in the New York Mission."

"What about the official rumor of a chemical booby trap in a subbasement, Anthony? Attributed to 'highly placed sources'?"

Marinetti smiled carefully. "You have to preserve your assets against the curious, even when they're half-destroyed and don't appear to have much utility." The god was fitting into the local routine very well. There was, he continued, a station outside Front Royal, Virginia. It had been discovered when its operator broadcast an active transmission to the departing fleet, demanding they return and evacuate him.

Fortunately, Agency people had found the god with his wrists slit before anything more compromising was sent, so the station's integrity was still intact. "Another asset," Marinetti observed during the helicopter flight to the station. "All the machinery seems standard, but we didn't want to destroy its usefulness by using it incorrectly. Like you said: subtleties and nuances. Your radio helps, but we still wouldn't presume to do anything more than listen. We've kept it clean and powered up. Do you think you can operate it?"

Slate said he thought he could. He had taken a few manuals from the stations he visited himself and believed he had a basic understanding of procedures. Marinetti showed him a hologram of the corpse, but Slate could not recognize it.

There had been little employment in Front Royal since the seasonal firestorms destroyed the forests around it. Then the gifted left and took with them the head of the largest local employer, a genetic engineering laboratory. Other disruptions followed.

The Sikorsky landed on a dusty softball field on the north side of town. An Agency operative accompanied by a regular Army sergeant drove them in, past looted storefronts and deserted streets where the sparkle of broken glass was sometimes bright enough to make them squint.

Marinetti noted how the soldier and the local agent looked at Slate. They stared, as people usually did at gods after they had noticed their perfection, but then their interest dulled until they turned away, distracted by something as ordinary as the appearance of a stray animal or a group of drifters. Then they would shake themselves, as if they had forgotten something both important and obvious, and forcibly return their attention to the god. The process would repeat itself, though each time with less intensity as if, though still a god, he was no longer perfect.

Slate should have been medically analyzed by now to see if

something objective was changing in him. Marinetti wondered if his ichor might show a reddish tinge or if fantasies of an Earthly death, rather than what passed for extinction among the members of his race, were invading his dreams.

The local agent showed them to a warehouse outside the town. The surveillance equipment was located in a room hidden behind stacks of fabricated sheet steel, now all turned the color of dried blood from rust. The room's entrance was protected by cleverly hinged panels. Search antennas were woven into the roof; a long-wave antenna covering ten acres was buried in the hills ten kilometers from town. Everything had functioned secretly until the god running it broke down.

Slate surveyed the room, referring randomly to the manuals he brought with him. Marinetti was not sure the god would know what to do, but he could see no reason to preserve the asset's sanctity any longer. After an hour, the god began to move switches and pass his hands over activation plates. Columns of lights moved across grid panels in apparent response. The video camera and directional mikes the local agent and the soldier had set up in one corner of the room recorded all of this. An AWACS ship orbited Front Royal seventy kilometers out, listening to both the warehouse and the remote long-wave antenna.

Marinetti had a hand monitor with a downlink to an Agency satellite. He held it discreetly, hoping the glow from its screen would not reflect off his features. The room was suffocatingly hot, and all three of the human beings were sweating heavily. The monitor showed Rane painting in his studio. Wisping shadows that might have been from smoke drifted across the eastern wall of the studio when the surveillance camera panned back. Then the sequence of advancing detail began, approaching the painting and penetrating its substance.

It was difficult to understand what was going on in the miniature screen. Even with the reduction to Persian miniature size and the pale, shifting colors of the liquid crystal display, it pulsed with compressed knowledge. Marinetti believed in it, even thought it had not yet told him what its truth concerned.

The figure of a god was easily discernible in the painting, despite the size of the screen. Marinetti then looked up at Slate, who was seated on an office stool in front of the transmitting console. *Does it look like him?* he asked himself so firmly that he wondered if he had spoken the question out loud. The agent and the soldier kept watching Slate, so he supposed he had not.

Then: *No. It's Slate who's looking like the figure in the painting. It was here before he was.* He shook his head, marveling at the certainty this impossible idea had instantly achieved in his mind. There was also a time to it now: *soon.*

Slate finished, pushed himself away from the console and turned off the illuminated devices. The soldier and the local agent took pictures of the settings and readouts. "All right. That's all I can do."

Marinetti looked at him questioningly.

"I told them the painting was in the National Gallery's basement in Washington."

The man was momentarily stunned. He had gotten too wrapped up in the interplay between the god and Rane's emerging picture. "Excuse me?"

Slate smiled tiredly, as if he had expected Marinetti to have figured it all out by himself. "They recognized me immediately. It was stupid to think they wouldn't. So I thought that whatever I said would be disbelieved. I'm a—what is the phrase I read somewhere?—'nonperson'—wonderful word, really—and not to be trusted. So I impulsively told them the truth in the hopes it would be disbelieved. Don't you think that was inventive, Anthony?"

Slate had said all this so ingenuously that Marinetti could not help but be disarmed. It was so childish. Surely he could have done something, anything more intelligent than that to buy time. The remote, professional part of Marinetti seethed at the creature, but he had not prepared him very well. *You can't let them go off by themselves. They'll bungle it every time. This inspiration probably came from the same place that he got the idea for the art show. Astounding. No wonder he was in their diplomatic corps.* Marinetti should have *told* him what to say; written him a script. Now it was too late.

"It was difficult to tell their reaction. My language's a little awkward after speaking English for so long. But there was a great deal of atonality at the end. I think they were confused. But that is probably the most we ... you could hope for." Unmistakable shame crossed his features, and this made him look more human than before. "This is treason now. Correct, Tony?"

Marinetti nodded, at least relieved that it was. He had seen the expression on the faces of honest, intelligent men before, often because of a professional triumph of his own. Respectful, funereal dignity had been the best pose to assume then.

"I've been reading that in your race's antiquity, the greatest error had been hubris. That was how one incurred the wrath of the 'gods.' Pride was the thing that offended them and invited ruin. But in this century and the one before it, the great sin was committed against the nation and was treason. That's where you got your newest Prometheuses: the Abels and Penkovskys and Erhards. Do you think that is correct, Anthony?"

Slate turned and walked out of the room without waiting for an answer. Marinetti followed along, his mind assaulted by the callousness of his old, Earthly trade, now magnified by the creature walking in front of him, his shoulders pushed down past the ideal geometries of Phidias by the weight of betrayal.

R ANE WAS SLEEPING ONLY A FEW HOURS EVERY DAY AND living on Earthly fruit and water, even though he distrusted the artificial stress this brought on. When he painted his portrait of Blake he had been stone sober and well fed; the inspiration had emerged from his own talent without any prodding. He had believed that the distractions of spiritual ecstasy or simple hunger would obscure understanding and distort technique.

But now he was inside of it and convinced he was transcending all his previous abilities. He had not taken his prosthetic glove off in days and could feel how the skeletal framework had worn away the skin where it wrapped around his fingers.

It began as an intricate structure of colors near the lower right corner, and Rane sensed meaning there after the second day of work. Things were not as they had been when he was painting *The Death of Blake*. They could not be. He was doing things that were impossible, even for one who had been able to perpetually animate Blake's assassination in that earlier work.

This only could have been experienced when the first true work was created. Such things cannot be newly discovered twice. But he still felt the focused precision of his movements and the catch of his breath as the picture revealed the previously unimagined. Once present, it assumed the certitude of truth.

The shape of a human's hand emerged against a cobalt background, where the still-darker outline of a ship or a building was implied. The hand had not existed in any form that morning. Then he painted it, and it communicated the knowledge that such a hand *would be held* in such a way, at such a place and specific time, for purposes that would be revealed by his continuing labor.

The creation of *Blake's Death* may have been something like that, after all. But all its truths had been known in advance: the identity of the subject, how the room had been furnished, the time, the power of his legacy to the race and the theories about why he was slain. Transforming all this into a form that would itself communicate such truths intact and bodily into the mind of a viewer had been a stupendous achievement. But this was pure discovery, far beyond all his prior artistic tricks of chronic perspective.

Can I really control the alignment of molecules of pigment with my hand? he asked the painting and whoever was eavesdropping. Electric servos on his brace whirred just loudly enough to be heard over his breathing and heartbeat. He touched his brush to a place where an instrument of unknown purpose awaited a still-unpainted operator and felt a moment of dissatisfaction. The powered framework around his hand committed a slight pressure as the brush contacted the painting just above the quantum level of physical actuality.

He brought his hand back from the painting and looked at the area carefully. Nothing had visibly changed, but excitement sparked through him and left behind, like warm ash, the knowledge that the instrument's operator would be human, rather than of his own race.

At times, however, Rane felt the certainty drain out of his movements, and the painting would keep its secrets no matter how he cursed it. Reproach and suicidal self-doubt then overtook him, forcing him to leave the studio until the feeling passed. The Agency people living in the townhouses on either side would always appear, offer him coffee and tell him to relax, that he was embarked on a great task and could not expect it to be easy. There was plenty of time, they told him in voices that were as anxious as his own.

He asked them to tell Marinetti that he appreciated the interest in what he was doing—was flattered by it—but the cameras were a distraction when the work was not going well.

Marinetti's people came into the studio the next morning, took down some panels on the wall facing the painting, and ostentatiously removed a number of boxes and cylinders.

Rane was convinced, however, that other sensors remained to pry into his abilities, and thus inadvertently prevent their return. He complained again but was assured everything had been stripped from the room.

Marinetti had decided to risk the lie, even if it only concerned one voice mike and two subminiature, stereoscopic cameras. The thought of not being able to watch the work's hourly progress, even if he could not probe any of its subtleties, was unacceptable.

Marinetti's people offered Rane women, but this irritated the artist even more than the presence of the cameras. Recreational drugs were ruled out because of ignorance about godly physiology and Marinetti's reluctance to test anything that might distort Rane's mind and accidently block the return of his abilities.

Marinetti was therefore confronted with a subject without any vices to exploit. At last, out of sheer distraction, he ordered Rane to be taken out and aired like a piece of mildewed furniture. A driver and armored limousine were provided, and Rane was urged to go sightseeing in certain areas of the capital. Sheets of ceramic armor showed through gaps in the car's interior trim; the blacked-out window glass was at least a centimeter thick. The air-conditioning ran all the time because of the October heat.

Rane asked to be taken to the Mall. He had a vague intention of seeing the triptych at the National Gallery.

A small armored car preceded them, anticipating their slow progress east on Constitution Avenue. An identical vehicle followed at an equal distance. Both had National Guard markings, but were cleaner and of a different type than most of the light Guard units that patrolled the city.

They were passing the Interior Department building when the driver touched his earpiece. "We may have to go home, Mr. Rane," the young man said when he was done listening. "There might be some difficulty ahead." The armored car behind them had moved up so there were only two private cars between them. The lead unit had pulled out of traffic and was waiting for them.

"Is it serious?" Rane usually deferred to the human beings around him, but the desire to see the triptych had deepened when the man indicated that it might not be possible.

The driver pointed through the windshield, adjusting a knob on the console to depolarize the glass for a better view. Smoke was curling up from behind the Capitol building in such a way that it appeared to be coming from the gutted Senate wing. "There's a disturbance by the Library of Congress. Some cars on fire."

" 'Disturbance'?"

The driver was embarrassed. "Yeah. Mob griping about the Library keeping books written by, you know, the gifted people that left with your . . . with the ships." The man touched his earphone again, listened and then shook his head. "Bullshit," he muttered. "Absolute bullshit."

Rane heard a muffled noise. He turned and saw the armored car behind them shoving an automobile out of the way, crushing its tail before taking up a position directly behind them. His own car had managed to inch up to where the other armored car was waiting. It pulled back onto the road in front of them.

People began running past them on the sidewalk and the Mall's hard-packed dirt, heading toward the smoke. The driver spoke into his microphone again, but Rane could not understand what he was saying from the back seat.

Sirens penetrated the car's interior, and a group of three heavy armored cars, unquestionably Guard units, ground past them on the center line of the street, brutally pushing other vehicles out of their way. Two tracked personnel carriers followed them.

"All right, sir. All right. Slight delay." The driver was looking all around, lightening the windows and then darkening them again. "We're going to have to leave. The Library's burning, and our people say it's getting ugly. Sorry about this."

The terror in the young man's voice penetrated Rane's mind and flowed into his hands, animating them. The skeletal handframe was at the studio, but he could move his fingers almost easily without them now. "Could we get nearer to the Library?"

The man spoke into his microphone and then listened to the secret Agency voices. "Seems like we don't have much choice." Rane looked north as they passed the next intersection and saw a cluster of blue and white D.C. police cars blocking off 9th Street. That street had been torn up where it crossed the Mall, so escape that way was out.

The armored cars which just passed them swerved across Constitution Avenue and turned around in front of the National Archives. The personnel carriers parked behind them. Troops piled out and began setting up equipment on the building's steps. Rane understood that documents of great local importance were stored there; nothing on the level of the triptych in terms of racial significance, however.

The driver's cursing intensified as did the strength in Rane's hands. This, he began to recall, was how he felt in front of Cavan's house and when he saw the street-murder in Philadelphia. Their observation healed him and created ways for the truth to reach his hands.

They passed by the National Gallery on their right as the traffic, by now almost half military or police, carried them sluggishly toward the Capitol. The smoke column rising behind it had grown thicker and there were helicopters circling it, just as there had been in New York when his race's Mission was defending itself.

"Awright!" the driver suddenly shouted and pounded his fist on the steering wheel. "We're outta here!" The automobile heaved to the right, jumped the curb and began driving across the Mall itself. The armored car in the lead speeded up, the movement of its turret back and forth across their path barely visible in the thick dust that boiled up in its wake. The other unit followed less than three meters behind their rear bumper; its turret was pointed backward, also traversing nervously from left to right.

They were almost across when the lead car fired its cannon into a cluster of people and vehicles blocking their entry onto Independence Avenue. The high-velocity shell hit a panel truck parked at the edge of the crowd. A blaze gathered around the rear of the vehicle for a second, but then the truck exploded in an enormous sphere of jellied fire. The driver yelled that it must have been carrying something illegal. People, some of them burning, scattered up and down the street, and the way was open to them.

R ANE WAS TREMBLING WITH EXCITEMENT WHEN THEY reached the studio on the Virginia side of the river. He was equally sickened by everything that he had seen. He purposely delayed at the curb and then, when the Agency people showed how upset they were by almost carrying him bodily inside, spent some more time talking with the driver and the uniformed personnel from the two armored cars that had escorted them all the way back. He was pleased at the steadiness of his voice, particularly when he heard how the humans' voices cracked and wavered.

They are all young, he thought looking at them. *They feel things slipping away from their control and comprehension.* Rane then identified the great need in the creatures around him and his corresponding responsibility to satisfy it. Rane was staggered by the egotism of these unspoken lyrics.

He accepted a beer from one of his keepers and drank it, smiling and talking despite its repulsive taste. He resolved to discuss all this with Slate, once the painting was done.

"O KAY. IT'S OFFICIAL. THEY'RE COMING DOWN, BUT there's no way to tell where." They were in the dining room. Timothy had made the dinner. Intermittent gunfire and the wind-roar of katyushas sounded far away in other parts of the city. "It sounds like London when I met your father, Tim." She blushed at this, as if it were an unintended intimacy.

Susan Marquez was at the table. She had gained some weight and looked healthier than she had when Timothy brought her to Washington. "Could your Mr. Cavan be on it? Do you think?" She looked back and forth between Timothy and his mother, clumsily playing the thirteen-year-old.

"No way to tell, dear. There were other ships in their fleet, and our people could be on any of them."

"Could we go see it when it lands?"

Linda Cavan wondered why they had to go through *that* again. *It seems inevitable that we should. But I wonder why?* "There's no indication they're really going to land. The whole thing might just be a low reconnaissance. Then back up into orbit to drive us all crazy for another few months."

"I think they'll come down. Here," the Marquez girl suggested. An explosion went off near enough to cause the windows to flex in their frames. Metal louvers automatically rotated shut over them.

"But why?" Linda Cavan really thought for a moment that the girl could tell her, and that it would be of great importance to her department.

"They came here first," the girl answered carefully, lining up the other reasons in order. "They had their biggest Mission here. They brought their art here, and that's where all the trouble started, anyway. A lot of their paintings and drawings are still here at the Gallery, aren't they? I guess they might want some of them back." She shifted her gaze from Linda Cavan's eyes to a point over her shoulder. "The pictures are very important. They were to me."

The intensity of the gunfire increased. Police sirens interwove the noise on the other side of the shuttered windows. Linda Cavan wished she had held out for an apartment opening onto one of the building's inner courts. "Place's breaking up," she whispered to herself, aware of how much more concerned she was with the night's violence than the two children at the table.

"Then maybe they ought to come here. Or come anywhere on Earth just to settle things down, or at least get everyone interested in the same thing again, even if it's fearing or hating them," Timothy said at last. "At least that would be better than more of this downhill slide."

"We're *not* sliding anywhere . . ."

"But if they do come down, we'll go and see them, won't we?" the Marquez girl asked, and Timothy Cavan answered that they would before his mother could say anything.

Timothy stayed up after the girl and his mother had gone to bed. He manually raised the window shutters so he could see the occasional flight of a rocket over the city. Helicopters and police ultralights flew lazily between smoke columns rising over the northern suburbs, illuminated pink and yellow from the fires underneath them.

He decided that his mother was correct: this was not a downhill slide. But it was a terrible confusion of power. There was something waiting to be formed out of it, and it required the reappearance of the gods. Without them above, preparing to descend into it, everything he saw would be mere civil war.

IT FINALLY RAINED ON NOVEMBER 10. A THICK BAND OF storm clouds covered the East Coast and prevented ground observation of the ship's descent. There was, however, plenty of video from the military and private aircraft that swarmed up to watch it.

It was, one commentator bitterly said, as if they had never left. The ship glistened and pulsed in the stratospheric sunlight, its gravitational fields making it impossible to discern its true shape or color. The field lensed objects behind it, so squadrons of ghostly aircraft appeared and then vanished above and below it when the alignment of the ship and an observer was right. Once, the ship achieved the same effect with the new moon.

It drifted down and emerged over Tarrytown, nearly invisible against the underside of the clouds. All the planned alerts had been sounded the prior evening, so there was nothing to be done, except for the continued shifting of forces to maintain the lines of attack and retreat relative to the ship. Evacuations were impossible, given the population densities the ship was passing over.

Rioting and joy erupted under it. Private aircraft flew up through the rain and were whirled about by the ship's fields or disintegrated when they came too close. Some exploded with enough violence to indicate that they had been carrying bombs or missiles; others just came apart in the air, their fuel atomizing and bursting into delicate, flaming webs that traced the fields' lines of force.

It was anticipated that the people on the ground would be uncontrollable. Troops and reliable police units secured especially important locations, primarily government, financial, communication, power and data transmission centers, but once this was done there was almost no one left to keep order. Hundreds of thousands of people spilled out into the glistening streets, staring up into the fine drizzle, waving flags, shooting guns or displaying personal icons, such as the mummified bodies of their children, miraculous paintings that wept ichor, or Ellis Island relics that were as incomprehensible to them as they surely would have been to the gods. Arguments over divinity grew into brawls that became riots engulfing entire neighborhoods. Godly agents, and—even more provocatively—returned members of the gifted were suddenly discovered on street corners, hiding in basements, or disguised as panhandlers, businesspeople doggedly going about their work despite the return of the gods, whores and lunatics. They were either swept away to places suitable for adoration or immolated on the spot.

Renegade National Guard batteries along the flight path opened fire on the ship. It was generally above their effective range, and even the shells that reached it simply detonated in whirling chrysanthemum patterns. Loyal Guard units or regular Air Force attack ships usually silenced them after a few minutes.

The NORAD/NATO staff at Cheyenne Mountain decorously averted their reconnaissance monitors from the ground and from the suicidal Pipers and Beechcrafts departing from Teterboro, Linden and Fairfield without clearance. They managed their interceptors and surveillance ships as if they and the descending spaceship were alone in the sky.

The Pentagon was half-abandoned to staff housing and more powerful civilian bureaus. The Navy had long before withdrawn to its impregnable island bases of Bermuda, Diego Garcia, Ulithi and Oahu. One-third of the Air Force's command structure lived and worked at Cheyenne Mountain, another third stayed constantly aloft, in relays, on board Looking Glass aircraft; only the remainder, along with the Secretary, stayed in Washington.

Marinetti had dropped by the Army room in the E Ring before driving to Langley the evening before. He found Judy Ireland there, and the two exchanged venomous glances. The atmosphere was strangely melancholy and impotent.

Things were more exciting at Langley. Marinetti had his own monitor in his office, as did every senior Agency person, so they would not have to guard their reactions against their colleagues' scrutiny. A smaller color monitor was on the wall beside it. That was all that was left of the surveillance suite in Rane's studio. Rane's back and shoulders occasionally lunged across the field of view; he was still working on the painting.

Slate had been brought up from the estate to watch with Marinetti, and the god was having his first drink with breakfast. "Well, they were going to come down eventually. You see? They started over New York. Perhaps they bought my stratagem."

The camera feeding the larger monitor panned over a crowded boulevard in the Bronx. Barricades of wrecked vehicles were burning on the street, their light dying down at intervals and then flaring up when people who had been pushed into them ignited. "The same thing's going to happen here, Anthony. At least my kind are not doing anything antagonistic. You see that. Even when they were shot at, they did not retaliate."

"The ship's invulnerable. Why should they?" Marinetti said, more impatiently then he had meant to.

"Not entirely, I think. But for all practical purposes it is. They musn't want to cause any great upheaval or conflict."

"They've got enough of that right now."

Slate shrugged, regaining his dignity by placing the drink at a distance on the table. "That is your own kind reacting. But what else could have been done? Their . . . our remaining staff on Earth is dead, killed, insane or . . . of suspect loyalty. What else was to be done but orbit and then come down as slowly as possible? Just as we did the first time—when your kind fell at our feet, and we had taken you up, told you that you should not be so needlessly impressed, that we were merely 'the gods,' desiring to visit this place for—how was it put then?—our mutual instruction and protection, and wishing only to carry out our work as unobtrusively as possible. Do you remember that, Anthony?'' Slate became wistful as he spoke, and that irritated Marinetti. It was bad enough that his stupid trick at Front Royal might have bought them some time after all.

Slate followed the man's gaze from his own eyes to the smaller monitor focused on Rane's painting. ''It's almost done, isn't it?'' he said, his voice coldly polished again. Shadows, presumably Rane's arms, flickered across the screen, seeming to leave the painting untouched; despite this, Slate could feel his mood and thoughts shift when he looked at the picture after each passage.

Slate blinked, and multitudes of previously invisible facts and identities poured from the screen. He *heard* a call, sung in both his own and Earthly languages, break loose from the televised image of the painting, even though there was no audio feed from the studio.

What has he done? Slate asked himself as he stood up, got his drink for balance and crossed the office to where the screen was. He looked closely enough to see the pointillist texture of the pixel groups, granular at first and then becoming smooth and detailed as one moved away from the surface, like Seurat's *Grande Jatte*.

''He's accomplished a lot,'' Marinetti said from across the room, without seeing Slate's reaction. ''He may even be finished. I don't know. But there's something very clear there. I can *see* that. Can't you, Slate?''

''Yes.'' Slate's voice was dry. He said the words in the Earthly manner, without the slightest hint of music. He looked again and saw a history of ferocious conquest erupt in front of him. It appeared in his mind as spontaneous knowledge. Nothing registered on its way through his senses and into memory. Instinctive barriers of linear cause and effect were erected and overcome, their prismatic fragments scattering the truth that emerged from the screen and amplifying its power. Thus, although all of it was clearly new, by the time he could warn himself of its acquisition, it had already become the past knowledge of unarguable facts and unassailable premises.

Slate could not hold his glass steady. *Is this what it had always been like for my friends, the ones who had understood the triptych? That isn't possible. I'm not looking at the real thing but a televised picture. And of something new. I still feel this way. How does this human being feel? Do I dare look at him and find out?*

He didn't have to. "He's done. *I* recognize the language. It's different from the triptych. He's taken his *Blake* and stretched it out past the limits of . . . genius." Marinetti had to force the word out. Geniuses inhabited self-created, ornamental worlds, appreciated by and ultimately useful only to aristocracies. The real world was built and advanced by craftsmen.

The larger screen now displayed the self-destruction of Harlem as the gods' ship approached. It was turning toward the rubble-garden on the Upper East Side where their Mission had been. Undulating waves of upturned black and yellow faces packed the streets below it, shouting and throwing things that trailed fiery streamers as they ascended and then fell back into the crowds and exploded.

"They bought your story, Slate." Any irritation he had with the alien was lost in his relief over the likelihood that the ship was going to waste time in New York instead of going directly to the National Gallery. Even an additional hour would be worth it.

Marinetti pointed at the smaller screen. The picture had changed again, even during the moment they had spent looking at the other monitor. *He has taught himself a new language! I must see it!* "Let's go. It might even tell us what to do next." Marinetti took his raincoat off the door hook and left the office.

"Shouldn't you do something else?" Slate asked stupidly, once he caught up with the taller man.

"Everyone in town's got their own contingency plan." He looked up and down the corridors. Doors were opening, and people clutching manila folders or ring notebooks were emerging and quickly walking in one direction or another. Slate noted how many of them were smiling.

"Yes," lowering his voice as they passed a security post.

"But you still haven't circulated the information about *why* they're coming down, have you? That would seem relevant."

"It isn't. Believe me. First, the Gallery's already under heavy security . . ."

"Not the maximum."

"It's tight enough. The triptych's not the only thing they left behind. For all we know, *The Death of Blake*'s the real prize for them. Second, I can't see what difference it'd make. So they want it? Big deal. Why not just ask for it back? Why all the imperial nonsense, sending the biggest ship back and making such a point of their silence? Do you think they have more in mind than just finding their precious painting, Slate? Have you told me everything that would be of interest?"

They entered an elevator and descended to the building's garages. "Do I know everything?" Marinetti repeated.

"Of course . . ."

"And there's nothing more about the the plot or conspiracy or whatever it was at home that blew up after the painting was gone that can affect us? Nothing else that you might have overheard but not mentioned yet?"

Marinetti led the way to a white delivery truck. Two Agency men stood beside the open front door. "You might as well tell me. Wentworth's been more helpful to us lately than he has to Ms. Ireland. He's untangled a few paragraphs of inter-ship communication the trans-Uranian net caught and sent back before your folks shut it down. They think members of the conspiracy came here along with the painting, don't they?"

Slate got into the truck and seated himself beside Marinetti. The other two men got into the front seat; a third was already inside, facing backward on a jump seat and cradling an automatic shotgun with a drum magazine; there were gun ports in the rear door and in each side panel. "There had been mention of something like that. But it was all indefinite and incomplete . . ." He let his voice trail away.

The truck moved toward the entrance camp. Water streamed down it and poured into a storm grate at the bottom. "Right. Your countrymen think you're part of it."

"Of course. But only by default. I'm still here, functioning and on cordial terms with the locals. We've already discussed how that adds up to treason in Earthly eyes. It would hardly be read any other way by my fellows."

"They think the same thing about Rane. But Rane really is a part of whatever happened at home, isn't he?"

Rane had always seemed so much the disconnected artist. The thought of Rane as a conspirator in the abduction of the race's icon was still as comical as it had been when he first realized what had happened. *But,* Slate continued to himself, *his greatest work had been about the killing of the man who created the triptych. Why hadn't that been noted in his psychological profile and been enough to prevent him from ever being sent here?* He shrugged inwardly. *Obviously: other conspirators had arranged for his selection. Marvelous. Wonderful to have all this unfold after it was too late. Always does in the foreign service.*

Light rain fell on the truck's windows as it left the building. It was the first in months, and the three agents, who were making a conscious effort to appear professional around Marinetti, could not suppress whistles of delight.

I**T WAS LATE AFTERNOON BEFORE THE SHIP STOPPED ABOVE** the ruins of the gods' New York Mission. Although it was still difficult to determine its true shape because of the gravitational vortices that swirled over its surface, its intimidating size was frighteningly apparent. Its bulk stopped the rain from falling on nearly all of the seven square blocks of the Upper East Side demolished during the Mission's self-defense.

Maddened crowds surged through the area, past old barricades of dragons' teeth the National Guard had erected during its week-long campaign to neutralize the Mission. It was a continuation of the same riot that had begun when the ship first emerged below the clouds, kilometers north of the city. The participants changed, but the hysterias the starship ignited were the same.

Most of the less developed countries had lately slipped back into a nineteenth-century level of technology and so were spared the immediate, visual spectacle of the ship's return. Radio commentary, no matter how eloquent or how colored with fear or rapture, could not convey more than a fraction of what was happening. But the rest of the world could *see*. Commercial television broadcast pictures of the horror as soon as it began in Tarrytown and then moved south, under the ship. That was allowed to continue for only an hour before it became apparent the transmissions were setting off other riots.

The civilian networks were ordered to cease transmission. Those that refused were summarily taken out by the regular services. Some of the networks had private planes. When these were forced down, they resorted to RPVs, but anti-radiation missiles honed in on their signals and destroyed either them or, more spectacularly, their ground stations. One by one the real-time broadcasts from New York were replaced by last year's bowl games, old movies or First Amendment outrage by commentators safely far away from Washington.

The government's own cameras and sensors kept blanketing the area. Since Linda Cavan's apartment building was inside State's fortified compound in Washington, her son and the Marquez girl could see much of what was appearing on the larger screens at the Department. The presentations were not as slick as those the commercial networks had been delivering, and they tended to stay at a great distance from the streets below the ship. The interest of the authorities was naturally with the ebb and flow of great masses of people rather than individuals. There were few close-ups of the mobs grinding up people or deciding which among them was a "gifted" infiltrating his way back into humanity. There was no need to offer people the opportunity to mouth incoherencies into a camera as tears and rainwater washed their upturned faces.

Infrared and satellite radar-imaging pictures taken through the clouds appeared at intervals on the apartment's set. Thick rivers of artificial color traced the mobs' paths along the streets and boulevards of New York and the cities around it: they also marked the districts that were on fire, or where the regular services were having an especially difficult time suppressing private stations or National Guard elements that were attacking the ship or taking advantage of its arrival to loot or settle old scores with rival units. The ship was identified as a pulsating black oval.

These pictures alternated rapidly with other transmissions from aircraft skimming the undersides of the clouds. Torrents of cryptic information ran across the bottom of the screen and up and down either side. Ordnance grids and isobaric patterns with significance only to specialists at the Department appeared for a few seconds, shifted scale and color and were then replaced by columns of figures.

The Marquez girl had been frightened at first, especially when the commercial networks were still broadcasting, each trying to outdo the other with examples of human irrationality. Timothy instructed himself to put a protective arm around her shoulders and say that this was unavoidable, that the ship was, at least, doing nothing destructive and that it would surely all be over soon.

His feelings cooled and hardened. The contempt he had felt toward the crowd near Hammonton returned once the private stations were off the air and he did not have to focus on an individual face or listen to a particular voice wailing about the end or the beginning of the world.

The Marquez girl must have experienced a similar change. "Can we get to New York?" she asked, her voice much steadier than it had been.

Timothy waved at the screen. A grid appeared, strung with pulsating red dots marking the ship's progress; each of the dots streamed coded information in yellow numbers and letters and were then replaced by a picture of the ship with a computer-generated overlay, hypothesizing its actual shape at that moment. "I'm not sure we have to. There's no reason for it to stay there. The Mission's destroyed and there can't be any gods left in the city. They would've come down somewhere remote, where they wouldn't have caused so much trouble, if they were only bringing back the gifted.''

The ship was hovering a hundred meters above the Mission, now just the largest pile of rubble in the area. It was getting dark, and it reflected the light of fires burning around it. Rocket grenades occasionally flew past, swerving to one side or exploding in bursts of startling color as the ship's fields fractured the detonations' light.

"Then what are they doing?" The girl resumed her questioning, though now with the voice of someone who thought she could actually find out.

"Searching." That was obvious to Timothy. "They've left something behind."

"Well, what? They've only left their people here. Like that Rane your mother keeps talking about. And Slate, and those that were with me at the camp. I can't even remember their names. And they left that building in New York, but there can't be anything still in it."

"It took care of itself pretty well, didn't it? Maybe there was something worth protecting inside." He did not want to be correct about that. He wanted the object of their search to be in Washington, where he was. "They've left some paintings behind. Remember? At the National Gallery."

The girl looked away from the screen. "I remember all of that. There was the crazy man and the dead one . . .''

"That was Rane's."

". . . and the woman that the men got so silly in front of. There was also a big one in three parts that I didn't pay much attention to, but I remember it now."

Timothy Cavan did too. It was supposed to have driven the gods into space, to search for the threat it warned against. He could not remember having understood it as effortlessly as he had the other paintings. But when he considered it now, he found the very clear knowledge of such a threat in his memory. But there was no power behind that truth. The reason for this might be that the threat was directed at the gods, not at humankind. *That's not all of it,* he continued to himself as he began looking for the keys to his mother's car. *An aggression can hurt bystanders just as easily as the target. If the gods are afraid, what should we be? We live in the same universe.*

"We should go." He turned the set off and motioned toward the door.

Marinetti HAD DROPPED ANY PRETENSE OF CONCEAL-ment. There were two regular Army tanks at each end of the street when they arrived at Rane's studio. Lighter armored units were parked at the other intersections or were slowly circling the block. All the houses on the street had been evacuated. It was possible that Judy Ireland or others like her might still be thinking about Rane, even at a time like this. They were going to have to move into the city, and the only safe way to do it was in force.

A regular Army colonel, taut and self-consciously precise, met them at the steps and told Marinetti that the ship was still occupied with the Mission ruins in New York. That city was doing a pretty good job of making a burnt offering of itself while the ship hovered impassively over the East Side.

Marinetti asked if the alien was alone. The colonel nodded and opened the door for them, glancing in surprise as Slate walked past.

Curtains were drawn over all the windows. There was government-issue furniture in the rooms, but no pictures on the walls or carpeting on the hardwood floors. The only evidence of habitation, aside from the mess in the kitchen, were piles of books against the living room walls and in the hallways. Most of them concerned Earthly history or political philosophy.

Marinetti led the way down a hallway and up two flights of stairs to the studio. He knocked, then walked in without waiting for an answer.

Although Marinetti had warned Slate about the change in the god's appearance, he was not prepared for the imperfections that had been inflicted on him. The alien was scarred and stooped. His skin was coarse; his hair had lightened and was greasy enough to be visibly furrowed from a comb. Rane's eyes retained their racial intensity, but the skin around them had been pulled and shaped to imply the acquisition of unnatural perceptions.

Rane had his intricately constructed hand-frame on. It was encrusted with tiny hinges, circuit boxes and hydraulic actuators. Braided power and data cables ran from the wrist cuff, up the god's arm and over his shoulder and then fell into a disorderly tangle behind him. They were finally collected into a louvered box, one meter square, against the far wall.

"It's good to see you again," Slate said politely in English. He was afraid of what the creature's voice would sound like.

Rane smiled and removed the hand-frame. He put it on a stool and went over to Slate and shook his hand in the Earthly manner. "You are looking well, Slate. Collaboration suits you."

The voice was normal, but Rane would have never dared to say such a thing to him before, even if it was true. Slate was more intrigued than irritated by the artist's presumption. "It seems that sort of thing has been rather harder on you." The god looked like something he would see in a welfare line in any Earthly city.

Slate was conscious of his own enduring perfection as he stared at the artist, wondering how far Rane had moved away from his race. *Much farther than I. Farther than I have any wish to be.*

"Anthony. You haven't been taking very good care of Rane." He turned around when Marinetti did not answer.

The painting was on the easel. Slate had been distracted by Rane's extraordinary appearance when he had entered and so had not looked at it. Now, it struck him solidly, forcing him to jerk his head away from it, as if he was preparing to receive a blow.

"It's finished?" he croaked. It was impossible that more could be done to it. Belief arced across the space separating him from the painting and entrenched itself at the foundations of his consciousness. It had not quite inflicted an unassailable truth on him, but he understood how it might do that to another, fractionally different mind. Even at this, it easily surpassed anything he had ever derived from Blake's great triptych.

Slate stepped closer until he was beside Marinetti. The human being had said nothing since they entered the room; he stood quietly, his hands behind him, regarding the painting with disturbing calm.

There were great washes of stars rising behind vague figures. Slate recognized some of the constellations as among those visible from Earth and then went on to locate more distant ones that would only have been visible from other worlds. He named some of them to himself, briefly pleased by his recognition until he realized that he had not previously known any of it. He had been *told* about these distant star formations by the painting. This must have been so, because when he blinked and looked still more closely he realized that the constellations he now *knew* were there were actually invisible to his eyes, either because of the distance Rane implied or because of the intervening dust lanes he had painted over the places where they certainly were.

Slate looked at Marinetti again and found him transfigured. The man had drawn himself up against the painting's assault. His hands were still clasped behind his back, but his shoulders were thrust forward and his arms were nearly trembling from the tension placed upon them. *What is he seeing?*

Slate concentrated and achieved some understanding of the figures in the lower half of the painting. They were mostly cast in lunar shadows or engulfed in the brilliant night that prevailed on worlds either close to the galactic core or so remote in space that there was only the galaxy itself taking up two-thirds of the night sky, and nothing else at all until an exiled sun arose for that world's morning. Yet the painting's *place* was certainly Earth, or, more precisely, the central world of human habitation.

Most of the hundreds of figures in the painting were human. They were depicted in poses of success and ability, either set apart from their companions in personal universes of their own making or absorbed by the manipulation of machines that were, themselves, just folds and densities of starlight in the painting.

Then, with a shock, Slate identified a god, even though its visible outline was no more distinct than the figures that surrounded it. A sense of personal subjugation emanated so strongly from that single figure that Slate felt the momentary urge to step away from the painting lest he be similarly enchained.

There were other races present, too, though he could not discover much to distinguish among them. Yet the instant he averted his eyes the figures acquired not only faces but names, families and histories that stretched back for generations. More remarkably, when Slate looked back to discover the slightest visual clue for the source of the information pouring into his mind, the individualities would be momentarily erased from the painting but not from his memory. When he looked back, each figure would return to his consciousness with a different name and story. But the race of the figures remained the same, as did the basic outlines of their histories.

The godly figure he saw was, by turns, a diplomat strikingly like himself, then a politician, a doctor, an engineer, a trader and, finally, a pilot. Each of these lives was poised to begin an irreversible descent into humiliation.

The other races were treated more sympathetically. But no matter when Slate forcibly slowed the parade of identities each figure broadcast, he was left with the conviction of defeat and exploitation. Some might be collaborators with the human figures in the painting; a greater number implied destinies of enslavement or extermination, though he could not understand enough of the painting to discover whether it was the races themselves or the humans who would be the agents of the promised tragedies.

The human figures were not so burdened. Although the fates of the other races were to be completed on the same field as theirs, these communicated a supreme unconcern. It was as if they could not be bothered and acknowledged the other races' existence only to the extent they unavoidably cluttered the painting's vastness.

All these beliefs were aimed at a vanishing point that was beyond Slate's comprehension. He felt relief at this. He had no more wish to be drawn into the painting's created truth than he did to partake of the one Blake's triptych had conjured ages ago. The price of this last measure of self-will was a great loneliness. He had not felt such a thing since the evacuations were completed and he was fleeing New York.

"You've surpassed yourself, Rane."

Rane bowed in acknowledgment from the edge of the diplomat's vision. Slate had to move his head before his eyes would leave the painting.

"I have accomplished the thing I was born for. I am not even sure this was my own work. The only way I can accept it is as the truth."

Marinetti unlocked his hands and let himself step back. "It is the truth. The truth that is going to happen soon." His breathing was deliberate. "It answers the questions your race posed." He stared into the painting, looking there for the next thing to say. "It answers Blake's painting. *Absolutely*."

"That was much of its intent," Rane answered quietly, savoring his triumph but obviously uneasy in its presence. "It is also a thing of this world. And of your kind, Anthony." He tentatively raised his right hand and then let it drop. "I can't explain more of it now. Perhaps after some rest . . ."

"You don't have to explain anything at all," Marinetti said, forcing brisk efficiency back into his voice. "It seems to have sufficient power of its own in that respect. You've created something of inestimable value. I . . ." His voice fell away from its enforced tone. "I don't envy you. Even if you have uncovered the truth."

"Which is?" Slate asked even though he had not intended to; he was close enough to grasping the answer himself to be afraid of it.

Marinetti turned to him with a tedious calm that he had

pulled over himself like a coat of mail. "*We* are now the threat Blake foretold. Isn't that true, Rane?"

The artist nodded in agreement. "Now you are." He was visibly tired, the final energies of creation draining away from him as they spoke.

When Marinetti resumed speaking it was unclear whether he was addressing the aliens or the painting itself. "Mission. Fate. Honor. Destiny. Every cliché that others are sent to die in the name of. All the reasons history promised us through the leaders' voices. But. . . . This is irrefutable! It can't be manipulated. It's constant and incorruptible. We're all seeing the same thing, aren't we, gentlemen? I'm seeing it more clearly than you—if you'll pardon me, Rane—but we're all being touched by the same thing. Aren't we?

"Oh, Jesus. Jesus. Was this how it was for your Blake and the first god who looked at what he'd done? Was this how the whole thing began? When your kind first began to live with his threat?"

"And," Rane continued the reasoning for Marinetti, "how are *your* kind is going to live with this?"

"This guarantee of triumph? It's *there* for anyone to see! Where everyone must see it!" Marinetti checked himself and looked away from the painting for the first time since they entered the studio. He quickly glanced at his watch and then all around, for he had momentarily forgotten his surroundings.

"All right. Yes." Marinetti turned around so he could not see it. Both Rane and Slate were surprised by this abrupt change and how forced it needed to be. "The . . . We should get this secured. Box it up. There ought to be a packing crate and materials downstairs. I'll have to ask you gentlemen to help. The people outside shouldn't see this."

"But why not?" Slate inquired. The idea of being allied with the human race grew more appealing as he looked at the painting and deciphered more of its meaning. *It cannot be illusion. I cannot hold it myself, but I can get near enough to touch its power!*

The idea that a mortal individual had created this work was

becoming incredible. Rane could not have had anything to do with it! *No one could. It has always been here, waiting for me to follow humans like Marinetti into it.*

Away from the painting, the man's gestures became nervous and poorly coordinated. "We can share it later. Now I just want to get this to the National Gallery. That will be the . . . correct place for it now."

Rane and Slate looked at each other, mystified.

"This has to be done," Marinetti said, equally threatening and pleading.

MARINETTI AND THE TWO GODS COVERED THE PAINTING with blankets and put it in a crate they found in the second upstairs bedroom.

Rane continued distancing himself from it. He spoke about how it looked to him and how its mysteries were so tantalizingly close but still beyond his sensibilities, as if he had had nothing to do with its creation.

Slate and Marinetti spoke the same way, too. The process of creation they had watched unfold on the television monitors was remembered, but was understood as the gradual discovery of something fully formed and complete, which they had been aware of all their lives.

Slate studied Rane's features. He wondered grotesquely if he should have his own skin roughened and scarred, and what other changes were medically feasible to help shed the godly perfection that was now so demonstrably valueless.

The three of them lugged the box out to the hallway where Marinetti ordered soldiers to put it in the waiting Agency truck. No one spoke to the two gods.

They followed the painting down and out onto the street. Marinetti spoke briefly to the officer in charge, concealing the difficulty he had controlling his voice. He was sweating despite the cooling rainfall and took off his suit coat. Then he and the two gods got into the truck with the painting.

One armored car pulled out in front of them; two more

aligned themselves behind. The four tanks that had been stationed at each end of the street took up positions at the front and back of the convoy.

They moved down the rain-polished streets, Federal-style townhouses and old elm trees on either side, their progress limited by the speed and size of the tanks. Slate could see curtains being pulled carefully away from windows as the convoy's passage probably rattled china or caused chandeliers inside to swing. The sky over Washington was sporadically illuminated by rocket trails and surface explosions.

The driver put on a set of earphones with a lip mike. He listened a moment and then informed Marinetti that the ship was still over the New York Mission; it had not taken any offensive action, but the mobs had set fire to at least ten percent of the city. Things were equally bad in the Bronx and Queens.

Slate, Rane and Marinetti were on the second bench seat; the agent with the shotgun was crouched in the rear, under the tilted crate with the painting in it. *They don't know,* Slate thought to himself, thrilled by the idea. *Just Rane and I know. Marinetti's the only human who knows and the only one who understands.*

He could not bring himself to ask Marinetti exactly what was being done. There was no time, even though minutes passed without anyone saying a word. If he ignored the approaching city and its flickering sky long enough to properly frame a question, he might miss something of importance.

All the men in the truck, including Marinetti, were looking intently around them. *Looking for what? For the ship? Ah . . . almost certainly for the ship, even though they had just been told it was still in New York.*

Rane had fallen asleep.

There was a Virginia state police roadblock on the west end of the Francis Scott Key Bridge. The officers hardly had time enough to move their barricades before the tanks drove past. They crossed over and drove into the city on K Street. Crowds packed the sidewalks, sometimes spilling into the roadway or side streets but otherwise relatively quiet and controlled. The driver remarked on this, and his companion in the front seat attributed it to the rain, the cooling temperature and the presence of more heavy armor than had been in New York. "They aren't used to foreigners up there, anyway," the man observed and then mumbled an apology back toward Rane and Slate.

They turned south onto 9th Street, toward the Mall. Slate stiffened as he saw the monumental buildings lining its northern edge and finally asked Marinetti why they were going there.

"It's the art. Correct?" Slate said stiffly. "If they're coming down to get the triptych, they're going to come here. Peacefully, if they can. They aren't going to bother with violence. That'd only risk losing the cornerstone of the race."

The possibility that the triptych might be destroyed was of little consequence to him. He had despised it long before he had ever heard of Earth. He was equally unconcerned by the thought that Rane's creation might be lost, though for entirely different reasons: *It cannot be destroyed. Any more than the freezing point of water can be "destroyed."* "And then?"

"Then we'll see." Marinetti looked at the passing buildings.

LINDA CAVAN HAD A TWO-YEAR-OLD MERCURY WITH yellow-coded license plates that allowed passage through most checkpoints. It also had a radio linked to the Department's local network, so Timothy could listen to its directives and updates.

The President, Cabinet and Congress had already removed themselves to secure locations, so there were no critical evacuations to carry out that evening. Getting the general population out of D.C. was no more feasible than it would have been in New York. Besides, it was the feeling that most of the people would decide to stay, to see if the gods had come back as their salvation or if they were truly worthy of the hatred generated by their departure.

"There's also the gifted," the Marquez girl pointed out as they drove into the city, her voice calm but her eyes opened wide and unblinking as they watched the military traffic on the street. "Your father may be coming back, Tim. That must mean something to you."

Timothy Cavan wondered what it should mean but could not decide.

"If not him, than maybe some others," she continued. "Y'know, a lot of people said things went really badly after the gifted left, but it was never the gods' fault. Maybe we just needed the gifted more than they did. Could that be true?"

"There were good people who went with them," he said to be polite. It was, however, correct, so he added: "We might've needed them someday, after all." The girl had apparently forgotten how she had spoken about the truly evil ones being taken along too.

"Like now?" she asked with misplaced hopefulness.

They passed the shell of the Library of Congress. Crowds had broken down the police barricades and climbed over its charred and partly collapsed walls. Others edged onto the street, oblivious to most of the traffic. Most were looking up into the fine drizzle.

He turned left on Constitution Avenue. There was a regular Army roadblock, through which the car's State Department plates allowed them to pass. The Capitol's ruined Senate wing rose above them. The rest of the building's lights were off.

Timothy Cavan could not see any reason for the checkpoint. If anything, the crowds were thicker here than they had been in front of the Capitol. Driving became impossible, despite perfunctory efforts by soldiers to clear a path when they saw the Department plates. He and the Marquez girl abandoned the car in the middle of the street.

For a moment he thought he had done something completely illogical. Then the contempt settled in, cooling his apprehensions and setting a comfortable distance between him and the brawling thousands pressing against them, threatening to make him and the Marquez girl just like them. *They* were waiting for the ship; *they* had nothing to do until then except wait and look up at the dripping sky.

The National Gallery was the only logical place for either

of them to escape the crowd. He mentioned this to the Marquez girl, and she stiffened at the suggestion. After all, she had died there. Timothy had done the same a hundred meters from its steps.

"The paintings are still there," he reminded her. "If the ship goes anywhere next, it should be there."

"Just like the last time." She sounded like any thirteen-year-old who knew she was obligated to fight off an approaching terror.

"No. I don't think so." He was leading her onto the Mall. The crowds had churned the dirt and dead grass into thick mud. "This has to be different. We know much more about everything now."

"We don't know *anything*. . . ."

"We know why they came the first time." He searched the ground for a less treacherous path. The observation logically followed: "That could be why they're coming back."

"Why? Looking for their horror again. You'd have thought they could have found one that suited them by now." So the girl was not going to lose her courage yet.

Couple of dead aristocrats. That's us, he muttered to himself, trying to control his thoughts.

The rain let up. Patches of night with stars embedded in it were visible through rents in the clouds. The breeze lost its moisture and came to remind Timothy Cavan of the springtime wind his parents had readily identified and said had been common when the world was not so warm.

Armor was concentrated at the corners of the Gallery: heavy wheeled vehicles, tanks, five self-propelled artillery pieces and a squadron of D.C. Police cruisers. Everything but the police units was regular Army.

Four Nissan limousines were hidden behind the tanks. At least one of them had Senate plates. Another black automobile joined them; this one looked as if it should be from the executive motor pool. A short, well-dressed man emerged. The driver and another man who had been in the front seat got out too, and the three of them proceeded quickly up the Gallery's steps. They spoke to an officer posted outside before entering.

After a minute, the sequence was repeated in reverse, although this time the central figure was older and taller than either of his companions. Instead of looking down at the steps and trying to avoid recognition by the crowd, this gentleman seemed nearly hypnotized by the sight of the night sky, so much so that the man on his right had to keep his hand on the other's elbow to guide him back down the steps to their automobile. Even then, the taller man stayed by the car while the door was held open for him, looking upward, his expression wavering between satisfaction and fright. He got in at last, and the limousine drove slowly onto the street, an armored car preceding it through the crowd.

"Important people?" the girl asked. None of the hundreds of people around them had paid any attention.

"I'm surprised there're any left in town. Maybe they're coming back to watch the show." If the triptych was still inside, it was reasonable that bewildered men of responsibility, charged with making decisions and not knowing what to do, would come and seek to renew their understanding of the gods by studying it. After all, as the men in the limousines must have been thinking, the human beings who really knew the answers had left with the gods. They, it was painfully obvious to them and their chauffeurs, were not among them.

Rolls of concertina wire with D.C. cops standing behind them guarded the bottom of the Gallery's steps. A police officer approached as they stepped out of the crowd and told them the Gallery was closed. The cop sounded anxious and weary. When the Marquez girl mentioned that she had just seen people going in and out, he hardened his voice and repeated the statement: "I said closed, goddammit! It's night and the monsters are coming back. What more d'ya need? Now move away." The officer motioned over his shoulder; two other cops hitched up their gunbelts and began to walk over.

Timothy stared at the man. There was no easy way into the Gallery and no time for bluffs or bribery. He had no idea if the ship would be content with New York or if it was really going to move on to the capital, but there was no reason for it to do anything else. Except leave. That would be unacceptable.

The other two officers joined the first. The largest one had sergeant's stripes. He assumed an attitude of condescension, but then his initial impression of Cavan's adolescence vanished. Timothy had watched this reaction before: older people glanced at him, picked up the tatters of youth clinging to him and began to frame their words accordingly; then, if they kept on looking, they perceived the rest.

The first cop began to plead. "Look. There's going to be nothing but trouble out here tonight. Take your sister home, will you? You seen what's going on up in New York? She shouldn't be around here." He was looking at the Marquez girl but confronted the same feelings he had with Cavan. This was more than he needed: "Awright, goddamnit! Back off!"

Cavan stepped into the crowd, but only far enough to be hidden from the cops; they immediately let their attention be distracted by something in the crowd or by the sky.

"We should try to get *in*. . . ." she complained above the mob's humming.

He moved around to the western edge of the steps, where the tanks were parked. Another distinguished person arrived and was being escorted through the wire. Cavan recognized Senator Dennis. He was supposed to be on board a Looking Glass.

Cavan followed the politician and his two guards. He actually got past the first coils of wire before one of the officers grabbed him from behind and hissed in his ear that he was getting goddamn sick and tired of his game, and if he wanted to look at the paintings he could goddamn come back in the morning when the world was straight again.

The cop felt Cavan's strength and how out of proportion it was to his apparent youth and vulnerability. The cop shoved him, as a test. When Timothy only wavered on his feet, the cop moved his free hand to the butt of his sidearm.

"There is no reason for trouble, Officer." The voice came

from the Gallery's steps and was difficult to hear over the crowd. Both Cavan and the officer turned and saw an ordinary man in a light raincoat walking toward them. A much larger individual wearing night-vision glasses and carrying a silenced machine pistol walked obediently behind him.

When the man reached them, he looked at Cavan and asked: "Timothy? Ah! It is certainly you. I thought you had been hurt or died. . . ."

"I had," Cavan answered ingenuously. The cop instantly released his grip as if he had just caught the scent of the grave.

"It is you?"

Cavan nodded. "And you're . . ."

"You do not remember?" The man stopped and ran his fingers over his face, tracing the outlines of another's. "But I have changed too. More than you have, on the outside. I am Rane."

The giant took a card from his breast pocket, showed it to the officer and motioned him away. The cop gratefully complied. "Mr. Rane, you should try to keep these things to yourself. At least until we're in a safe place." The man appeared as nervous as the officer despite his size and weapon. "We should get back inside, sir. The ship . . ."

"The ship is still in New York, but has abandoned the Mission's ruins and ascended five kilometers over the city. Did you know that, Timothy?"

Cavan answered that he did not.

"This is . . . ?" Rane half-bowed until his face was even with the girl's. "This is the Marquez girl." The god's appearance was completely human. The bewilderment and sorrow in his expression were mortal; only his lyric voice betrayed his origins. "My protector is correct. Please come in." He proceeded up the steps with his hand on Cavan's arm before the Agency operative could say anything to the contrary.

Rane walked like one who was consciously testing the limits of his environment. At the top of the steps he said, "I have something I must show you. You, at least."

The large man spoke to the Army officer at the door. It

opened, and they walked into the Gallery. Only the security lights and a few temporary floodlights on tripods illuminated the interior. A sign to the right announced an exhibition of "The Republican Works of Jacques-Louis David"; the hall beyond it was empty.

The gallery on his left, where the gods' first exhibition had been, was similarly bare, but a number of packing crates of various sizes were assembled in the middle of the floor. A forklift truck was parked behind them.

The Marquez girl sighed and repeated the elaborate exercise required to suppress her fear. Armed guards in groups of two or three were posted at intervals in the entrance hall and in the gallery where the packing crates were. They mostly stood back in the shadows, rocking on their heels or pacing back and forth. A larger cluster of people, including the well-dressed ones that had arrived in the limousines, were grouped around three or four open crates. Occasionally someone coughed, and the sound was magnified by the Gallery's uninhabited spaces.

"Is the triptych in some of those? Still here?" the girl asked as Rane led them into the exhibition hall.

"It is."

"They're coming back for it?"

"That is what is anticipated."

"Mr. Rane," the giant behind them quietly pleaded. "These things are still sensitive. At the highest classification, as Mr. Marinetti explained."

Rane hardly cared. "That cannot make any difference now, can it? Besides, I have one of my own works here and I would like to think they are coming back as much for it as for Blake's masterpiece."

"Is your own *Death* still here?"

"Yes. Blake's painting would be incomplete without it." He pointed to an opened crate with a number of dignitaries grouped in front of it. "That would be one panel, if I was told the truth."

"It's not a ship's copy?" It seemed impossible that it had

not been noticed when all the gods were on Earth; perhaps they
had been distracted in those days.

Rane smiled in his new, Earthly way. His artificially coarsened skin wrinkled amiably. "But now I have a masterpiece
of my own."

"The picture of Blake?"

"Not at all. Would you like to see it?"

"You've been working?"

"Yes." He turned to their escort and appeared relieved to
find him at the other side of the hall, waiting to talk to Marinetti
and too far away to stop them. Rane walked over to a medium-
sized crate and pried one side off with a crowbar. The god
adjusted a tripod light to shine into the box.

Cavan felt the floor drive up into his legs. An impression
of multiple stories being simultaneously told and comprehended rushed through his senses, converged and planted ir-
revocable triumph in his mind. Ships and figures of human
beings rode colored avenues of thought, identified a future
within measurable reach and set the destinies of all other races,
the gods among them.

Rane already had his hand gently poised above the Marquez
girl's mouth, but she suppressed any audible reaction by herself.

A *time* followed the knowledge of ships and races. It made
and then instantaneously kept a promise to him that everything
it portended would be fulfilled within his lifetime, if not within
the decade. Cavan focused his attention and found the painting's moment gaining clarity, as if it were coming closer,
traveling against the normal current of time to meet him, rather
than waiting, aloof, in the manner of all other promised destinies.

The tripod light was knocked over, but even in the gloom
he continued to acquire information from the painting. It radiated its own illumination until the giant and another armed
man slammed the crate shut.

"This isn't allowed!" Their escort was quivering with rage.
"Mr. Marinetti's the only person to view that box's contents,

and you are not under any circumstances . . ." The man was trying to hold his voice in check so the bigwigs on the other side of the hall would not notice any trouble.

"Mr. Marinetti is also aware that it is my painting," Rane interrupted. He had lost every outward semblance of his race. "If it has been brought here for display after the other works are gone, then I fail to see what is the problem."

"It'll be leaving with them." Marinetti had come up behind the two armed men, his voice flattened by the effort to control it. "Did you get a good look at it, Mr. Cavan?" Slate was standing beside him, shadows from the emergency lights sculpting the idealized contours of his face.

"Only for a second."

"Did your friend?" Slate gestured at the Marquez girl, who was rubbing her fists against her eyes.

"I did," she answered herself. "I didn't understand."

"You must have understood something, though?" Marinetti asked. His concern was obvious. Slate betrayed nothing.

Timothy Cavan tilted his head and nearly smiled; it already seemed as if he had known the painting's rough dimensions since childhood. It was now as indispensable to his conception of physical reality as gravity. "I wouldn't have ever believed that we . . . would follow such paths!"

Marinetti quickly stepped around the armed guards and placed himself directly in front of Cavan. He kept moving forward, and the younger man retreated before him until they were three meters away from the others. "It wasn't necessary to look at that," Marinetti hissed.

"Not necessary to see what will happen to us? Not necessary to *know* that we'll win? After years of the gods and of . . ." He waved his hands at the mob outside the Gallery's doors. "Years and years of *that*? How can it not be necessary? It's *going to happen*." Cavan's voice was soaring upward, led on by the process of rediscovery he could already apply to the painting's memory. He could almost grasp the name of first victory; it had been knowledge hidden behind a star, a millimeter across, placed in the painting's upper right-hand corner.

Distinguished faces ducked around the crates on the other side of the hall, trying to see who was speaking so heatedly.

Sadness, animated by rage that was not really directed at Cavan, drew the corners of Marinetti's mouth down and narrowed his eyes. "This must be kept secret."

"How? Impossible! That's like saying the sun's a secret."

Marinetti raised his hand to ask for quiet. "It *is* a secret. So far. There are only three human beings who have seen that picture. You and I and possibly the girl, though I don't know what it means to her yet. There're surveillance pictures and analyses that've been circulated, but they can't compare with *seeing* what Rane's just done!" Marinetti's voice broke away and chased his own memory of the painting. Then he stopped talking, inhaled sharply and looked at the darkened ceiling.

He raised his hand again, but this time it was in apology. "I *know* what the painting is. I've looked at it for half an hour. You saw it for five seconds and mostly in shadow. I know it better than Rane does. He made it but I don't think he's retained the . . . languages he used. But I also know that we can't do anything about it *right now*. So . . ."

Cavan was shaken by this suggestion that Rane's prophecy could be thwarted. "But it *will* come true."

"When, Cavan?" Marinetti asked patiently.

The younger man was flustered by the question. "Very . . . very *soon*."

"But not goddamn *now*! We *can't* do anything *now*. We have no ships, no skills. We won't have the science for at least a generation, even if that painting does to us what Blake's did to the gods! We're not as patient as the gods, Cavan. We'll be chasing victory instead of trying to meet an invincible threat as far away from home as possible. Our promise could die of starvation in less than the time required to fulfill it. It could burn itself out on Earth before we could ever leave." He snapped his fingers to signify the conflagration of hope.

"But if we have the reason to begin, Marinetti, who knows how quickly the work could go! That's what they had, and it got them out into the universe quickly enough." Cavan struggled against the awful suspicion the older man had planted.

"They didn't want to meet the threat, dammit! They didn't want to meet us! But *we* look at this new painting, and we *want* . . ." He stopped again, breathing more heavily than he knew he should. "And if you don't work to hold its knowledge away from you, there's going to be a chrome-plated fury to be off and chasing them trapped inside of us."

"You're wrong. This has to be seen so we can begin the work." He was unable to understand how Marinetti could have been exposed to the painting and still talk the way he did. The older man must be consumed with the desire to keep it for himself. "I think the others should see."

People moved cautiously around the crates and approached them. Cavan recognized Senator Dennis and recalled the man's humiliation in the same hall. That had been years ago. The politician had come back tonight because he still believed in the paintings, and especially in the triptych. He may have been told it was the real one.

"He should know. People like him must see it," Cavan said to Marinetti; but he whispered it, unsure if he was correct.

"He can't! No one else can! If they do, it'll only make it harder to let go of it. Christ! It's almost impossible for me to do it now. Don't make it any more difficult! Please." Anguish suffused Marinetti's voice. He seemed to be fighting so many battles at once.

The Senator was about to say something to them. Marinetti had already begun to face him, but a distant thunderclap caused him to close his mouth and look up at the Gallery's windows. Violent purple luminescence flickered outside, showing that every one of the panes was suddenly veined with networks of fractures.

Then the background rumbling of the crowd swelled and broke into the Gallery. Some of the armed guards in the entry hall trotted to the main doors, one of them speaking into a handset and the others checking the actions on their weapons.

The Agency operative who had followed them up the steps with Rane was listening to his own radio. The portion of his face that was visible below the night glasses were ashen. "It's appeared in local airspace, Mr. Marinetti."

Marinetti was relieved by the diversion. "I should have been informed when it left New York."

"There was no time, sir. Langley reports a simultaneous dematerialization at New York and appearance here over Dulles. There's a lot of damage in both cities, but more here where the event happened closer to the ground."

A roar penetrated the building, half cheer and half panicked shout. "It may be visible now," the man said unnecessarily. "Clouds are mostly gone. Visibility's fifty kilometers." Then he dropped the hand with the radio to his side and pointed his goggles at Marinetti. "Is this possible? We going to go through that shit all over again, sir?" Rane was not included in the question.

Cavan almost said something about the painting and how this time things would be unimaginably different.

Slate said, "No. They are not going to stay this time."

"Then what the hell are they coming for, sir? This goddamn time?" The man was insubordinate and he knew it; he loathed the fear that was controlling his speech. Cavan thought of breaking the spell by showing the man Rane's painting. It could be that simple. Five seconds, and he would *know* what Timothy did.

Marinetti stopped Cavan. "They are coming, Mr. Steinner, for their art. The beauty they mistakenly left behind." He pointed at the crates behind him. "In which they place great . . . decisive importance. They are also coming for the 'traitors to their race.' " Slate winced as Marinetti said this, but otherwise kept his supernatural composure.

Rane overheard. "I did not know about that," he said as he walked toward them. "Have they used any names?"

"Wentworth wrung it out of transmissions from the ship last night. They've mentioned yours."

"Mine?" Slate asked, losing some divinity in the process.

"We don't think so. But there's a lot that Wentworth's still working on. They want all their works and Rane plus some

others. I've only heard of two of the others before. The rest
are new."

Beams of prismatic light fanned into the Gallery through the
windows. The human roaring grew again.

The agent put the radio to his ear and listened. "It's in sight,
descending. There's some violence starting around College
Park and Greenbelt, but everything else's under control."

"Any transmissions?"

"Yes, sir. Plain language: they will retrieve their art and
they want the traitors. They'll leave as soon as this is done."

"What will happen if it's not?" Slate's voice was under
better control than Marinetti's.

"There was only the statement that it *will* be done, Mr.
Slate."

"They won't risk destroying the triptych."

"*We*, Slate, will not risk destroying the city to keep it."

"Then what about the new painting? Rane's? We can't give
that up!" Sudden desperation invaded Slate's voice. He had
settled upon his new allegiance and did not want it to renounce
it so soon. *Would that,* Slate wondered to himself, *be how the
humans felt when we left them? When the gifted left them?*

The building began to resonate from the ship's local field.
The rest of the armed men moved into the main hallway, while
the dignitaries like Senator Dennis lost interest in the triptych
or with what was going on between Marinetti and the others.
They circled about with their bodyguards, unsuccessfully looking for someone of greater authority to defer to.

Marinetti gestured to his people, who discreetly closed the
crate with part of Blake's triptych inside.

The low resonance died down along with the noise from the
mobs outside.

The giant, Steinner, was leaning against a wall, whimpering,
Cavan could understand some of his words: "I *don't* want
them back. Any of them. Not the gods or the gifted. I just
want . . . them to leave. Please make them do that. . . . Please."

That's how we'll be if they take the painting with them!
Cavan was convinced of that. It could not be allowed to happen.

"Mr. Marinetti," he began, speaking more quietly. "I . . ."

Marinetti flinched when the youth put his hand on his shoulder. Then, as Cavan was carefully placing his words, he swung around and struck him in the stomach with his fist. Cavan only bent slightly under the impact. Marinetti had hit the carapace of scar tissue; it had an internal structure that was as hard as bone.

Marinetti held his hand up in front of him and closed his other hand over it. His face showed only casual surprise. "I believe that it is best to let them take all of this." The pain evened out his voice; it sounded normal again.

"Rane, too?" Cavan asked incredulously. "He's a genius! Prometheus stealing fire for mankind!"

"Prometheus ended up chained to a rock where vultures devoured his liver every day forever," Marinetti answered in the same level tone. "We cannot keep the painting's promise right now. We'll destroy ourselves trying."

"Then hide it! Keep it safe! No one knows about it but you and me! And Slate and Rane, and they're on our side now, aren't they? The girl won't say anything. She doesn't understand." Cavan heard his own disarray.

Marinetti opened his mouth to speak again, and it seemed as if he uttered a dense, muffled explosion that threw aside the Gallery's main doors and thrust a scarlet light into the entrance hall. All the temporary lights in the building were knocked out.

"Oh, Jesus!" Cavan heard Steinner behind him. "Not again!" Then came the sound of the man dragging himself back to his feet and shuffling toward the entrance hall where he would be needed.

Smoke billowed into the Gallery. The floor was textured with fragments of the brass doors, glass and marble splinters. The Marquez girl was sitting on the ground, her legs crossed and both hands resting in her lap. She must have wandered away and been hit by the concussion. A deep laceration ran down from her left cheek into a tear in the collar of her dress.

He could see the glass fragments embedded in the wound and gently picked out the ones that were large enough to grasp. The girl evinced no pain as he did this. She was bleeding, and Cavan noticed despairingly that it was clear ichor, colored red from the doorway light. He touched the liquid with his fingertips, feeling its warm, oily consistency. It smelled like honey.

His ears were ringing from the explosion, but he should have been able to hear the crowd. *Have they all been killed?* Such a thing was possible.

Marinetti bent over the boy and the wounded girl. "This has to be given up, Timothy. We can't do anything now." He was speaking carefully, so he could be understood against the pulsing quiet. "The only way its promise can be endured without attempting somthing we just aren't capable of yet is to let the gods take it away."

The outside light sank to a lavender hue. Then chromium filaments, like Tesla coil radiance, arced through the acrid dust. Cavan thought he was dying all over again.

Marinetti kept talking at the same metronomic pace. "The *only* thing to do is to let them take it away, out to Jupiter, and hope the gifted will see it and act. You have to understand. It's the only thing to do. The only thing we're *able* to do now. If the gifted *see* it, they must understand. They're out there, in the middle of the gods. *They'll know what to do, and they will be able to carry it out.* Either that or they'll be destroyed along with the painting. Then only we will know what was lost."

The enormity of Marinetti's proposal loomed at some great distance from Cavan, its details indistinct and contradictory. "Has this been cleared?" was the only thing Cavan could think of to ask; he used his mother's State Department voice.

"Not entirely." Then: "No. Not at all."

"But . . . ?"

"It is *right*, Timothy. It's the only way both we and the painting can have a chance of surviving."

"I understand that it . . ." He corrected himself: "That we

and it must survive.'' He thought of the painting on a faraway ship, illuminated by the diminished light of the sun. The painting's certainty spilled into his vision; for a moment its prospective loss was bearable.

''I've explained the painting to Rane, and he agrees. He doesn't think of himself as its creator, you know. He's as distant from it as we are from the triptych. I hadn't anticipated their desire to get him back too, though.''

Rane was standing apathetically behind them, near the packing crates. He may have been smiling, but it was difficult to tell in the pale light. Slate was not around.

A soldier shouted and the armed men who had approached nearest the entrance began carefully walking backward away from it until they were either inside the darkness at the other end of the main hall or flattened against the walls behind pilasters.

The smoke thinned away. Against Cavan's expectations, the presence of the mob outside failed to reassert itself. The world beyond the Gallery's portico might just as well have been vacant.

Then a god appeared, gliding up the inclination of granite steps on a large repulsion sled that barely fit through the main doorway. Cavan shut his eyes and placed his left hand over the girl's. He was struck by the irrational fear that the gods would choose this moment to appear in their own true form and that it would be one of unimaginable horror. *That would be consistent*, he thought feverishly. *It would make their ordained destruction easier.* He opened his eyes.

They were as they had been before, but the chill of space clung to them more obviously this time. The backlighting from the city lights across the Mall exaggerated their size and etched their features to the point of abstraction: serene, beyond the touch of human concerns but acutely self-aware.

There were five of them, each one on a sled. They entered the hall in a line. One of the soldiers raised his rifle, whereupon the god in the lead said in a sepulchral voice that violence would be inappropriate. The power of their ship, it continued, was committed to their protection.

The regular Army officer in charge said something, and the rifle came down.

"We wish to recover our works. They are important to us. We should not have departed without them."

Cavan felt the stirrings of old emotions at the sound of the god's voice, now sharpened by the promise of their eventual subjugation.

Marinetti suddenly stepped forward. "They've been prepared for you." No one was ready to say anything else. "Please take them. We know why they are needed."

The gods' expressions were impossible to decipher, but one or two of them turned questioningly to a companion. "We also demand the traitor."

"Is that necessary?" Marinetti knew perfectly well that it was.

"It is indispensable. We believe you have one of our race named Rane in your company." The god had trouble with the name in English, breaking the syllable into fractured, musical notes.

A voice called out from the other, darkened end of the entrance hall. "I am ready to go home."

But Rane was still leaning against the wall a short distance behind them. He had said nothing.

Slate then walked out of the shadows toward the gods, drooping his shoulders in imitation of abject defeat. "You wish to take me and my works away from this world?" he said in English so the people in the hall could understand.

The god on the lead sled dismounted and went over to him. It had a notebook in one hand and a box the size of a deck of cards with lights coursing over its surface in the other. "You are Rane?"

"Of course."

"I had believed that your appearance would be somewhat different," the other creature said doubtfully.

"Perform a genotype." Slate held out his arm but the other god waved it away impatiently.

"We cannot do that here. There are facilities for that on the home-ship."

"Then I am Rane."

"You are still not . . ."

"I am Rane, who took the painting from home and created the imitation."

The other god visibly quailed at this and abruptly asked Slate to stop. "But is it here? Is it?"

Slate pointed toward the exhibition hall, and the human beings in it backed against the walls as if his hand directed a thunderbolt. He walked stiffly toward the crates. The other god walked carefully behind him with his sled following obediently. The other four gods and sleds joined them.

Each of the gods in turn looked at Rane's scarred figure propped up against the wall as they passed. Nothing detectable passed between them. The artist had withdrawn from their plane of reference through surgery and his devastating act of creation.

Cavan glanced at Marinetti and saw the terrible relief on his face: *This should not be done. Even though Slate understands nearly as much of it as we do, he did not make it. But let him play this out.*

The gods clipped reference units to the ends of the crates and then guided them with hand controllers up and onto the repulsion sleds. The box with Rane's new painting was loaded along with the rest. Marinetti and Cavan both stiffened as it was lifted on board.

The three largest crates, containing the triptych, were conspicuously left until last. The gods walked slowly around them as they were lifted by the reference units, touching them reverently and at times placing their foreheads against the rough surfaces, closing their eyes and trembling from the communion.

They're taking it away! Cavan beat down his panic. *Only we will remember it! Could Rane, if he's actually left behind, make another one? Is that too much to ask for?* He looked over at Rane and knew that it probably was.

Slate was talking to the gods. After a brief exchange, he left them and walked over to Marinetti and Cavan. "Please take care of Rane," he whispered hurriedly. "He made that, and he deserves something for it. Some peace, if nothing else."

"This is preposterous!" Marinetti hissed. "This farce of yours is going to last about one day before you're recognized or one of your shit-for-brains colleagues catches on."

"Nevertheless, the decision is correct. At worst, I'll be gone and Rane will be saved. They will not come back just for him. At best, I can make sure the gifted see it."

"You'll do that?"

"Rane can't," he answered, sadly inclining his head toward the recently made human being against the wall. "They said they need a traitor and won't leave without one. I qualify."

"This isn't *required!*"

Slate returned to the gods and stepped onto the lead sled. The first god eyed him suspiciously, then shrugged as a human would. They drifted through the doorway and dropped below the level of the portico.

Instantly, a low roaring, like wind coming over prairie lands, rose from outside and blew into the entrance hall. Cavan half-expected the noise to kick up a storm of dust and granulated plaster from the floor. But it was only the sound of worshipful awe and detestation from the crowd outside, utterly silent for the hour since the gods landed.

He should go and watch them depart. *With our masterwork!* The noise pushed against him, even against the pull of Rane's stolen painting.

Marinetti recovered his power of movement first. He uttered a cry, like that of a child who realized the persistence of an error his seniors had been anciently blinded to. Then he heaved himself forward, as if his feet were weighted.

Cavan looked at the older man. His internal war had become a personal Armageddon. Conflicting emotions, all mediated by varieties of self-hatred, conflict and duty, animated his features.

"Anthony?" Rane was behind them. He sounded unaware of his surroundings.

"Your work is leaving," the other managed to say.

"That was what we had agreed should happen. Remember?" Marinetti stared and then nodded dumbly. "Yes. Agreed. Agreed."

Hope opened in Cavan's heart that Marinetti would suddenly stop, turn around and reveal another part of his plan that would keep the painting on Earth.

Marinetti disappeared down the steps. Cavan followed, not daring to quicken his pace, soldiers and assorted dignataries following at a distance.

He reached the Gallery's doorway. There was no moon, but the government buildings and the gods' ship cast their own cool, lunar light over the hundreds of thousands of people jammed together on the Mall. The only things disrupting the vast topography of heads and shoulders were occasional arms thrust up holding flags or rifles and unable, because of the throng, to put them down again.

The crowd had drawn apart to form an avenue twenty meters wide to the gods' ship. There were bodies scattered in the cleared space; some were trampled into bloody pulps while others were intact. Some quivered reflexively as the sleds passed over them.

Marinetti followed the gods down the avenue. He seemed unaware of the mass of human observation that became attached to him once the gods passed a given point. Cavan could not understand how the man resisted calling out to those around him, to *tell* them what was concealed in one of the crates and what it promised.

Marinetti walked carefully, stepping over the corpses that littered the path, holding his arms at his sides. But then he stopped and suddenly swept up his right arm.

Cavan heard a series of rapid clicks behind his left ear. Marinetti's arm continued its arc, reaching around in back of him as if he were trying to touch a spot between his shoulder blades. Then he pitched forward. No one in the surrounding mob seemed to notice.

A wisp of acrid smoke drifted by Cavan. He looked to his left and saw the giant, Steinner, kneeling with his silenced machine pistol held in both hands, still pointed at Marinetti.

The gods reached the ship and passed inside. Its gravitational anomalies captured the lights around it, dim arrays of spectrographic radiation flowing along its surface. As always, it was impossible to tell its shape.

The avenue narrowed and then disappeared. Marinetti's body was lost with the others. The oceanic bellowing of the thousands rose as they turned toward the ship and hurled at it whatever they had stored up during the years since the gods had first landed. *Everything*, Cavan thought exhaustedly, *except the promise of what the fools let them take away*. The words threatened to force tears from his eyes. *It's gone. It can't go. It's been here forever*.

Steinner recovered his voice with the execution of his instructions; rationality was restored to his limited universe. "Mr. Marinetti ordered me to do that, Mr. Cavan. He said that if he followed he could not be trusted to respect his plan."

"You're allowed to do that?" Cavan asked distractedly.

"The correct priorities were all invoked, Mr. Cavan. This was fully authorized. It must have been."

"Of course." Rane had walked out onto the portico behind them. "He could not bear to live without it. Do you think we can, Timothy?"

"Who? You and me?"

"And the Marquez girl."

"She's young."

"Not so young as to have already died."

"That may be. She doesn't have human blood any more. Did you know that, Rane?"

"No. Is the same true for you?"

"I haven't been wounded yet, so I don't know." The gods' ship lifted up. The crowd's noise rose to a cheer or bestial howl. "What about you? Would you bleed red blood now if you were hurt?"

"Will Slate when they discover him? That cannot take long." The god's voice quavered with shame and relief.

The ship jumped, almost too quickly to follow. It stabilized at a thousand meters above the Mall, then leapt up again toward the zenith and was gone. Ten seconds had elapsed. Nothing like that had been demonstrated during the course of their first visit, or even during evacuations carried out under shellfire. At least it did not cause the destruction it had at Dulles when it arrived.

"They are still capable of more than we can imagine. We would invite an apocalypse if we moved against them today, when we are so unprepared," Rane said.

The noise of the crowd ebbed again. The silence became complete, attaining a physical density that immersed the city. It was the four-o'clock-in-the-morning sound of the city again, intensified by the contradictory suggestion of an approaching wilderness. "Listen," Steinner whispered.

Cavan counted his breath: five seconds, ten, thirty, a full minute until there was a shout, far away and heard only because the west facade of the Capitol reflected it back toward the Gallery's portico. A response came from across the Mall. Then a gunshot, the beginning of a siren wail from an armored unit that ended abruptly; then more sounds, all explosively disruptive and not at all like the monotone that had just attended the gods' departure.

"We should get inside, Mr. Cavan." Cavan and Rane followed Steinner. A line of armed men formed across the threshold once they passed, even though there was no reason to suppose the mob might storm the Gallery. Everything outside indicated self-destruction that would confine itself to the Mall's open spaces.

"Now there are only you and I and the girl," Rane said.

"She and I are freaks," Cavan muttered, all of his foreignness descending on him at once. "You were the creator."

Rane shivered in the damp warmth. He traced the scarified

imprint where the powered frame had been attached to his right hand. "I cannot think of it that way."

"Can you . . . function without it? Without your kind?" Cavan asked hopelessly.

Rane considered the question for nearly half a minute, then smiled wanly. "Yes. If only to wait for the human being who will paint *The Death of Rane*. I deserve that much."

A̲T FIRST HE HAD FELT ONLY REMORSE AND SELF-recrimination. Treason had been everywhere among the Nobel Prize winners, social activists of the purest kind, artists of unlimited potential and leaders he had joined, and every one of them had been immersed in a depression so profound that the gods kept them in a light narcotic stupor for a week after they left Earth.

That was replaced by an athletic feeling of imminent discovery once the orbit of Mars had been traversed. Wives and children, schools of political philosophy and nations were all diminished by the distances they travelled. The gods politely tolerated this quiet excitement. They were as remotely gracious as they had been on Earth: they also spent as much time scanning the welkin around their ships for evidence of the threat their seminal painting had promised them as they always had.

He had feared dimensions of space before he left because he presumed they would be magnified by the limitations of the ships they would be confined in. But the gods conveyed themselves about the heavens in spacious vessels, and the home-ship itself was equipped with magical forests and miniature oceans evocative of their own worlds. That ship's libraries were opened to the gifted, and they were provided with the devices necessary to render all the gods' works into the tongues of humankind.

Lately, however, an impatience grew in him. He was able to separate this from his original feelings of betrayal and desertion, but that did not diminish it.

They waited for months on the home-ship. The gods said

that one of the fleet had been sent back to Earth to recover some important articles inadvertently left behind. They would resume their journey home as soon as it rejoined them.

Cavan watched this ship's arrival from a deck one kilometer above the home-ship's main entrance port. Cargo was unloaded, assurances were given that they would depart the solar system soon and most of the gifted returned to their studies.

Another week passed, however, with no movement. At the end of this period, Andrew Cavan was approached by a god and asked, if he pleased, to speak to a traitor to his race. Cavan stared at the perfect creature, remotely astounded that it did not sense the question's irony, and then consented.

He was being asked to do this, the god explained as he guided Cavan down corridors and lift-ways to an inner deck, because he had been with an Earthly government and might have some insight into personalities of this sort.

They passed down a corridor that was much narrower than the ones he had become used to elsewhere on the home-ship. The light was rationed and moisture condensed on the metal walls. Heavily armed gods, something he had never seen before, were posted at fifty-meter intervals.

He was led through a reinforced door into an even more dimly lit room. Inside was an open framework with the distorted figure of a god suspended in its center. Probes were attached to it from the frame's perimeter. Traces of ichor ran down from the places where the supporting rods pierced its flesh.

"What is this?" Cavan asked, turning aside so he did not have to look after he realized it still had eyes.

"As I explained: it is one who stayed too long on your world. His reticence has compelled us to undertake unaccustomed measures to discover his true motives. But we are not confident he has told us the truth. Would you please inquire of him further?"

Cavan looked at the god in bewilderment. "And ask him . . . ?"

"He has been psychologically prepared to be receptive to

your questions. That required a corresponding strengthening
of his ability to resist our entreaties. It is a novel tactic, but
your presence here allows us to exploit it.'' The god smiled,
and Cavan tried to fit it into his memory of Marinetti and the
other Direct-Action people he had been forced to work with
on Earth.

The victim's features were terribly distorted, but Cavan
thought there were one or two points of recognition. He shook
the feeling away; even if they were there, he did not want to
be sure.

He inclined his head and ignored the smell of necrotic tissue
long enough to ask the creature what he had done on Earth.
Instead of answering, it asked him to come closer, where his
escort might not hear. The god looked at Cavan understand-
ingly: he was trusted, and they had anticipated this. The alien
left the room.

When they were alone, the tortured god told Cavan that he
must look at all the works of art the gods had brought back
from Earth. Every single one, because the mutually exclusive
destinies of both their races were contained in them. Its words
were uttered one at time, without any particular sentence structure.

Then it appeared to die. An alarm sounded in the corridor
and the god who had brought Cavan to the room rushed in
with a squad of armed gods to assist him.

When he was debriefed, the gods questioning him merely
agreed with the statement of the importance of their art and
then asked more earnestly if there wasn't something more useful that the traitor might have confided in him. The room had
been completely wired, of course, so his answers were accepted. He was cautioned against disclosing what he had wit-
nessed to any of the other gifted.

He wandered about the home-ship for the next two days,
not at all reassured by its departure from the Jovian parking
orbit. The gods told him that the return to their home worlds
would require about three months of subjective time for him;

it was impossible to be precise because the human perception of time was so different from theirs.

Cavan began frequenting the home-ship's bridge and studying drawings of its layout he found in the libraries. Some of the other gifted were doing the same thing, though they sometimes confessed to each other their embarrassment with what they were doing; surely, the wonders of the larger universe were of greater interest than even the marvels of the gods' vast flagship.

After they had left the solar system, Cavan and the rest of the gifted were invited to the ship's main lecture hall. There, in a room a half a kilometer long with walls encrusted with gold and blue titanium reliefs of incomprehensible mythologies, they were shown the triptych that some of them had seen at the National Gallery and told, through nearly endless circumlocutions, that this work was the primary reason they had come to Earth in the first place. The human audience acted suitably impressed but was otherwise mystified by the ceremony.

Cavan returned to that deck some time later. The triptych had been removed to a more secure place, but the rest of the works the gods had recovered were still there. He found the insane scholar and the woman who had driven Senator Dennis mad with adolescent desire. The memories they evoked carried traces of his son with them, but he was able to disregard them.

The traitor had asked him to look at all of the works. He dutifully went through the crates, one at a time. Some were mere daubings that impressed him no more than they had on Earth. Others were just as powerful as they had been when he and his son had looked at them for the first time. The few gods working in the shadowed perimeters of the immense hall were uninterested in what he was doing.

He found *The Death of Blake* and for a moment drew a connection between it and the traitor he had spoken to.

Next he opened a crate with a painting he did not remember in it. It seemed to be indecipherably dark at first. Then he pried the crate open so the light from the hall's terraced galleries could illuminate it. He looked again and found all the promised glory of humankind reflected back from its surface.

Cavan's mind was instantly cleansed of all admiration for the gods. In its place were pity and the certitude of their defeat. He surveyed the limitations of the home-ship and its potential to assist in the commencement of the required assault. *It could be used*, he decided as he sought out his companions to share his discovery. *It must be used*. The painting had explained how.